Robert Herrick, Edward Everett Hale

Selections from the Poetry of Robert Herrick

Robert Herrick, Edward Everett Hale

Selections from the Poetry of Robert Herrick

ISBN/EAN: 9783337277116

Printed in Europe, USA, Canada, Australia, Japan

Cover: Foto ©Andreas Hilbeck / pixelio.de

More available books at **www.hansebooks.com**

𝕬𝖙𝖍𝖊𝖓𝖆𝖚𝖒 𝕻𝖗𝖊𝖘𝖘 𝕾𝖊𝖗𝖎𝖊𝖘

SELECTIONS

FROM THE POETRY OF

ROBERT HERRICK

EDITED BY

EDWARD EVERETT HALE, Jr., Ph.D. (Halle)

PROFESSOR OF ENGLISH IN THE STATE UNIVERSITY OF IOWA

BOSTON, U.S.A.

GINN & COMPANY, PUBLISHERS

1895

PREFACE.

THIS volume of selections is meant as well for those readers who are content to enjoy Herrick's poetry as for those who desire to study a little the things which they have enjoyed. With such a double object there have been certain difficulties ; some things which are interesting to the student are very dry to the lover of poetry, and something might be said on the other side as well. Some concessions have to be made to each necessity. I have tried to give all Herrick's best poems ; but I have also, by including some that are by no means his best, aimed at giving an idea of his work that would be fairly accurate as well as pleasing. I have not thought it necessary to preserve the original and often erroneous spelling and punctuation; but it has seemed well to follow it where it really tells us something about the pronunciation, whether for the sake of the metre or for other reasons. I have tried to point out some of the things which are delightful in Herrick's poetry; but I have not shunned the discussion of several matters which may seem aridly scholastic. I have also omitted a few lines here and there, as is indicated by the numbering.

I have been aided by the studies of several of my predecessors who are mentioned in the Bibliography, and must especially acknowledge the help I have had from the work of Dr. Grosart and Mr. Pollard. Their editions are referred to so often that I have used merely the initials G. and P. I may also remark here that the abbreviation *Diss.* refers to the Dissertation mentioned on p. lxx, and that poems are referred to by the number in Mr. Pollard's edition.

Lastly, I am glad to mention the kindness of my colleague Professor A. N. Currier, who has always been ready to aid my recollections of the Latin poets whom Herrick admired so much, and, most particularly, that of Professor G. L. Kittredge, who has helped me with many a reference not only to the Latin but to English poets as well, and whose suggestions throughout have been of the greatest value.

STATE UNIVERSITY OF IOWA,
April 4th, 1895.

CONTENTS.

—•◦•—

INTRODUCTION.

I. ON THE LIFE OF HERRICK.

ALMOST all editors are zealous to give us a Life of their author, — to tell when he was born, what he did, how he lived, and when he died. About a poet these are among the least necessary things to know, and more especially about a lyric poet. What we really want to know is what kind of man he was and what kind of poetry he wrote. In so far as his birth, and parentage, and education, and friendships, and occupations, and so forth, — in so far as facts about these things help us to know him and his poetry, they are good. Otherwise they are matters of minor curiosity. We may, therefore, be thankful that concerning Herrick we know a little as to these matters, and only a little. We know enough on the main points, and not too much concerning the trivialities; we know so little that we must depend chiefly on his work, and so much that we can on the whole apprehend his work very well.

What little there is to say of Herrick's life without invoking the aid of his poetry, though not very interesting, does at least give us the main facts. His various editors have been somewhat successful in finding the names of his parents, his brothers and sisters, of his uncles and aunts, and of a good many friends and connections. They have fixed, too, the main events of his life down to the year 1648, after which we are sadly in the dark. But it cannot be said that the chronicle offers many remarkable circumstances. It is hard to make it much more than a list of names and dates. It is not until we get to his poetry that Herrick becomes a real man. Such as it is, however, the narrative runs thus: —

Nicholas Herrick, of Leicester, the son of John (who spelled his name Eyrick), sometime mayor of that city, came to London a dozen years or so before William Shakespeare, and there became a goldsmith. There, too, he married. His wife was apparently of good family, and had at any rate connections of position in the city. Married in 1582, they had seven[1] children, the eldest born three years after the marriage, the youngest only fifteen months before the death of his father. This youngest born was Robert Herrick, and his birthday was August 24, 1591. Little more than a year afterward Nicholas Herrick was killed by a fall from a high window. Whatever may have been the real cause, there was suspicion that the death was a suicide, on which account a good sum had to be paid to the High Almoner to buy off the legal claim that thus existed upon all that was left behind. As it was, however, the widow was left in what seem fairly comfortable circumstances. The estate was about £5000, or, as money was worth then, something like $125,000 of American money of the present day. Nicholas Herrick's brothers were made guardians of the children and managers of their share of the property. William Herrick, who became subsequently Sir William, was, like Nicholas, a goldsmith, and to him in course of time was Robert apprenticed for ten years. He probably had some schooling, but what it was cannot be said. Dr. Grosart thinks he may have gone to Westminster.

What sort of prentice the future poet made we do not know. We do know, however, that in 1614, some years

[1] Tradition adds an eighth, said to be younger than Robert.

before his time was up, he desired to stop being a prentice and go to the University. His uncle seems to have
made no opposition, and he entered as Fellow Commoner
at St. John's College, Cambridge, being at that time
twenty-one years of age.

As to Herrick's university life we are not left wholly
in the dark, for to this period belong the only products of
his pen preserved to us besides his poems. There are a
number of charming letters from the future poet (probably more or less of a poet then, too) addressed to his
uncle and guardian. They are all of one tenor; they all
sound a note that one can easily imagine in the letters of
a student to his guardian. Herrick was not without humor in his university days. "Before you unsealed my
letter (right worshipful) it cannot be doubted but you had
perfect knowledge of the essence of my writing before
you read it; for custom hath made you expert in my plain-
song (mitte pecuniam), that being the cause *sine quâ non*,
or the power that gives life and being to each matter."
Sometimes Herrick asks for his usual allowance, sometimes he hopes that an advance can be made him, sometimes he seems to hope there will be a bit over and above
the £40 a year that was apparently the sum to which,
like Goldsmith's Pastor, he found himself entitled. · In
spite of money's being worth more in Herrick's time than
nowadays, in spite of Herrick's having only himself to
care for, he seems never to have felt comfortably off. At
any rate, he moved in a year or so over to Trinity Hall,
where the expenses were less than at St. John's, and
there, in 1617, he took his Bachelor's degree, and three
years later his Master's. In 1620 he returned to London.

What Herrick did in London and how he supported
himself cannot now be said with any accuracy. There is
no doubt, however, that, whatever else he did, he began

now to become known as a poet. At this time Ben Jonson was a sort of Dictator in the Republic of Letters, and it is evident from references in the *Hesperides* that Herrick made one of the group of younger poets who gathered round the great man, received rules from him at the Devil Tavern, and, to speak technically, were "sealed of the tribe of Ben." Other friends of Herrick we hear of, but not so many as to give us any clear notion of his life. Mr. Hazlitt thinks that he had some place in the Chapel Royal, and the conjecture is by no means unlikely.

Whether or no he held any such position, he seems to have had at this time or later some connection with distinguished persons at Court, especially with Endymion Porter, groom of the bedchamber under Charles I. Porter was a patron of literature and the arts, and Herrick always alludes to him as to his Mæcenas. Other patrons, too, Herrick seems to have had; for at that time men of letters depended for support, not as to-day upon the fancy of the public, but upon the liberality of wealthy men. But since we cannot be sure, as will appear later, what poems Herrick wrote at just this period, and since outside evidence is lacking, we cannot form any very definite notion of this time of his life.

At court and at the tavern Herrick passed some of his time in London, and probably did very many interesting things there and elsewhere of which we now shall never know. But he seems to have sought an independence, and to have turned to the church. When he was ordained is not known, but in 1627 he was appointed chaplain to the fruitless expedition to the Isle of Ré, and in 1629 he was named to the vicarage of Dean Prior in Devonshire.[1]

---

[1] Dean Prior lies between Plymouth and Exeter, nearer the former, and some little distance to the south of Dartmoor Forest.

We might almost say that here Herrick's life begins. For nineteen years he was Vicar of Dean Prior, and in those nineteen years he wrote many of his poems, collected and corrected others, and at the end of that period published the book which has made him immortal. Of the book we shall speak later; here we may content ourselves with saying that for his Devonshire life it is almost our only authority. It is certainly sufficient authority for practical purposes. It is true that it is only with the greatest difficulty that we can screw out any definite facts,[1] but it must always be remembered that definite facts are not the things we want most in the case of a poet. We know that Herrick lived at his vicarage for nineteen years on a stipend of £50 (equal to about $1250 of the present day), and that in 1648 he was dispossessed for Royalist opinions. We know that he had a housekeeper named Prudence Baldwin, a spaniel named Tracy, and a sparrow named Phil, and, according to tradition, a pig which he taught to drink from a silver tankard, as a type perhaps of his consideration of his parishioners. Further (again following tradition), we know that he sometimes became disgusted with his Devonshire life, flung his sermons in the faces of his congregation, and went home to write rather nasty epigrams upon them to vent his wrath. We know, too, of a number of his friends, — Endymion Porter as before, Sir Clipsby Crewe, Sir Edward Giles, of Dean Court near by, and others, many of them persons of consideration in their day.

But certainly such material as we have here is of far less interest than that afforded us by even a few of his poems. *His Winding Sheet* (517) and *A Thanksgiving to God for His House* (*N.N.* 47) give us more that we really

---

[1] With what difficulty, the writer's Dissertation, spoken of later (p. lxx), bears emphatic witness.

want than any number of names and dates. *A New Year's Gift sent to Sir Simeon Steward* (319) or *The Hock-Cart* (250) reconcile us easily to a very plentiful lack of definite facts.

Herrick lived in Devonshire, then, for nineteen years, at the end of which time, in 1648, he was dispossessed of his vicarage by the Puritans, and presumably returned to London. In London he must at first have busied himself chiefly about publishing his poems; the idea had been long in his mind, but never before had he been able to put it into effect. They were published in rather a thick and dumpy little quarto in the year 1648, and with the publication Herrick vanishes from us like a lamp extinguished in darkness. A few rumors concerning the following years are preserved, but none seem worthy of restatement here. When the king came to his own again, Herrick also returned to what had been his own. He went back to Devonshire in 1662 as vicar of Dean Prior, where he died in 1674.

Such, in rather compressed form, is the story of Herrick's life, as far as outside sources give it to us. Some elaboration and conjecture could be added. Mr. Hazlitt, Dr. Grosart, and Mr. Pollard, in their editions, offer us a good deal more that is of interest about Herrick's family and friends and about Herrick's literary activity. But after all, the only thing that makes Herrick real to us is his *Hesperides*, and without that a hundred pages of detail concerning friends and manuscripts could not interest us in him. No one will desire to linger long over such matters before proceeding to Herrick's poetry; no one, except perhaps (to borrow Swinburne's excellent phrase) "the sturdy student who tackles his Herrick as a schoolboy is expected to tackle his Horace" (P. I, xii), and even the sturdy student may not find it amiss to proceed at once ; his welfare is provided for in foot-notes, and his wits will not be allowed to rust.

With the exception of a few poems found here and there, first collected by Hazlitt,[1] Herrick's work is all included in two collections, one of poetry entitled *Hesperides,* and the other of religious verse called *Noble Numbers.*[2] The two were published in the same book, though the *Noble Numbers* has a separate title-page, which is dated 1647, while the *Hesperides* title-page bears date 1648. A single glance at the book is enough to see that we have in it not only most delightful poetry, but a most delightful poet. Herrick takes at once a personal aspect.

On this matter there is one difficulty, — a difficulty which would hardly be worthy of note in just this place[3] were it not that it has led several Herrick lovers somewhat astray. It lies in the fact that the poems of the *Hesperides* (there are more than eleven hundred of them) are printed in one grand confusion, to which no one has as yet succeeded in finding the clue. And the consequence is that in comparatively few cases can we affix a date to this poem or that. This matter, which seems at first a mere scholarly bother, is really of some importance ; for the

---

[1] They may be found in G. or P., and are as follows : *The Description of a Woman, His Daughter's Dowry, His Farewell unto Poetry, A Carol presented to Dr. Williams, His Mistress to him at his Farewell, Upon Parting, Upon Master Fletcher's Incomparable Plays, The New Charon,* and the *Epitaph on the Tomb of Sir Edward Giles,* — this last, by the way, first printed from the church at Dean Prior by Dr. Grosart.

[2] Speaking exactly, the name *Hesperides* is given on the title-page to *The Works both Human and Divine* (see p. lxvi), but it is more commonly confined to the secular poems.

[3] To the student it is of course important. I have thought it better to reserve any particular discussion of the matter until later (pp. xlviii–liv).

poems of the *Hesperides* seem so inconsistent that, unless we can form some conception of different times of composition, they present to us discordances which are really more ridiculous than serious, but which we should be glad to avoid. For the present it will be enough to bear this fact in mind, and with such caution to turn at once to a consideration of Herrick's poetry.

II. THE HESPERIDES.

Best loved, I think, if not best known of all Herrick's poems, are such as celebrate the old-time customs of the country year. They are the truest English pastorals that we have. Whether it be but an invitation to Anthea to the wake (763) or some more formal praise of country life for Endymion Porter (664), the atmosphere is always in harmony and the touch is always true.[1]

From Yule around again to Yule, the due celebration of the country calendar was dear to the poet, and we feel that we never touch his life more surely than when

---

[1] Perhaps absolute accuracy would compel us to make exceptions of the very few cases in these poems where Herrick gives way to the fashion of his time, and writes of "enamell'd meads" (664) or "damask'd meadows" (106). Such expressions are very rare in those poems of Herrick which seem inspired by the country. In 577 there are a number and so in some other poems, but these poems have not the country atmosphere, and there are other reasons for supposing them to be earlier than Herrick's life in Devonshire, v. p. lii. As to the fashion itself, it was not uncommon in the days of Charles I., as one may see by reading Carew. We may even find examples in Milton's *Arcades* and *Comus*. Nowadays such artificial imagery generally strikes us as in false taste. Tennyson's "slow dropping veils of thinnest lawn" in the *Lotus Eaters*, called forth some comment on this very ground.

we read the verses thereby inspired. "Sweet Country life," he writes,

> " to such unknown
> Whose lives are others', not their own,
> But serving courts and cities, be
> Less happy, less enjoying thee."

In this poem to Endymion Porter (664) thus so well begun, he compresses the cheerful round of times transshifting into a few lines.

> " For sports, for pageantry, and plays,
> Thou hast thy eves and holidays,
> Thy wakes, thy quintels, here thou hast,
> Thy Maypoles too with garlands grac'd,
> Thy morris-dance, thy Whitsun-ale,
> Thy shearing-feast, which never fail,
> Thy harvest home, thy wassail bowl, ·
> That's toss'd up after fox-i'-th'-hole,
> Thy mummeries, thy Twelf-tide kings
> And queens, thy Christmas revellings — "[1]

These lines might almost serve us as a list of Herrick's country poems, for wake, quintel, and maypole, wassail bowl and harvest home, Christmas and Twelfthtide revellings, each called forth a special verse, and some more than one. The succession of Christmas holly, box at Candlemas, Easter yew and Whitsun birch, was sung by him. The horses of the hock-cart, decked with white linen and crowned with garlands of oak-leaves, were objects of his care. He sees to it that future ages shall understand the true ingredients of the wassail bowl, nor was he above immortalizing those potent charms which

---

[1] The best illustrations of these poems of Herrick's are to be found in Brand, *Popular Antiquities* (ed. Ellis., 3 vols., London, 1846), often quoted in the Notes. Herrick did Brand good service in illustrating the country customs of England, and now the debt is well repaid by the wealth of illustration that Brand affords Herrick.

prevent the night-hag's entangling the horses' tails, or enable the maids the more easily to light the fire.

In the longer eclogues there is sometimes a touch of Horace.[1]   When he compares his brother's happy lot with that of the industrious merchant

> "who for to find
> Gold runneth to the Western. Inde,"

we have a dim recollection of the Odes.[2]

But Herrick's love for the country went far deeper than mere elegant classicism.   To Endymion Porter (664) he writes :

> "Yet thou dost know
> That the best compost for the lands
> Is the wise master's feet and hands."

This is an old English proverb and rings as true as

> "The smell of morning's milk and cream " (375).

Whoever will read Herrick's reminiscences of Marlowe's "Come live with me" (*To Phillis*, 523) will see how much more substantial were the delights offered by the later poet, — more substantial, and, we may add, more of them.

English Pastorals may these poems be called, and that in the truest sense of the word.   But it is not to be thought that Herrick, trained in the atmosphere of the

---

[1] The best authority in the matter of Herrick's indebtedness to the classics is A. W. Pollard, whose edition of Herrick is full of the most interesting comparisons with passages from Latin and Greek. Mr. Pollard provides much, but he has evidently more of the same kind in reserve, and it is rather tantalizing that the limits of his edition did not allow him to be as detailed in his illustration as would apparently have been easy for him.   On this poem see his edition, I, 267.

[2] Made more definite, the recollection would perhaps be of *Od.* I, i, 17.   Compare also the following lines of the poem (106).

Universities, and in the somewhat conventional school of the Elizabethan lyrists, would not have conceived of other pastorals, less homely in character, and less genuine in their ring. Even in the truer sort there is not wanting some mention of Phyllis and Themilis. So there are others, too, less redolent of the harvest fields of Devonshire, which celebrate the shepherds and shepherdesses of that vaguely mythic Arcadia which has been in all literary periods a favorite wandering-place for poetic fancies. Shortly after his coming into Devonshire, Herrick celebrated the birth of Prince Charles in a *Pastoral* (213; cf. the note), which was set by Mr. Nic: Laniere, and presented to the king. The speakers are Mirtillo, Amintas, and Amarillis, who bear a garland, an oaten pipe, and a sheephook, as gifts to the infant prince. In another Pastoral (422) sung before the king, Mirtillo bewails the loss of Amarillis to the sympathetic consolation of Montano and Silvio, his companions. In another, *A Bucolic; or Discourse of Neat-herds* (718), two rival swains contend in song and with the pipe, while Lalage listens to adjudge the victory. And in another Bucolic (986) Lacon endeavors with but ill success to console Thyrsis for the loss of a lovely steer, bitten and killed by a mad dog. Conventional these pastorals certainly are and largely lacking in the qualities which make the others delightful. But because they were written by Herrick they have a certain charm and a naturalness, which makes them by no means uninteresting. The local color, at least, is generally true, and had we no other pastorals of the more truly country quality, we might well be half-satisfied with these.

As every one knows Herrick as the poet of old-time custom and tradition, so also are we apt to think of him as the poet of revelry and good-companionship. Perhaps as well known as any of the poet's presumed characteristics is a cheerfully bacchanalian tendency. "'To Live Merrily and to trust to Good Verses'" is, in many minds, the motto of the poet's life. Not wholly consistent with the gravity of the priestly character, the delight in conviviality is looked on with kindly indulgence by the poet's admirers, and taken to be a minor failing that we can very well excuse. Now it is quite true that the general tone of Herrick's work is cheerful; true also that some of his poems are distinctly bacchanalian. *A Lyric to Mirth* (111) is characteristic. So also *The Welcome to Sack* (197), and *The Farewell* (128), and *A Bacchanalian Verse* (655). But most of these, I incline to think, must have been the product of his London life, or of his years in Cambridge. Not that our poet, when he left the delights of London life for Devonshire, lost all desire or liking for the pleasures of conviviality. He was doubtless as good a companion as ever. But there is nothing to show that he was more devoted to conviviality than would be proper enough even in a clergyman of to-day, let alone one in his own freer time. He still wrote an ode to Bacchus now and then, or in his poems raised the thyrse, but on the whole he must have taken more delight in the simple country pleasures which had then, perhaps, all the charm for him of novelty. It is more reasonable and agrees better with such little evidence as we possess to think of Herrick's real excesses as past and gone with his younger days, when he was, perhaps, one of those sealed of the Tribe of Ben, and made one of the company at "those lyric feasts, made at the Sun, the Dog, the Triple Tun." [1]

---

[1] Such also was the opinion of Dr. Grosart, but on grounds which appear to me insufficient. Dr. Grosart seems to assume (I, lxxi, clxxi) that it would have been more natural if such poems of revelry

But if the poet paid further rites to Bacchus only in form, to Venus he was perhaps more faithful. Of all Herrick's many charming verses, few are more charming than the best of the multitude written to his "many dainty mistresses." Many indeed they were (if they were at all); the list is a long one, beginning with the immortal Julia and coming down to vague Irenes and Myrrhas. And very charming are they too, Anthea, Perilla, Corinna, and many others. But none is more than an alluring figure half remembered from the glimpses of a dream. It is as though we really wandered in that beautiful western garden where the golden apples hung, and saw the wood-nymphs here and there among the trees, beautiful but shy. Julia alone stays to be seen.[1]

had been written before Herrick entered the ministry of the Gospel, and then chides Mr. Edmund Gosse (I, cxciii) for having allowed himself to be deceived by the minglement of earlier and later poems in the *Hesperides.* My own grounds for believing most of these out-and-out bacchanalian poems to be early are somewhat different, and cannot very well be rehearsed here (*Diss.*, §§ 6–9, especially pp. 37, 49, 50). In the place cited I tried to date certain poems by reference to external facts, by metrical peculiarities, and by some other consid-erations, and finding among the poems, which for such reasons could be placed before 1629, a certain similarity not found in those which came later, I added to them some other poems which I could not otherwise date. By such means I found that most of the poems in which the convivial note is most loud were to be judged early, and as this result agreed with what would otherwise have seemed natural, as well as with the tone of the *Farewell to Poetry*, I arrived at the opinion expressed above.

[1] Mr. Edmund Gosse (*Seventeenth Century Studies*, p. 123) thinks that Julia was actually Herrick's mistress, that she bore him a daughter, and that she "died or passed away before Herrick left Cambridge." As to the last point there is not much ground for argument. But I must confess that *His Daughter's Dowry* does not seem to me any more reason for giving the poet a daughter than is *His Age*, 333 (stanzas 12, 15, 16), for providing him with a son. Both son and daughter are, to my mind, most likely imaginary.

Of Julia we may form some notion if we like, for Herrick loved to write of her. He celebrates her petticoat pounced with stars, her hair bundled up in a golden net, her glittering silks shot with silver, her curious laces, and her lawny ferns, the soft perfumes that accompanied her. We may even imagine her beauty, or, at least, the poet is willing to help us out :

342. "UPON HIS JULIA.

Will ye heare, what I can say
Briefly of my Julia?
Black and rowling is her eye,
Double chinn'd, and forehead high :
Lips she has, all ruby red,
Cheeks like creame enclareted :
And a nose that is the grace
And proscenium of her face.
So that we may guess by these,
The other parts will richly please."

He writes of gifts that passed between them, a ring or a pomander bracelet, of Julia's illness and recovery, of his absence from her. Julia he connects with his curious mythical imaginings, with his glowing zeal for that strange cult of his, concerning which there is more to be said later. And Julia is the object of endless little poems embodying numberless lover's conceits as to her pearly teeth, her ruby lips, her delicate skin, her sweet breath, and what not.

As to whether there ever was a Julia one may believe pretty much as one desires. We can learn but little from the poems. It is more than probable that Herrick at one time and another in his life felt the scourge of Venus, and more than probable too is it that the object of his devotion inspired him to verse. So far one can go with the utmost safety. But to assume that all the poems to Julia represent actualities, to assume even that they are all addressed to the same real person or to any real person at all, and then to seek to reconstruct the old and long-lost fact from its ashes, all this is beyond the function of criticism or beyond its power. It seems uncritical to imagine that the Julia to whom the three-score and odd poems were addressed had no real prototype. But it is equally uncritical to imagine that all the poems in question were addressed to one and the same real person. We can put our finger here and there on certain of the poems to Julia, to Anthea, to Electra, and say with certainty, "This was a real woman." But farther we cannot go save in fancy.

And as food for fancy, these poems provide us with much that is of Herrick's best. *The Nightpiece to Julia* (621) and the lines *To Anthea* (267) are among the most often quoted of the poet's work. Only less fine and exquisite are the serious lines *To Perilla* (14), the looked-for farewell *To his Lovely Mistresses* (636), and the fine morning song, *Corinna's going a-Maying* (178). To tell the truth, little is gained (save scientific accuracy) by knowing whether there were real Julias and Antheas or not. Indeed, curiosity in such matters is rather apt to blind us to the poetry in our search for the reality. One gains the true pleasure from them without bother as to whether there ever were or were not some one whom the poet loved, and loved to think of as Julia, or Anthea, or Perilla. No footnote "This is a fact" is needed.

But whether there were or were not those to whom these many poems were written, no such doubt attaches to another set of poems, numerous though hardly so interesting, namely, those written by Herrick to his friends. These were the poems which, so Grosart thinks, were designed by the poet for a special collection for his

Book of the Just (Wks. I, cxiv-cxx, cxxii). I have already tried, elsewhere, to show that there is no evidence to convince us that Herrick ever designed any collection of this sort. But though no formal collection was ever planned, it is hardly to be doubted that Herrick often thought with pleasure of the circle of his friends and of the poems he had written to celebrate their glories. And a very gracious and interesting collection is thus made. Although the poems themselves are, as a whole, far inferior to those of which we have just spoken, yet they have a human interest that makes them fascinating. A recent article[1] discusses many of those to whom these poems were written, and we shall have merely to call attention in the notes to the chief matters of interest.

If there be one thing noticeable in these poems, and one thing interesting, it is the poet's estimate of himself and of his verse. Horatian here, as in many other respects,[2] the poet felt a pleasant satisfaction in thinking that those whom he chose for friends, received by virtue of that choice a brevet for immortality. He may often

---

[1] By A. W. Pollard, *Macmillan's Magazine*, LXVII, 142.

[2] That Herrick resembled Horace in some ways, if not in others, needs very little illustration. His editors have pointed out the resemblance of his poetic quality to Martial and Catullus. As far as the formal qualities of their poetry are concerned, Horace and Herrick have not much in common; but in spirit they have a great deal. How much of the similarity we may set down to conscious imitation on the part of the younger poet may be a matter of question, although I am inclined to think but little. When we say Herrick's temper was Horatian, we mean that he loved a simple country life better than a more formal courtly existence, that he was devoted to many lovely mistresses and to many friends and patrons, that he looked forward to death with melancholy certainty, but that he firmly trusted to the excellence of his work to give him immortality. Each poet had much that the other lacked, but there was much also in common.

have felt, too, when with those who were richer or of nobler birth than himself, with those who were in those days his patrons, that the time would come when the balance would hang the other way and he should be able to return with splendid interest the favors received in this world.

Mingled with such a feeling was, for a time at least, the more or less frank imitation of Ben Jonson and the tradition of the Tribe of Ben. But this the difference in circumstances made less important. For Herrick in his best days was not a great poet surrounded by lesser lights, but rather a poet who lived by himself, whose friends were rather men of the world than men of letters. Now and then he speaks of his "righteous Tribe," but the expression is clearly but a reminiscence of the days of the Devil Tavern. The chief thought was that of his chosen friends his genius made a group, a gathering, which after-ages would gladly know and hold in mind, and this fancy of his expressed itself in varying poetic forms. Sometimes the circle of his friends is a City set with Heroes, sometimes a Calendar of rare Saintships, sometimes a Gem in an eternal Coronet. Sometimes they form his righteous Tribe, sometimes he thinks of them as Stars in a Poetic Firmament. Or they are a Plantation or a College. His poems, written for them, he calls a Poetic Liturgy or a Testament.[1] And for this Liturgy, this Testament, he has naturally an affectionate feeling, indeed for all his verses and for his book. Not every day, nor time of day, was fit to write, nor was every day fit to read. The good spirit must be present or the poet's effort was vain. And the reader, too, must be well tempered and attuned to the poet's work. As was

[1] For some discussion of this question, v. G., I, cxviii; P., I, 314, and *Diss.*, pp. 12-15.

more customary then than nowadays, his verses got abroad, were copied and passed from hand to hand ; some were published in a more or less fragmentary form. And so he gathered them together for publishing and prepared to send them forth into the world. He looked upon his collection as one would look upon a favorite child about to start out in the world to make his fortune. He hopes that there will be such as will be kind to it, and bespeaks the patronage of his friends and of other souls akin to his. So also does he somewhat fear an evil reception at the hands of the ill-disposed, and against this he steels his heart and calls down various evils on the unappreciative.

6. "TO THE SOUR READER.

> If thou dislik'st the piece thou light'st on first,
> Think that of all, that I have writ, the worst:
> But if thou read'st my Book unto the end,
> And still dost this, and that verse, reprehend,
> O perverse man ! If all disgustful be,
> The extreme scab take thee and thine for me."

Even a worse lot is not absent from his mind. Books come to other uses than merely to be read, and so may his. He sometimes conjures up sad pictures (846, 962, 1127), the fire, the grocer's shop, the careless reader.

In general, however, Herrick trusted to his verse to find a good reception, and believed that his book could take care of itself, and not only of itself but of its maker as well. Not only should his friends have immortality, but far more would he himself remain in the minds of men, his name engraven on a pillar more enduring than many of those set up for such as in their day had had much greater fame than his.[1]

---

[1] It is worth noting as characteristic of the poetry of the time, poetry largely marked by fashion and by fancy, that the last poem

These poems border closely upon the autobiographical. Nor are there lacking many more strictly of such a character. More even than most lyric poets does Herrick take his readers into his confidence, or perhaps we ought to say that in minor matters he is more garrulous and confidential. We have many poems in which he celebrates the circumstances of his domestic life. Mostly do these seem to be poems of Devonshire; they give us the life of the vicar, rather than the student's life, or the young poet's in London. We hear much of his content in the country and of his grange or private wealth. He lived, as has already been said, with Prudence Baldwin, his housekeeper, with Tracy, his spaniel, Phil, the sparrow, with the goose and the kitling, and, if tradition tells aright, with that convivial pig, whose name is unknown and whom the poet seemed to think unworthy of immortality.

In his parsonage in Devonshire, Herrick lived a pleasant, peaceful life, — a life which he heartily enjoyed despite the recurrence now and then of the reminiscence of wilder days of unrestrained mirth. The simple things of the country were a great delight to him and he heartily loved the old-fashioned country ways. Still it cannot be denied that at times he hated Devonshire with a fierce and bitter hatred. There is no doubtful sound in some half a dozen poems.[1]

in the *Hesperides*, the poem in which Herrick expresses the idea just mentioned, is written in the actual form of a pillar. So one of the last poems in the *Noble Numbers* is in the form of a cross. Readers of contemporary poetry will not be at a loss for illustrations. We may note particularly *Easter Wings* and *The Altar*, by George Herbert, as examples of the same fashion influencing a mind of very different character.

[1] 51, 86, 278, 458, 715.

458. "UPON HIMSELF.

Come leave this loathed country-life, and then
Grow up to be a Roman Citizen.
Those mites of time, which yet remain unspent,
Waste thou in that most civil government.
Get their comportment, and the gliding tongue
Of those mild men, thou art to live among:
Then being seated in that smoother Sphere
Decree thy everlasting topic there.
And to the farm-house ne'er return at all,
Though granges do not love thee, cities shall."

And in another poem, written it may be on his final
return to London, we have the same thought:

715. "HIS RETURN TO LONDON.

From the dull confines of the drooping West,
To see the day spring from the pregnant East,
Ravish'd in spirit, I come . . .
. . . I am a free-born Roman; suffer then,
That I amongst you live a citizen.
London my home is, though by hard fate sent
Into a long and irksome banishment;
Yet since call'd back, henceforward let me be,
O native country, repossess'd by thee!
For, rather than I'll to the West return,
I'll beg of thee first here to have mine urn.
Weak I am grown, and must in short time fall,
Give thou my sacred reliques burial."

Rather more importance than they deserve has been
given to such poems, or rather, no effort has been made
to reconcile them with those which express feelings quite
the reverse. It may be that no explanation is necessary,
and yet a word or two will not be out of place. Such
differences of feeling may be thought of in several ways.
It is not impossible that the poems expressing delight in
the country were all written in the earlier years of his

life in Devonshire and the others in later years. We may hold that the poet was at first charmed, but that in time he became weary. Or precisely the contrary may have been the case. He may at first have been constantly longing to return to London, but on a longer stay and a truer sympathy he may have given up his earlier hatred and become filled with a feeling quite the reverse. Or, again, it is perfectly comprehensible that both series of poems should have been the fruit of the same series of years. A man of moods will think his surroundings first detestable and then delightful, or *vice versa*, not only in the course of a single year, but in the course of a single day. We must remember that these poems of Herrick are not necessarily the record of continued thought or feeling. A single half-hour of despondency may have stamped itself into eternity by a fortunate verse, and so outweigh months of less expressive pleasure. Some such view as this last seems, on the whole, most comprehensible. Herrick sometimes hated Devonshire, sometimes loved it. We might think that it depended on the weather, were it not that the poems which express disgust are far fewer than we should then imagine.

So we must not allow these examples of impatience, or of a temper colored by the blues, to do more than modify our notion of Herrick's attachment to the country. The instances of his thorough delight and appreciation are far too many. He was evidently delighted in the sights and sounds of country life, in its sport and in its labor, in all the great things and little which went to make up the daily round.

Mr. Gosse has noticed that Herrick's pleasure in country scenery is almost entirely of the domestic sort. To tell the truth, we should hardly expect to find in Herrick's day and generation the same pleasure in the wildness and ruggedness of natural scenery that exists in ours. The most beautiful country sight to Herrick, whether in Devonshire or elsewhere, lay in the country flowers. Perhaps he had a garden of his own. But we never hear anything of his cultivating it, and it may well be fancied that the poet was wise enough to know that for one who loves flowers in a poetical way only, a friend's garden is as good as one's own and oftentimes better.

In his earlier days, it may have been that Herrick loved to imagine how

> " All the shrubs, with sparkling spangles, show
> Like morning sun-shine tinselling the dew.
> Here, in green meadowes, sits eternall May,
> Purfling the margents, while perpetual day
> So double gilds the air, as that no night
> Can ever rust th' enamel of the light." [1]

And in such a time and temper it was enough, we may think, to have the conventional wreaths of roses and myrtles and lilies, or the crowns of ivy and laurel and bays. But in after years, I take it, his affections grew, and in the garden of his thoughts, at least, he had great luxuriance. The primrose ("the sweet Infanta of the year"), the gilliflower (does he call it July flower in jest?) and the marigold he had, and a many others too, wall-flowers and daffodils, rosemary and rue, pansies and pinks, tulips and hyacinths, violets and daisies, jessamine and cowslips, eglantine and honeysuckle and sweet-briar and woodbine. A stretch of the imagination was it, perhaps, when he would have orange flowers and almond blossoms for Lady Abdie (375).

A favorite fancy with Herrick was of a sort of evolution more poetical in a sense than that of Darwin, though

---

[1] *The Apparition of his Mistress* (577).

not so well substantiated by the order of the universe.
He writes:

> 505. "HOW MARIGOLDS CAME YELLOW.
>
> Jealous girls these sometimes were,
> While they liv'd, or lasted here:
> Turn'd to flowers still they be
> Yellow mark'd for jealousy."

So also he tells us how roses first came red (where he
offers two hypotheses) and lilies white. So also can he
tell us of the wall-flower, how it came first and why it had
its name. He found out how violets came blue and
primroses green: he even formulates a theory of *Why
Flowers change Color* (37). So far did his love of science
carry him. In general, however, he was well content to
enjoy the flowers' loveliness without care for their origin.

And not only in their beauty but in their fragrance.
Herrick, in common with many other poets, took a keen
delight in the beautiful things that appeal to the senses.
But though many other poets have enjoyed such things
as please the eye and the ear, and even the touch, Herrick stands almost alone among the poets in his leaning
to the delights of perfume. In this characteristic he
resembled Mahomet. Like the gardens of paradise, Herrick's *Hesperides* is pervaded by the odor of burning incense and fragrant gums. Between the trees and under
the golden apples passes the beautiful Julia, dispensing
aromatics from her rustling silks.

> " How can I choose but love and follow her
> Whose shadow smells like milder pomander!
> How can I choose but kisse her, whence does come
> The storax, spikenard, myrrh, and ladanum." (487.)

A pomander, by the way, was a mixture of perfume
carried in a silver ball: Julia, who was, doubtless, well

aware of her poet's fancies, sent Herrick a pomander bracelet. The right pomander, it appears, was made of labdanum, benzoin, both storaxes, ambergris, civet, and musk. For civet Herrick seems to have had no especial affection, and for aught we know he was acquainted with one kind of storax only. But in the other ingredients mentioned he delighted, as also in balm ("the Arabian dew" he calls it), galbanum, cassia, frankincense and myrrh. His imagination went back to the costly spikenard of ancient days, and he loved to chafe a bit of amber until it gave forth its warm fragrance. In fact, Herrick was clearly an amateur in perfumes. But not only the perfumes of commerce were his joy, ambergris from the West Indies and gums from the East, but everywhere about him in the country did he revel in all the many opportunities given by flower and fruit. Most fragrant of all his poems are the lines *To the Most Fair and Lovely Mistress Anne Soame* (375), which are heavy with essence of jessamine, with orange-flowers and almond-blossoms, not forgetting, on the one hand, the amber bracelet and the maiden pomander, or, on the other, "the smell of morning's milk and cream," or "of roasted warden or baked pear."[1] Nor was he unconscious of his peculiar sensibility, as witness the lines in 98, *Being once Blind, his Request to Biancha:*

[1] The argument that Herrick cared for perfumes is of course based largely on the frequency with which he mentions them. Compare the *Hesperides* with all Shakespeare's plays, for instance. Further it may be held that although reference to the more commonly known perfumes argues but little (for such allusion might readily be conventional), yet the noticing such odors as, for example, in the last half of the verses to Lady Abdie, shows that the sense of smell was far more developed with him than with most men. The goddess Isis, who at one time absorbed some of his attention, appears to have been especially fascinating through her fragrance (cf. note to 197).

> "Go then afore, and I shall well
> Follow thy perfumes by the smell."

His love for perfumes was greater than his love for music, and yet there are not a few little poems scattered here and there which show that the poet was at least not unacquainted with musical pleasures. He seems to have known the best composers of the day, either personally or by reputation. His songs were set by Henry Lawes and by Ramsey, and he refers to William Lawes, Dr. Wilson, Lanier, and Gouter. And whatever knowledge of music or feeling for it he might have had, he once or twice found a very perfect expression for what he heard, as in the lines *To Music to becalm his Fever* (227):

> " Fall on me like a silent dew,
>   Or like those maiden showers,
> Which by the peep of day, do strew
>   A baptime o'er the flowers."

Julia could sing and play, it would appear, — the poet thinks of her walking in her chamber

> "Melting melodious words to lutes of amber."

There is not very much in the *Hesperides* that reminds us that Herrick was a clergyman. Indeed, according to our modern conception of the priestly character, his poetry, as far as we have already spoken of it, is not merely secular in quality, but even unclerical. Later we shall turn our attention to the *Noble Numbers*, or the poems with which Herrick sought to make amends, as it were, for the unpriestly character of the *Hesperides*. We shall see that, though not by any means the equals of his secular poetry, they are at least sincere, and they do indicate a religious side of his character of which without them we should·have hardly dreamed. But although a sincere religious seriousness may well have been either a phase in Herrick's life or a thread running through his whole character, it will be readily acknowledged that we find in his temper and his work little of that glowing zeal which marks Herbert, or of that religious ecstasy which marks Crashaw. Some of Herrick's work is seriously devout, but there is little religious enthusiasm. Yet the time was one when religious enthusiasm was in the air.

It seems to me that Herrick's nature had its devotional side, but that he found little in the church of which he was a priest which called it forth. Had he been a Roman Catholic, the case might very possibly have been different; but as it was, it seems evident that the religious side of his nature found little expression in the directions which appear to us to have been the most natural. There is no reason to suppose that Herrick slighted the duties of his position; but, except for the few poems in the *Noble Numbers* which ring true, there is little reason to suppose that he went into those duties heart and soul. It was not that there was no opportunity, it was that somehow Herrick never saw the opportunity. So the devotional side of his character frittered itself away. Occasionally it rose to the seriousness of the lines *To his Sweet Saviour* (*N. N.*, 77); occasionally, perhaps, he put his heart into the traditional usages of the country, finding there expression for the feeling that might have been turned elsewhere, — and occasionally his religious emotion was strangely turned and formed by the strength of his own fancy.

To Herrick the two greatest things of life were Love and Death, — and his mind turned constantly to the thought of one or the other. And finding in his own religion no true satisfaction for his whole feeling, it would really seem as though he had sometimes fancied, half-seriously, half in sport, a strange cult of imaginary deities in the ritual of whose service, had it ever existed, he might have found a satisfaction which was given to him nowhere else. More than a fancy this could not be, and yet it gives the feeling to some of the most curious and even, in some cases, the most sincere of his poems.

Several times he bids his mistress to remember the proper funeral rites when he shall die., The lines *To Perilla* (14) certainly have strength of feeling behind them, and certainly that feeling is neither Christian nor what we should call pagan. *To Anthea* (22) is less earnest, but it may be mentioned as well. So *His Charge to Julia* (629). But the other verses *To Anthea* (55) are again full of emotion. It is true that the main thought of these poems is one which might well exist in any serious-minded man, and which is observable elsewhere in Herrick. Still the curious definiteness of circumstance, the prescribing of these strange ceremonies, invented or borrowed from any source, is a different note.

As with death, so with love. In "Love's Religion"[1] Julia was *Flaminica Dialis*, and the poem written to her with that name (541) is very curious. Even if written before taking orders (Mr. Gosse thinks it was), the last two lines are such as strike the attention, to say nothing more. As Julia was the Queen Priest, so was Herrick the *Rex Sacrorum* (*To Julia*, 976). There were altars erected to the mysterious gods, — altars which must be served with diligence and devotion under pain of high displeasure (cf. also *To Electra*, 838). In *The Sacrifice* (872) he gives us a snatch of the ritual, and in *To Groves* (451) we have a hint of the martyrology and the calendar of saints.

To take these poems seriously would of course be folly. Herrick might bring into his verse strange allusions to

[1] The phrase occurs in the lines *To his Mistresses* (38).

some mystic cult whose gods were Love and Death, but he never believed in any such strange gods. No, nor did he ever seriously conceive them. But so many poems as we have in this strange strain show us an inarticulate passion, an emotional nature, which, could it have found the right channel, would have grown strong and vigorous. These religious dreams were dreams and nothing more, but not the dreams of a Christian nor dreams of the gods of Greece and Rome. His gods were the shadowy figures of his own fancy. They were like the terrible imaginings of a child in the dark: he knows to a certainty that no one is there and yet feels sure that some one is.

As here Herrick seems to have gods of his own, so in yet a greater degree had he his own private gods to guard his household. More properly speaking there was his one household god or Lar. Perhaps he too obtained with the poet an affectionate reality: "Jocund Lar" (427) or "Lucky Lar" (333) he calls him, or the "Good Demon" (334). But sometimes he thinks of more than one, the Lares (478) or Closet Gods (654).

To the gods of Greece and Rome, or, more properly speaking, of Rome only, Herrick paid proper poetic worship, and of them he made the conventional use. He even went a step farther and wrote a little cycle of poems, one to each of the greater gods, promising that if they would be auspicious he would offer appropriate sacrifice: to Apollo, swans; to Bacchus, daffodils; to Neptune, a tunnyfish; to Venus, myrtles; to Juno, a peacock; to Mars, a wolf; and to Minerva, a broadfaced owl. So also to Aesculapius was a verse dedicated when the poet was in great grief over the illness of Prudence Baldwin. He promised a cock if she should recover, and let us hope he paid the vow, for Prudence did not die (just then), but lived on for thirty years or more.

With whatever unction Herrick celebrated the rites of the church on those occasions which are ever recurrent in life, he was at least careful that the muses at such seasons should not remain unforgotten. Hence we have a number of Epithalamia and a number of Epitaphs, and among them are some very characteristic poems. Bachelor though he was, and though he sometimes swore he would never curtail his freedom by taking a wife, yet Herrick was warm-hearted and of a loving nature. To him a marriage among his friends seems to have been the occasion for true delight and happiness. Lover as he often was, the ideal beauty and sweetness of the union of two lovers had a powerful effect upon him, an effect which, had he been of stronger and nobler mind, would have produced finer poems, but which, as it was, has given us some of the best specimens of a form of poetry now almost neglected. And as the thought of marriage had for him a great fascination, so also did the thought of death exercise over his mind a domination no less imperious than the other because it appears more subdued. We have already seen that he often thought of his own end. Sometimes it was so far only as to write a little verse to the Robin Redbreast to take care of him when he could no longer take care of himself, or to the Cypresses to grow beside his grave, or to the grave-digger, called in kindly wise the bedmaker, and sometimes it was merely in a line or two coming at the end of a poem in a lighter vein. One of his longer poems, wherein he celebrates his pleasure in his home and in his friend John Wickes, begins with an imitation of " Eheu fugaces." So, often thoughtful of his own end, Herrick was moved, too, by the death of others. The titles of his Epitaphs are significant and pathetic. *Upon a Child; Upon a Virgin; Upon a Maid that Died the Day She was*

Married; Upon a Lady that Died in Childbed and left a Daughter behind Her; Upon a Sober Matron; Upon an Old Man, a Residentiary. If Herrick was always impressed in his own case with the necessity of death, so in the case of others did he always see the pathos. It needs no great effort of the imagination to think of the old vicar who delighted so keenly in so many of the charming things of the charming world about him, gazing wistfully forward to the necessary end, brought continually to his mind by the passing of those to whom death must have come as a stranger.

Another set of poems in the *Hesperides*, — and poems they are, almost unique in English literature, — are the Gnomic Couplets or Sententious Distichs. Wise sayings are these: sometimes we find quatrains, but, as a rule, some aphorism is compressed into two lines that might almost make a stone for the mosaic of Pope. Of these little snatches there are in the *Hesperides* several hundred. They deserve far more the name " epigram " than do the quatrains to which that name is usually given (v. inf. lxiv, lxv). For the quatrains are, on the whole, entirely lacking in that concise point which we nowadays consider necessary to the epigram, whereas the couplets usually possess that characteristic to a marked degree.

I am inclined to think that these couplets were largely written toward the end of Herrick's life in Devonshire.[1] But whenever they were written they are an element in the *Hesperides* which has been passed over with too little

---

[1] See *Diss.*, pp. 44 ff. The points of evidence are that they occur sparely in the earlier part of the book, but with great frequency toward the end; that there are very many of them in the *Noble Numbers*, presumably written, to speak generally, after the *Hesperides;* that they agree in versification with Herrick's later views on verse; and that they are more in accord with the temper of middle years than with that of youth.

comment. Wholly aside from any value in subject matter, they offer evidence of a certain characteristic of Herrick's mode of expression which is important. I mean the ability to put an idea into concise and clear-cut utterance, the same ability that is such a marked characteristic of the genius of Pope and of the other poets who are usually thought of in connection with Pope. Of this there will be more to say in another place; at present it is of more interest to note the ground covered by these little poems. A great number are reflections called forth by the political events of the time. And as such they are of value in determining how Herrick stood on the great questions which in his day divided England. It has always been a common opinion, first, that Herrick stood almost entirely aloof from the controversy of his time, and, second, that he was an ardent and devoted Royalist. Although these views will by no means be reversed on a careful reading of his sententious utterances on politics, yet such a reading will give us a more accurate idea of what is meant by such statements than we have previously had. Undoubtedly, when we compare Herrick with Milton or Marvell, on the one hand, or with Suckling or Lovelace, on the other, we may say that he stood aloof from the quarrels of his time, as far at least as action is concerned. But as to the field of thought, we shall see from these couplets that the stormy state of things about him by no means left him unaffected.[1] It is true that it will not do to infer his opinions wholesale from these couplets. Doubtless they were not infrequently the expression of some notion that took his fancy for the time being, and could be hardly said to make up a part of his serious opinion (P., I, xxv). But where there are so many evi-

[1] See also *The Bad Season makes the Poet Sad* (614) and *Upon the Troublesome Times* (598).

dences of consideration as here, we cannot well say that the poet was wholly unmoved. To tell the truth, Herrick seems to have had opinions that were quite definite, if not extraordinary. He was a Royalist, in that he was loyal always to the person of the king. A Royalist, also, in that he approved theoretically of the royal power. But that he was an undiscriminating Royalist, a Royalist who backed the king in everything, good or bad, a firm believer that "the king can do no wrong," cannot be maintained. He had strong opinions on the duty of kings toward their people.

782. MODERATION.

In things a moderation keep,
Kings ought to shear, not skin their sheep.

863. KINGS AND TYRANTS.

Twixt kings and tyrants there's this difference known :
Kings seek their subjects' good ; tyrants their own.

1000. PATIENCE IN PRINCES.

Kings must not use the axe for each offence :
Princes cure some faults by their patience.

1067. GENTLENESS.

That Prince must govern with a gentle hand,
Who will have love comply with his command.

It is true that there were many who held such views, theoretically, along with so strict an adherence to the "Divine right" that they approved every act of the actually reigning sovereign. It may be that Herrick was such a one. He was most certainly no republican : he had no desire for a government by the people.

538. ILL GOVERNMENT.

Preposterous is that government and rude,
When kings obey the wilder multitude.

345. THE POWER IN THE PEOPLE.

Let kings command and do the best they may,
The saucy subjects still will bear the sway.

It was natural that Herrick should have been a Royalist ; for so many of the beautiful things that he loved seemed to belong by right to the Royalists rather than to the Puritans. But we must not believe that it was only through emotional sympathy that he was loyal to the king : he had evidently given good thought to the subject.

There are many other subjects for these gnomic couplets, although none so constantly recurrent as the political situation of the day. The Horatian "Carpe Diem" supplies a few, not unnaturally; there are several on The Golden Mean. Some on the End rather than the Wayside, some on the Power of Money, some on Fame. In the *Noble Numbers* there are a number on Sin, of which two at least are worth remembering :

N. N., 37. SIN SEEN.

When once the sin has fully acted been,
Then is the horror of the trespass seen.

N. N., 86. SIN.

Sin leads the way, but as it goes, it feels
The following plague still treading on his heels.

A greater number are on sorrow and the bearing of grief ; gentle and resigned are these, some in the *Noble*

Numbers, but more in the *Hesperides;* and, lastly, there are not a few on Love, of which the best are, perhaps, 29 and 841.

We should, to-day, call such poems epigrams. But in the study of Herrick, the word "epigram" is a technical term. The poet himself applied it to a class of poems which have given his admirers much trouble. These so-called epigrams, of which there are a good number, are quatrains on various real or imaginary people, detailing each one some disagreeable personal peculiarity. They are often nasty (and that in the American sense); no other word gives their quality exactly. They are not merely coarse; they are not all indecent, but they are almost invariably nasty. It is the tradition that Herrick amused himself by writing these epigrams on his parishioners, but it is merely a tradition, and one without much foundation.[1] We have printed some specimens of them (183, 188, 206, 273, 420, 436, 503, 579, 706) that the reader might not be without means to satisfy himself on this point ; but a few are enough.

Other editors have been puzzled to know just what to do with them. Dr. Grosart, although he prints them all, feels bound to assert that Herrick never meant them for publication, that it was the publisher who insisted on using them (I, cxxi, cxxii). Mr. Pollard omits them all that they may be printed in a detachable appendix (a sort of a poetical pigsty: one pities the compositor who had to set them up in their unrelieved nastiness). Mr. Edmund Gosse says that "it must be confessed . . . that

---

[1] It is not very likely that a parish like Dean would have had so very many very disagreeable people in it as must be inferred if these epigrams have any basis in fact. If it had really so many, we need not be surprised that Herrick in time became weary of it, in spite of its beauty.

they greatly spoil the general complexion of the book." Mr. Henry Morley, so far as I know, is the only editor who has anything to say for them. "There is truth in the close contact of a playful sense of ugliness with the most delicate perception of all forms of beauty. Herrick's epigrams on running eyes and rotten teeth and the like, are such exaggerations as may often have tumbled out spontaneously in the course of playful talk, and, if they pleased him well enough, were duly entered in his book. In a healthy mind, this whimsical sense of deformity may be but the other side of a fine sense of beauty." (*Hesp.*, ed. Morley, p. 7.) Except for the suggestion that Herrick may have written more epigrams than have been preserved to us, this view seems the most satisfactory. Some such idea occurred also to Swinburne, who says, in his preface to Mr. Pollard's edition (I, xii): "It was doubtless in order to relieve this saccharine and 'mellisonant' monotony that he thought fit to intersperse these interminable droppings of natural or artificial perfumes with others of the rankest and most intolerable odor." But Swinburne does not think highly of the mixture. "A diet," he says, "of alternate sweetmeats and emetics is for the average of eaters and drinkers no less unpalatable than unwholesome." The fact is that Herrick wrote the epigrams, and that fact we cannot explain away. In part, we may set them down to a difference in feeling on certain matters on the part of the seventeenth century and the nineteenth. But even after so much has been done, even after Mr. Morley's views, Herrick's epigrams are rather a bitter pill for a lover of the poet to swallow, or rather not so much a bitter as a very badtasting one.

Although Herrick was a clergyman, yet his verse in the *Hesperides*, is, as has been said, generally not merely secular in quality but even exceedingly unclerical, according to our common conception of the priestly character. Herrick's gnomic distichs, his epitaphs, his poems to friends are not out of keeping with his office of vicar, but the main line of thought of most of the others is not precisely what we should expect of one in holy orders.

Of this discrepancy Herrick was well aware. He calls attention to it in the first poem of the *Noble Numbers*. The *Noble Numbers* are his religious verses, a separate collection altogether, published between the same covers as the *Hesperides*. At the very outset Herrick opposes these pious offerings to the more profane verse which has gone before: he makes his *Confession* (*N. N.*, 1) and his *Prayer for Absolution* (*N. N.*, 2). If the *Hesperides* is found evil, he hopes that the *Noble Numbers* will be found to make amends. With such a feeling it is a bit strange that Herrick published both, — perhaps he had at one time the notion of publishing the *Noble Numbers* only. Certainly they have a separate title-page, a different date, and independent pagination. The date is 1647. Now Herrick was ejected from his vicarage in 1648. It may be that while he was vicar he thought only of publishing his pious poems, having given up his earlier ideas of printing all his work: on losing his position he might have had many reasons which would lead him to publish all the poems he had. If there were ever doubt in his mind, it was a lucky chance for us and for his fame, which led him to publish what he did.

In whatever way the poems were published, we have in the *Noble Numbers* Herrick's sacred verse, and that as a part of his whole production. It must be confessed that it is on the whole a most inferior part, inferior in thought and inferior in handling. There are, it is true, poems which have such coloring as reminds us of the *Hesperides*. It was with these poems in mind that Mr. Edmund Gosse wrote: "Where the *Noble Numbers* are most readable is where they are most secular." Such poems do give us the idea of singing "hymns of faultless orthodoxy, with a loud and lusty voice, to the old pagan airs." Indeed the whole criticism on the *Noble Numbers* in *Seventeenth Century Studies* is sound and gives one the right idea. With a few exceptions, the *Noble Numbers* is little more than an attempt to turn the Garden of the Hesperides into a Cathedral close. There are couplets on points of theology which will balance the everyday distichs. There are sacred songs on the Circumcision or the Nativity, set and sung before the King like the pastorals of more secular character. We have the same quaint and experimental metres in both books. We have sometimes the same method (a very common one, it must be admitted), as for instance in *To Find God* (*N. N.*, 3) and *His Protestation to Perilla* (154) or *Impossibilities to his Friends* (198).

The result is in very few cases fortunate. There are hardly a dozen of the *Noble Numbers* that come up even to the average excellence of the *Hesperides*. These few it is not easy to characterize for they differ in kind and have by no means the like qualities. I should name as the best, for those who wish to study them: *The Widow's Tears*, 123; *The Dirge of Jephthah's Daughter*, 83; *Upon Time*, 38 (with a touch that reminds one of Herbert); *A Thanksgiving to God for his House*, 47 (cf. *His Winding Sheet*, 517); *To his Saviour, a Child;* 59, *To his Sweet Saviour*, 77 (which has something of the character of the best Elizabethan sonnets); *His Wish to God*, 115; *The Bellman,* 121. These are devotional poems of a high order, but unfortunately Herrick did not often reach such a level. Either it was but rarely that his imagination turned in such directions (perhaps he wrote the *Noble Numbers* on Sundays and the *Hesperides* on week days), or else it may be that it was only toward the close of his life in Devonshire that Herrick really began to feel a certain emptiness and vanity in his earlier work and that his mind really turned into serious channels. There are several reasons which support such a view as this latter. I am inclined to believe that the *Noble Numbers* were the last written poems : the poet was trying a new vein and, as it turned out, no very successful one.

IV. THE CHRONOLOGICAL EVIDENCE OF HERRICK'S POEMS.

Such then are the poems of Herrick that he presented to the world in his book. Some few others he wrote (as has been remarked on page xvii) but it is by his book that he is really and sufficiently represented. And what does his book tell us of his life? This is the first question that the scholar must ask himself, if only to get it out of the way and leave room for a freer enjoyment of the poems themselves.

Here there are somewhat varying views. As a rule those interested in the matter have been well content merely to draw this or that inference from this or that poem, and to produce, as a result, a portrait of the poet as fanciful as it was charming. Until the *Memorial Introduction* of Dr. Grosart, hardly any attempt was made to deal with the *Hesperides* critically. And yet there are few books which need more careful criticism, if we desire to obtain any information that we can rely on. It is easy enough to enjoy the *Hesperides*, but to learn anything of Herrick from his book is not so simple a matter. For the *Hesperides* is a garden without order and without arrangement. The poems of, it may be, thirty years and more appear in the most glorious confusion and with the most tantalizing silence as to their origin. When it is doubtful if Herrick were twenty or forty when he wrote one or another poem, when we do not know if two poems were written the same year or with an interval of a quarter of a century, it is quite obvious that we cannot be too cautious in drawing inferences.

In this confusion Dr. Grosart endeavored to establish some order. He formed a theory as to the different elements which make up the book as we have it, a theory for which he presented the bases in pp. cxii–cxxviii of his *Memorial Introduction.*

Concerning the views of Dr. Grosart, I have elsewhere expressed myself quite fully.[1] A careful examination of his argument seemed to show that his results were not justified. Even had they been wholly borne out, they would not have helped us very much in the question in hand. I do not know that, even at best, we shall be very much helped ; but we may at least take precaution against going astray. In such a study it is necessary to be resolute in not assuming what we desire to prove. Herrick's character is to be the result, not the basis. We cannot begin by saying, It would be most likely that a man like Herrick would have written this, or this, at such and such a time. Intellectual self-respect compels us to take the trouble to find something

[1] *Diss.,* § 4.

more substantial. Until we have otherwise determined enough poems to get an idea of the poet's character, we cannot rightly infer the date of a poem therefrom. We must first proceed by other means. Now other means are by no means numerous. A good many poems may be dated with some exactness on account of allusions to known events. *Upon his Sister-in-law, Mistress Elizabeth Herrick* (72), would have been written in 1643, the year in which Mistress Herrick died. *To the King upon his Coming with his Army into the West* (77) would naturally have been written in 1644, the year in which the expedition in question took place. Dr. Grosart and Mr. Pollard have done much toward determining such dates and I have gratefully availed myself of their work in this direction. It is also possible to say, to a limited extent, "such and such a poem is more likely to have been written in Devonshire, — or in London." But here we must not be too eager. It seems as though *The Hock-cart* (250) or *The Wake* (763) must have been written in Devonshire. So *A Frolic* (584) or *To Live Merrily* (201) should have been written during his tavern life in London. But this mode of determining is less certain.

Another help comes from a study of Herrick's versification. Everybody is familiar with the literary change of heart which sent the verse of Shakespeare out of fashion in favor of the verse of Pope. A comparison of Herrick's longer poems shows development in the same direction (pp. lvii, lviii), and so gives us conjecturally the approximate date of a good many of his longer poems. Another form of evidence, pointed out also by Mr. Pollard, lies in the general distribution of the poems. It seems probable that the greater number of poems in the first part of the *Hesperides* were written before Herrick had put together his collections in 1640, and that most of the others were written afterward. Mr. Pollard's argument is based on the presence of poems which can be dated early, in the first part only, and on the lack of MS. copies of poems in the last half. My own argument, which was made before I had seen Mr. Pollard's edition, rests chiefly upon a comparison of the poems in the latter part of the book with the Introductory Verse, and upon the prevalence of Gnomic Poems in the latter part of the *Hesperides* and in the *Noble Numbers* (*Diss.*, p. 44).

From such preliminary work as this, we may, I believe, date enough poems to give us the general drift of the poet's development. I am myself accustomed to think of three periods; having for dividing points the years 1629 and 1640. I would gladly have ground for dividing the first period into two, one of the poet's university days, the other of his days in London, but I find no special reasons. The second period includes his Devonshire life down to the time when, in 1640, he planned to publish his poems. The last would embrace the time between 1640 and the final publishing.

Of these points of division, the first is, of course, of such a nature as might readily have been expected to work a change in the feeling and character of the poet. Up to that time he had been a student at Cambridge and a young poet in London. Afterward he was a country vicar in a distant part of England. That his earlier work should be marked by qualities of exuberance and license which are not so noticeable later would be but natural. The second point of time, however, is quite arbitrary, and is chosen only because it is possible in many cases to infer that a poem comes before it or after. The gathering together of his poems for publication is, of course, a point in Herrick's life, but not such a point as necessarily marks a change in his character and way of looking at things. But some point of time must be chosen to separate the poems of Herrick's earlier mood from those which came later, and this is a convenient one to choose.

The poems which can be definitely assigned to the first period are such as bear out the conclusion we might naturally have come to without them. The two poems on Sack (128, 197), *The Farewell to Poetry* (p. 133), *The Apparition* (577), *His Daughter's Dowry, The Cruel Maid* (159), are poems all of a piece in character as well as in versification. In versification they are the work of the admirer of Jonson ; in character they are decidedly secular to say the least. The more we read them, the more are we inclined to agree with Dr. Grosart, though on different grounds, that the great number of Herrick's erotic and bacchanalian poems belong here. We are not surprised that the other evidence should put in this period the two fine Epithalamia, *To Sir Southwell and his Lady* (149), and *On Sir Clipseby Crew and his Lady* (283), which have a warmth and glow to them that is hardly in harmony with the more self-restrained character of the Devonshire poems. Here, too, would I put the fine *Corinna's going a-Maying* (178).

After he had been in Devonshire for ten years or so, Herrick gathered together his poems with a view to publication. The book was even entered in the Stationers' Register, but was not published. We can form some idea of its contents (p. li), and excluding such as we believe to have been written in Cambridge or London, we have the poems which give us our notion of Herrick during the first years of his stay in Devonshire. It is from these poems that we get the idea of Herrick the country-lover. Here come the poems on country customs and country pleasures. They are fresh and happy poems:

the poet is in love with his surroundings. If we must put here any of the poems expressing disgust of Devonshire, we may believe that they represent transitory moods rather than a prevalent temper. Whoever will read *The Hock-cart* (250), *The Wake* (763), *The Country Life* (664), *His Content in the Country* (554), *To Mrs. Anne Soame* (375), *To the Maids* (618), and *To Phillis* (523), will, I believe, have little difficulty in believing that they were written in Devonshire. And it is these poems which show especially the more restrained and indeed confined versification which we have thought characteristic of Herrick's later manner. I believe, also, that a general restraint and control will be observed in the thought and the handling.

In the later years, between 1640 and 1648, the poems take on a graver tone. The characteristic Devonshire poems have been already written: those that come at the end of the *Hesperides* are by no means among the best. The early freshness seems largely lost and we have apparently many of the sententious distichs. The *Noble Numbers*, too, would in great part seem to belong here. Here, too, come not a few poems to public persons or on public events, which latter at this time sometimes had their depressing influence on the poet. The poems on "loathed Devonshire" would hardly be so much out of place here as earlier. It may well be that Herrick was by no means sorry to be superseded.

If what has been said does not supply us with very full material for making out our poet's life, and character, it does at least one thing worth doing. It shows some rational ground for dispelling some of the contradictions that have long existed in our ideas of Herrick as a man. Herrick loved Devonshire and hated it: we have seen that there is good reason to suppose that the poems which express his affection were the product of his earlier years in his vicarage, and that later a graver tone prevails which might often have deepened into disgust. Herrick enjoyed a simple country life and yet delighted in wild orgies. But we have seen that there is good reason to suppose that the bacchanalia belong to his life in London or Cambridge, the poems of the country life to the first years in Devonshire. In some such way, too, may we think of the curious difference in Herrick's religious poetry. Some of the most secular was probably written while in London or early in Devonshire. And the most theological are all of a piece with the sententious couplets which were probably the fruit of his last years in Devonshire.

But it would be futile as well as foolish to try to make out a character for Herrick which should reduce him to the dead level of what we may imagine properly consistent. He was of a quick, emotional nature, feeling one thing now, another later. He could doubtless write, in the morning, one of the prettiest of his poems on flowers or to one of his girls, and in the evening turn out an epigram of the nastiest kind. Or else he could feel to the full the sweet gentleness of his own vicarage and of his country life, and in another hour he could pen some lines boisterous with reminiscence of his London days. One day he was calmly delighted with Devonshire, and the next he was disgusted with it. It is the good side of a study of Herrick that with the material at hand, we can never be very dogmatic; we must always leave the final imagining to each separate reader. But the general groundwork that can be settled is by no means useless, even though it do not accomplish everything.

One of the satisfying and refreshing things about Her-rick's poetry is his facility in verse-form. His words seem to bubble into metre with the spontaneous ease of a bird. Although the greater part of his work is in common forms, yet there is enough in freer mood to show that his ingenuity in this particular was practically inexhaustible, or, more accurately, that his imagination was never weary of creating new forms for his fancies.

His verse-forms vary from the conventional couplet or the stanza with alternate rhyme, to a freedom of construction that reminds one of a modern ode. And yet this freedom is never licentious ; the same structure is often carried through stanza after stanza with masterly regularity and ease. And, in writing couplets or stanzas of alternate rhyme, Herrick by no means confined himself to one given form ; we have decasyllabics, octosyllabics, and so down even to the dissyllabic triplets of 477, *Upon his Departure Hence.* Nor was he content with such diversity : even in the common following rhyme he varies the metre so as to produce the grave effect of *His Winding Sheet* (517), or *A Thanksgiving to God for His House* (*N. N.*, 47) ; the reminiscence of the classic elegiac as in *A Country Life* (106), or *A Panegyric to Sir Lewis Pemberton* (377) ; the elaborate stanzaic forms of *A Nuptial Song* (283), or *His Age* (336) ; or the delicate coloring of *To the Yew and Cypress* (280), or *The Primrose* (582). In like manner, but not with such variety, does he use the alternate rhyme, as in *Upon Julia's Hair* (486), or *His Grange* (726). Some forms where the versification may seem at first wholly unrestrained will be regularly repeated in recurring stanzas, as in *To Laurels* (89), *An Ode to Endymion Porter* (185), *To Primroses* (257),

or *To Daffodils* (316).   Somewhat less elaborate in stanzaic structure are the lines to *Clipseby Crew* (546), to
Ben Jonson (913), *To Blossoms* (469).   Now and then we
have just a snatch at the end of some decasyllabics, as
in *A Pastoral* (422), or *To a Gentlewoman* (164).   In
The Tear (123) the form is used with peculiar happiness
in the first stanza.   So also in *To Music* (227).

Two minor curiosities may be mentioned.   Several
times Herrick divides a word and rhymes with the first
syllable, as in

> " Spice-
> ing the chaste air with fumes of Paradise."
>
> *—A Nuptial Song* (283), st. 2 (cf. also st. 6).

There are also a number of examples in *Oberon's Feast*
(444).   And rarely he rhymes following words within the
line, as

> " Two smelling, swelling, bashful cherrylets"

or

> "a virgin merry, cherry-lip'd."
>
> *— The Description of a Woman,* lines 20 and 22.

But all such enumeration and comment does little
more than call attention to what any one can readily
enough appreciate without criticism.

Swinburne says of Herrick : " The apparent or external
variety of his versification is, I should suppose, incomparable," and here most people would incline to agree
with him, excepting perhaps from the comparison Swinburne himself.   It does not seem to me that he is so
happy in his view that Herrick's "more ambitious or
pretentious lyrics are merely magnified or prolonged
songs."   With such a judgment we can only agree by
throwing out of consideration a good number of Herrick's longer poems, which are not songs and have no
resemblance to songs.   It may be that Swinburne does

throw these out of consideration, for he uses the word
"lyrics," and these are certainly not lyrics. There are
a number of Herrick's longer poems written in the decasyllabic couplet, not his best work, perhaps, but, as will
be seen at a glance, very characteristic. Aside from the
question of their poetic value, however, these poems are
of interest to the student of literary history for the light
they throw on the development in the seventeenth century of that famous form which in its variations has been
almost an index of the poetic excellence of its time. As
is well known, the result of that century was that the running freedom of the Elizabethans became the formal
elegance of Pope. Concerning the exact history of the
change there have been various opinions, but no one
would be astonished to see that the tendency showed
itself in the poetry of Herrick. For such as are interested in the matter, I transfer from a former publication
a table showing the frequency of run-on lines and couplets in Herrick's longer poems. The poems selected are
all written either in decasyllabic or octosyllabic couplets,
and are more than twenty lines in length. From shorter
poems it seemed hardly fair to form an opinion in either
direction. The percentages are made by dividing the
number of run-on couplets and midstopped lines by the
number of couplets, and are useful, of course, only for
comparative purposes.

		Percentage of mid-stopped lines.	Percentage of overrun couplets.
577	The Apparition	52	33
293	Oberon's Feast	50	22
444	Oberon's Palace	43	33
128	The Welcome to Sack	43	21
197	His Farewell to Sack	40	35
136	The Suspicion	37	28
	His Farewell unto Poetry	37	15

	Percentage of mid-stopped lines.	Percentage of overrun couplets.
467 The Parting Verse	29	30
157 The Cruel Maid	25	33
His Daughter's Dowry	11	16
319 A New Year's Gift	9	8
664 The Country Life	4	3
N. N. 263 Good Friday	3	2
223 The Temple	2	6
N. N. 230 His Meditation Upon Death	1	0
672 A Paranaeticall	13	0
182 The Captived Bee	11	0
523 To Phillis	0	11
618 To the Maids	0	11
640 The Beggar to Mab	0	8
The Description of a Woman	0	3
554 His Content in the Country	0	0
375 To Mrs. Anne Soame	0	0
250 The Hock Cart	0	0
763 The Wake	0	0
2 To His Muse	0	0

In the *Dissertation* often cited, I used this table as a help toward laying down bases for chronology. It seemed natural to suppose that the difference might represent a development : if so, it would be also natural that the development should be in the line of the progress during the century. The poems with most run-on couplets would then be earlier. Those with none would be later. This opinion is somewhat confirmed by the large proportion of gnomic couplets in the latter part of the *Hesperides*. Mr. Pollard (II, 291) supposes that the poems in the latter half of the book were, as a rule, written later. From different reasoning, I came independently to the same result (*Diss.*, § 8). The habit of writing these little distichs would have tended to make his pentameter couplets more "correct"; or it may be that the correctness of his pentameter turned him to writing the distichs. In either case it seems to me probable that, as Herrick grew older, he changed his ideas, or at least his practice, as to enjambement to some degree, though, of course, he never reached the smooth-clipped characteristics of Pope, or even of Waller. Nor is it probable that he would have cared to do so, had he conceived of such versification.

Although it will not be possible to present here any detailed study of Herrick's vocabulary, yet it will not be out of place to note a few points, which, with the glossary of uncommon words, will do something to indicate to the linguistic student what interest may attach to Herrick's poetry in this respect.

Most noteworthy is Herrick's freedom in word formation. Undoubtedly the English language was by no means so stiff at that time as it has since become. Even a very little reading of Elizabethan English will show a flexibility of language which allowed new formations with a frequency now uncommon. It would almost seem, however, that Herrick availed himself of the possibilities of word-formation with greater freedom than most of his contemporaries. It is not possible at present to be sure whether some special form were or were not coined by Herrick : in the following list there are probably a good number of words which may be found in other authors, but many of them are undoubtedly new formations.

1. *Verbs compounded with* be-. Bedangling, 944 ; befringed, *D. W.*;[1] behung, 336; bepearled, 582; bepimpled, 108 ; bepranked, 523 ; bescattered, *D. W.;* beset, *N. N.*, 96 ; beshivered, *N. N.*, 3 ; bestrewed, 506; besmears, 201 ; bespangling, 178; bestrutted, 293; bewearied, 336; bestroking, 283; bewash, 1028 ; besweetened, 293; bethwack, 1053.

---

[1] *The Description of a Woman.*

2. *Verbs compounded with* circum-. Circumbinds, 223; circum-crossed, 653; circumflanked, 747; circumfused, 179; circummortal, 445; circumspangle, 806; circumvolving, 169; circumwalk, 35 : *cf.*, also, circumgyration, 968; circumspacious, 924.

3. *Verbs compounded with* inter-. Interplaced, 986; intertalked, 268.

4. *Verbs compounded with* re-. Reaspire, 98; reconverse, 698; recollect, 722, 962; redelivers, 323; repossess, 963; resojourn, 86; reworn, 148 : *cf.*, also, remeeting, 355.

5. *Diminutives in* -let. Armilet, 47; cherrylet, *D. W.;* flagonet, 784; flosculet, 316; nervelet, 41; niplet, 190; pipkinet, *N. N.*, 130; rubylet, 654; trammelet, *D. W.;* thronelet, 210; zonulet, 35.

6. *Diminutives in* -ling. Firstling, 36; fondling, 23; kitling, 106, 200, 336, 444; shepherdling, 2 (*cf.* 523 and p. lxi); steerling, 718; sweetling, 635; youngling, 250, 257, 283, 377, 577, 635, 664.

7. *Nouns in* -ment. Affrightment, *N. N.*, 263; designment, 926; divorcement, 197; justment, 82.

8. *Nouns in* -ship. Babyship, 213; dukeship, 266; kingship, 213; queenship, 88; saintship, 498.

9. *Feminines in* -ess. Disposeress, 718; neatherdess, 986; rectress, 1082; spartaness, 142. *Cf.* also poetress, 265.

10. *Nouns compounded with* fore-. Foreleader, 979; foreshows, 124; foresounds, 319.

11. *Adjectives compounded with* un-. Undreadful, 323; un-smooth, 571; *N. N.*, 137; unsober, 592; unsoft, 748.

Such examples as these show a freedom in the handling of material that is practically an artistic characteristic.

The subject of new word formations is one which has some rather curious by-paths. There are a few words in Herrick's poetry which seem to illustrate what is commonly known as contamination. In *To Live Merrily and to Trust to Good Verses* (201) we find the curious word *immensive :* —

> "Then this *immensive* cup
> Of aromatic wine,
> Catullus, I quaff up
> To that terce muse of thine."

And again in 687 we have the expression "this *immensive* sphere."

Such words occur in conversation not so infrequently as one might think: the speaker has two ideas or two words in his mind, and mingles them in his expression into one. But in literature they are more rare. Such is the word *slantindicular*, sometimes to be heard in America, and to be found in *Martin Chuzzlewit*. Such the word *eloquential*, which I have heard used in conversation for *eloquent*, and *consequential*. Such the word *withstrain*, which I have seen in writing to express *withstand* and *restrain*. Such a word is *frowl*, such *quib*. They are used once on the spur of the moment, and if noticed are corrected. For other examples see Carroll, *Through the Looking-glass*, pp. 126, 128; Paul, *Principien der Sprachgeschichte*, chap. viii, §§ 242–245; and Wheeler, *Analogy, and its Scope in Language*, p. 8.

Immensive seems to have been thrown out by Herrick because it sounded like *immense* and like *expansive*, both of which ideas he may have had in mind. *Zonulet* (114), although properly enough formed as a double diminutive from *zone*, is used with a distinct reminiscence of the meaning of *amulet*. So in *shepharling* (fem.), 523 36, he may have had *shepherdess* and *darling*, although shephardling, 2 12, is one of Herrick's favorite diminutives. In the version of 283 in the Harleian MS., 6917 (printed by Mr. Pollard, I, 291) we find in st. 16 [9] "the *fragrous* bride." It was changed in the *Hesperides* to *fragrant*. But the first word has the effect of *odorous* as well as of *fragrant*.

Such words as these, although they appear at first merely whimsical, are yet of a certain philological value. They may have been used consciously, in which case they indicate hardly more than ingenuity on the part of the writer, and flexibility on the part of the language. But they may have been used unconsciously; in which case we see the poet with his mind absorbed in his idea, striking out, as it were, a new, unifying, and meaningful expression.

Another characteristic of the English of Herrick's day, — or at least of a great part of the published English, — is also distinctly marked in his poetry, namely, the use of words borrowed from the Latin in the Latin sense.

The importation of Latin words into English was begun systematically about one hundred years before Herrick's time by Sir Thomas Elyot. Although the principle was strongly opposed by Sir John Cheke and others, yet there were not a few writers in the sixteenth century who adopted the idea, so that by 1600 "inkhorn terms," as they had been called by Wilson, were by no means uncommon. Bacon's work abounds in them, and after Bacon, Jeremy Taylor, Sir Thomas Browne and Milton. Of these borrowings many have been retained, usually with a change of meaning, commonly in the direction of tropical signification. "He had a star to *illustrate* his birth," says Jeremy Taylor. "Coming into an inn," says Lord Herbert of Cherbury, "I found my fame had *prevented* my coming thither." "On the other side, *Incensed* with indignation Satan stood Unterrified," says Milton. "The contempt of death from corporal *animosity*," says Sir Thomas Browne. "After a few minutes' refreshment [they] *determine* in loathing," says South.

Examples of this very common practice may be found in Herrick also, of which the following are a number: candid, 445, 900; circumstants, 197; continent, 506, 742; convinces, 197; cunctation, 746, 922; determine, 577; effused, 636; errs, 83; errors, 444; instant, 319;. indignation, 871; lations, 133; lautitious, 785; mel, 370;

perspire, 644; reiterate, 1030; regredience, 658; resident, 521; retorted, 201; transpire, 375, 577.

These are not so different from the examples that
might be quoted from contemporaries. They are, however, perhaps worth noting because Herrick was not a
learned writer like Jeremy Taylor, Sir Thomas Browne,
or Milton. Other lyrists of his day, Herbert, Crashaw,
Suckling, are hardly so Latinized in diction.

VI. HERRICK THE POET.

So much for various things of interest from various
points of view concerning Herrick's poetry. I hope that
something has been said which will resolve questions
which may come up in reading the selections which follow; I hope, too, that such information as there may be
will in no wise divert attention from the real sources of
delight which every lover of poetry will find in the
Hesperides. For this is the main thing; information concerning chronology and language and other such matters
is of no great moment if we do not really feel the charm
of our poet, and there will be not a few who know and
love their Herrick, who really care but little for such
matters as are apt to occupy the attention of the scholar.

Herrick is distinctively a poet from whom to receive
pleasure. He is not necessarily to be studied; he is to
be enjoyed. Doubtless many who love his verses will be
led on by an honorable curiosity to desire to know this
and that concerning the man and his work. But the
poetic enjoyment is the main thing. Herrick is a very
individual poet. He has something about him which
lifts him out of the crowd of Jacobean and Caroline

lyrists, such as Carew and Suckling, nor do we think of him as on precisely the same level as his predecessors the Elizabethans. His poems have a certain air of distinction. Many of them are trivial enough, doubtless, but they are never quite commonplace. Some of them are coarse, but he is rarely vulgar. It is hard precisely to define his quality, but I think Mr. Palgrave has come the nearest to it. Hard to define, it may be, but not I think hard to feel.

True, Herrick is not to be called a poet of the first order. He has no part of that spiritual insight which perceives axiomatic reality in what to the ordinary mind was a blank range of circumstances. His work does not inspire and uplift, save as the work of any artist inspires and uplifts, not by any particular enunciations, but by its special quality of absolute expression. He deals with simple matters in a very simple way, — it is his perfection of lyric expression that has made so many of his poems masterpieces.

Mr. Coventry Patmore, in speaking of the intellect and imagination of a recent poet, calls Herrick a "splendid insect." [1] It will probably be admitted that Herrick is not remarkable for his powerful intellect nor for his quickening imagination. Perhaps the poet's lovers will not so willingly incline to think of him as a splendid insect. Doubtless he has little enough in common with certain long-legged fliers of gaudy spottings and streakings, nor with those magnificent but amorphous-looking beetles with antler mandibles, nor yet with the venomous and slim-waisted varieties with which we have sometimes come in contact. But an entomologist might see much resemblance to the *Phaneus carnifex*, for instance, which burrs about among the South American flowers in subdued lustre of green and ruddy gold, whose iridescence comes

[1] *Religio Poetæ*, p. 202.

not from any superficial pigment but from the very nature of his being.

And yet I think we are better off with no figure of speech between ourselves and the poet. Whether he be the riotous young fellow in London, or the country vicar in his first enthusiasm for the lovely things around him, or in the more sober days of his later life he always has for us the distinctive character of the artist, his own power of feeling and his own innate discrimination, and his own peculiar process of distilling from the great mixture of impressions that would seem common to all, the drops of clear quintessence, aureate and fragrant.

VII. BIBLIOGRAPHY.

Herrick's poems were originally published in 1648, just before the execution of Charles I. Then came the Commonwealth, the Restoration, and the Eighteenth Century, during all which time no second edition was called for; and indeed, so far as we can judge, the first edition was not much read. Not till almost the beginning of the nineteenth century did the poet begin to feel the first glow of that immortality he had so often promised himself. Those were the charming days when our older literature was in a sense an untrodden field, when one could turn to the Elizabethans and to Chaucer with the fresh excitement of a new discoverer. As far as Herrick was concerned, Sylvanus Urban began the revival in 1796 and 1797, followed in 1804 by Nathan Drake in his *Literary Hours*, and since that day we have had a baker's dozen of "Complete Works," not to speak of the volumes of selections.

The following list gives all the editions of Herrick's complete works and the most important volumes of selections. It was made at the British Museum, and, having compared it with Dr. Grosart's (I, vii–xi), I hope that it is tolerably complete and correct. Besides the editions of his works there is not much Herrick literature, and what there is is chiefly periodical, and so may be easily found in Poole's *Index.* A few remarks on the chief articles are added.

[Editions of complete works, even if expurgated, are numbered 1, 2, 3, etc. Volumes of selections are marked A, B, C, etc. I have not thought it necessary in all cases to give the complete title.]

1. Hesperides: or, The Works both Humane and Divine of Robert Herrick, Esq. Ovid, *Effugient avidos Carmina nostra Rogos.* London. Printed for *John Williams* and *Francis Eglesfield.* 1648.

   This is the original edition. It includes both the *Hesperides* and the *Noble Numbers,* the latter with a separate title-page, dated 1647, and separate pagination.

A. Select Poems from the Hesperides: with remarks by J. Nott. 8vo. Bristol, 1810.

   This is the first result of the reawakened interest in Herrick, and the means of much of the subsequent interest.

2. The Works of Robert Herrick. Edited with a Biographical Notice by T. Maitland. 2 vols., 8vo. Edinburgh, 1823.

B. Selections from the Hesperides, etc., by Charles Short. London, 1839.

3. Hesperides, or Works both Human and Divine of Robert Herrick. Edited by H. G. Clarke. 2 vols., 16mo. London, 1844.

   Issued in Clarke's Cabinet Series.

4. Hesperides, or Works both Human and Divine, etc. With a Memoir by S. W. Singer. 8vo. London, 1846.

> Published by Pickering. It is practically the same as 2.

C. Selections from Herrick for Translation into Latin Verse by A. J. Macleane. 16mo. London, 1848.

5, 6. Dr. Grosart notes that "other complete editions appeared in 1850 and 1852 — each in two volumes." But these I have not myself seen.

7. Hesperides; or, the Works both Humane and Divine of Robert Herrick, Esq. 2 vols., 8vo. Boston, 1856.

> This is Little and Brown's revision of Pickering (4).

8. The Poetical Works of Robert Herrick. With a Biographical Memoir by E. Walford. 8vo. London, 1859.

9. Hesperides: Poems and other Remains of Robert Herrick, now first collected. Edited by W. C. Hazlitt. 2 vols. London, 1869.

> Here were first collected a number of poems by Herrick which did not appear in the *Hesperides* or *Noble Numbers.* Hazlitt was the first editor to get much beyond what had been done by Maitland and Nott.

10. The Complete Poems of Robert Herrick. Edited by Alexander B. Grosart, D.D. 3 vols., 8vo. London, 1876.

> This edition contains an elaborate " Memorial Introduction," a literatim text, copious Notes, and a " Glossorial Index." It has the merits and faults of most of Dr. Grosart's work. No student of Herrick can afford to neglect it, and every student who uses it will find a good deal to disagree with and a good deal that will annoy him. Dr. Grosart's work is not distinguished by scholarly accuracy, or by critical insight. But his

intimate familiarity with the literature of the time, his untiring diligence, and his warm devotion to his subject have made his work of great value. In spite of all objections his edition is the standard.

D.   Favorite Poems by Robert Herrick. 32mo. Boston, 1877.

     This contains sixty-six of the best-known poems.

E.   Chrysomela. A Selection from the Lyrical Poems of Robert Herrick, arranged with notes by Francis Turner Palgrave. 16mo. London, 1877.

     One of the Golden Treasury Series. Mr. Palgrave's gift at making selections is remarkable and well known. The introduction is far and away the best criticism on Herrick that has been written. " Herrick," says Mr. Palgrave, " is the best commentator on Herrick." This is true so far as the poems themselves are concerned, but whoever neglects Mr. Palgrave's comment will lose what in its own way is equally good. He considers chiefly the relation of Herrick to the men of letters of his own day and of antiquity, and thus comes to his particular characteristics.

F.   Selections, etc. With Illustrations by E. A. Abbey, and a Memoir by Austin Dobson. 4to. New York, 1882, and London, 1883.

     Both memoir and illustrations are well known to Herrick lovers.

11.   Hesperides: or Works both Human and Divine of Robert Herrick. With an Introduction by Henry Morley. 8vo. London, 1883.

     This is the volume in Morley's Universal Library. It gives a text (with slight expurgation) and puts into the few pages of introduction a great deal that is good.

G.   Herrick. Edited by H. P. Horne in the Canterbury Poets. 16mo. London, 1887.

     The Introduction and Notes have a good many independent and interesting remarks and conjectures.

12. The Hesperides and Noble Numbers. Edited by Alfred Pollard, with a Preface by A. C. Swinburne. sm. 8vo. London and New York, 1891.

This edition has a Life by Mr. Pollard and Notes, which have been, as will be seen, of the greatest assistance to me. Mr. Swinburne's preface is slight, but has a number of suggestive remarks. Mr. Pollard's work is the most thorough that has been done on the subject. His edition does not, of course, include all that is of value in Dr. Grosart's, but he goes beyond Grosart in several directions, and is far more scholarly and accurate. The chief points illustrated by his Life and Notes are Herrick's friends, Herrick's reminiscences of the classics, and the MS. versions of Herrick's poetry. The poems are here for the first time numbered, and the numbering has been followed in the present selection, although I have been unable to find what poems Mr. Pollard would number 402 and 448. "This numbering," he says in the editor's note, "renders it possible to print the Epigrams [v. p. xliv foll.]. which successive editors have joined in deploring, in a detachable appendix, their place in the original being indicated by the numeration." In the copy which I have used (and I suppose in the rest of the edition) the Appendix is not only detachable but detached, and the text is as a consequence expurgated. In this particular it differs somewhat from 11. Mr. Morley omitted whatever he considered licentious, and retained much that most people would consider nasty. Mr. Pollard seems to have omitted what was nasty, and has retained a good deal that is licentious.

Mr. Pollard gives the idea of one confined for space. It is a pity that he could not have taken all the room that he desired, for he would then have made what might well stand as the final edition of Herrick. As it is, his edition is, within its limits, far more useful than Dr. Grosart's.

13. The poetical works of Robert Herrick. Edited by George Saintsbury. 2 vols., 12mo. London, 1893.

This is one of the "Aldine Poets." It presents a good text and the notes have been minimised.

The chief work on Herrick has been done by his editors. In addition, however, to the introductions to the editions mentioned, the following articles may be noted:

Early articles by "Sylvanus Urban" and Nathan Drake, as above.

In the *Quarterly Review* for August, 1810, and the *Retrospective Review* for August, 1822, are interesting articles, the first containing a good deal of information about Herrick's Devonshire surroundings, and the latter distinguished by the taste of its selections and its critical remarks.

Edmund Gosse: Robert Herrick. In Seventeenth Century Studies, 2d ed., London, 1885. With this it is well to read Mr. Gosse's Introduction to the selections from Herrick in Ward's *English Poets* (4 vols., 8vo, London and New York, 1881), vol. ii, pp. 124–129. I have had occasion to differ from some of Mr. Gosse's conclusions, but the essay is one of the best things on the subject, and should certainly be read by any one interested. It was first published in the *Cornhill Magazine*.

By the present editor: Die chronologische Anordnung der Dichtungen Robert Herricks. Halle a. S., 1892. This is a study made with a view of ascertaining the principles that must obtain in any attempt to draw inferences from Herrick's poetry concerning Herrick's life.

Alfred Pollard: The Friends of Herrick. Macmillan's Magazine, August, 1893. Presents more fully than it was possible in his edition the results of Mr. Pollard's studies on the persons alluded to in the *Hesperides*. In this direction Mr. Pollard is chief authority, and his work cannot be neglected.

A SELECTION

FROM

HESPERIDES:

THE WORKS BOTH HUMAN AND DIVINE

OF

ROBERT HERRICK.

WELL may my book come forth like public day,
When such a light as You are leads the way,
Who are my work's creator and alone
The flame of it and the expansion.
And look how all those heavenly lamps acquire   5
Light from the sun, that inexhausted fire :
So all my morn and evening stars from You
Have their existence, and their influence too.
Full is my book of glories ; but all these
By You become immortal substances.   10

HESPERIDES.

1. THE ARGUMENT OF HIS BOOK.

I SING of brooks, of blossoms, birds and bowers,
Of April, May, of June, and July-flowers ;
I sing of may-poles, hock-carts, wassails, wakes,
Of bridegrooms, brides, and of their bridal-cakes;
I write of youth, of love, and have access   5
By these, to sing of cleanly wantonness ;
I sing of dews, of rains, and piece by piece,
Of balm, of oil, of spice, and amber-greece ;
I sing of times trans-shifting ; and I write
How roses first came red, and lilies white.   10
I write of groves, of twilights, and I sing
The court of Mab and of the Fairie King.
I write of Hell ; I sing, and ever shall,
Of Heaven, and hope to have it after all.

2. TO HIS MUSE.

WHITHER, mad maiden, wilt thou roam ?
Far safer 'twere to stay at home ;
Where thou may'st sit, and piping please
The poor and private cottages,
Since coats and hamlets best agree   5
With this thy meaner minstrelsy.
There with the reed thou may'st express
The shepherd's fleecy happiness,
And with thy Eclogues intermix
Some smooth and harmless Bucolics.   10

There, on a hillock, thou may'st sing
Unto a handsome shepherdling,
Or to a girl, that keeps the neat,
With breath more sweet than violet.
There, there, perhaps, such lines as these   15
May take the simple villages.
But for the court, the country wit
Is despicable unto it.
Stay then at home, and do not go
Or fly abroad to seek for woe.   20
Contempts in courts and cities dwell ;
No critic haunts the poor man's cell,
Where thou may'st hear thine own lines read,
By no one tongue there censured.
That man's unwise will search for ill,   25
And may prevent it sitting still.

3. TO HIS BOOK.

WHILE thou didst keep thy candor undefil'd
Dearly I lov'd thee, as my first-born child ;
But when I saw thee wantonly to roam
From house to house, and never stay at home,
I brake my bonds of love and bade thee go,   5
Regardless whether well thou sped'st or no.
On with thy fortunes then, whate'er they be ;
If good I'll smile, if bad I'll sigh for thee.

8.   WHEN HE WOULD HAVE HIS VERSES READ.

IN sober mornings do not thou rehearse
The holy incantation of a verse ;
But when that men have both well drunk and fed,
Let my enchantments then be sung or read.

When laurel spirts i'th' fire, and when the hearth 5
Smiles to itself, and gilds the roof with mirth ;
When up the thyrse is rais'd, and when the sound ·
Of sacred orgies flies around, around ;
When the rose reigns, and locks with ointments shine,
Let rigid Cato read these lines of mine. 10

12. NO BASHFULNESS IN BEGGING.

To get thine ends, lay bashfulness aside ;
Who fears to ask, doth teach to be deny'd.

14. TO PERILLA.

AH, my Perilla ! do'st thou grieve to see
Me, day by day, to steal away from thee ?
Age calls me hence, and my grey hairs bid come
And haste away to mine eternal home ;
'Twill not be long, Perilla, after this, 5
That I must give thee the supremest kiss :
Dead when I am, first cast in salt, and bring
Part of the cream from that religious spring ;
With which, Perilla, wash my hands and feet ;
That done, then wind me in that very sheet 10
Which wrapt thy smooth limbs, when thou didst implore
The gods' protection but the night before,
Follow me weeping to my turf, and there
Let fall a primrose, and with it a tear :
Then lastly, let some weekly-strewings be 15
.Devoted to the memory of me ;
Then shall my ghost not walk about, but keep
Still in the cool and silent shades of sleep.

22. TO ANTHEA.

IF, dear Anthea, my hard fate it be
To live some few sad howers after thee,
Thy sacred corse with odors I will burn,
And with my laurel crown thy golden urn.
Then holding up there such religious things   5
As were (time past) thy holy filletings
Near to thy reverend pitcher I will fall
Down dead for grief, and end my woes withal ;
So three in one small plat of ground shall lie,
Anthea, Herrick, and his poetry.   10

23. THE WEEPING CHERRY.

· I SAW a cherry weep, and why ?
   Why wept it ?   But for shame
Because my Julia's lip was by,
   And did out-red the same.
But, pretty fondling, let not fall   5
   A tear at all for that
Which rubies, corals, scarlets, all
   For tincture, wonder at.

25. THE DIFFERENCE BETWIXT KINGS AND SUBJECTS.

'TWIXT kings and subjects there's this mighty odds :
Subjects are taught by men ; kings, by the gods.

29. LOVE, WHAT IT IS.

LOVE is a circle, that doth restless move
In the same sweet eternity of love.

32. THE POMANDER BRACELET.

To me my Julia lately sent
A bracelet, richly redolent ;
The beads I kiss'd, but most lov'd her
That did perfume the pomander.

35. HIS SAILING FROM JULIA.

WHEN that day comes, whose evening says I'm gone
Unto that wat'ry desolation,
Devoutly to thy closet-gods then pray,
That my wing'd ship may meet no remora.
Those deities which circum-walk the seas, 5
And look upon our dreadful passages,
Will from all dangers re-deliver me
For one drink-offering poured out by thee.
Mercy and Truth live with thee! and forbear,
In my short absence, to unsluice a tear ; 10
But yet, for love's sake, let thy lips do this,
Give my dead picture one engend'ring kiss ;
Work that to life, and let me ever dwell
In thy remembrance, Julia.   So farewell.

36. HOW THE WALL-FLOWER CAME FIRST, AND WHY SO CALLED.

WHY this flower is now call'd so,
List', sweet maids, and you shall know.
Understand, this firstling was
Once a brisk and bonny lass,
Kept as close as Danae was ; 5
Who a sprightly springall lov'd,
And to have it fully prov'd,
Up she got upon a wall,
Tempting down to slide withal ;

But the silken twist untied,   10
So she fell ; and bruis'd, she died.
Love, in pity of the deed,
And her loving-luckless speed,
Turn'd her to this plant, we call
Now The Flower of the Wall.   15

39.   UPON THE LOSS OF HIS MISTRESSES.

I HAVE lost, and lately, these
Many dainty mistresses :
Stately Julia, prime of all ;
Sapho next, a principal ;
Smooth Anthea, for a skin   5
White and heaven-like crystalline ;
Sweet Electra, and the choice
Myrha, for the lute and voice.
Next, Corinna, for her wit, ·
And the graceful use of it ;   10
With Perilla : all are gone,
Only Herrick's left alone,
For to number sorrow by
Their departures hence, and die.

47.   THE PARCÆ ; OR, THREE DAINTY DESTINIES.
      THE ARMILET.

THREE lovely sisters working were,
   As they were closely set,
Of soft and dainty maiden-hair,
   A curious Armilet.
I, smiling, ask'd them what they did,   5
   Fair destinies all three,
Who told me they had drawn a thread
   Of life, and 'twas for me.

They showed me then how fine 'twas spun :
　　And I reply'd thereto,　　　　　10
I care not now how soon 'tis done,
　　Or cut, if cut by you.

50. TO ROBIN REDBREAST.

LAID out for dead, let thy last kindness be
With leaves and moss-work for to cover me ;
And while the wood-nymphs my cold corpse inter,
Sing thou my dirge, sweet-warbling chorister.
For epitaph, in foliage next write this :　　5
Here, here the tomb of Robin Herrick is !

51. DISCONTENTS IN DEVON.

MORE discontents I never had,
　　Since I was born, than here ;
Where I have been, and still am sad,
　　In this dull Devonshire.
Yet, justly too, I must confess,　　　　5
　　I ne'er invented such
Ennobled numbers for the press,
　　Than where I loath'd so much.

53. CHERRY-RIPE.

CHERRY-RIPE, ripe, ripe, I cry,
Full and fair ones ; come and buy ;
If so be you ask me where
They do grow?　I answer, there,
Where my Julia's lips do smile ;　　　　5
There's the land or cherry-isle,
Whose plantations fully show
All the year where cherries grow.

54. TO HIS MISTRESSES.

PUT up your silks, and piece by piece,
Give them the scent of amber-greece;
And for your breaths, too, let them smell
Ambrosia-like, or nectarel;
While other gums their sweets perspire,
By your own jewels set on fire.

55. TO ANTHEA.

Now is the time when all the lights wax dim,
And thou, Anthea, must withdraw from him
Who was thy servant.   Dearest, bury me
Under that Holy-oak or Gospel-tree;
Where, though thou see'st not, thou may'st think upon
Me, when thou yearly go'st procession;
Or, for mine honor, lay me in that tomb
In which thy sacred reliques shall have room;
For my embalming, sweetest, there will be
No spices wanting when I'm laid by thee.

57. DREAMS.

HERE we are all by day; by night w'are hurl'd
By dreams, each one into a sev'ral world.

58. AMBITION.

IN man, ambition is the common'st thing;
Each one by nature loves to be a king.

59. HIS REQUEST TO JULIA.

JULIA, if I chance to die
Ere I print my poetry,

I most humbly thee desire
To commit it to the fire ;
Better 'twere my book were dead,   5
Than to live not perfected.

67. UPON JULIA'S VOICE.

So smooth, so sweet, so silv'ry is thy voice,
As, could they hear, the damn'd would make no noise,
But listen to thee, walking in thy chamber,
Melting melodious words to lutes of amber.

70. THE SUCCESSION OF THE FOUR SWEET MONTHS.

First, April, she with mellow showers
Opens the way for early flowers ;
Then after her comes smiling May,
In a more rich and sweet array ;
Next enters June, and brings us more   5
Gems than those two that went before ;
Then, lastly, July comes, and she
More wealth brings in than all those three.

77. TO THE KING, UPON HIS COMING WITH HIS ARMY INTO THE WEST.

Welcome, most welcome to our vows and us,
Most great and universal genius !
The drooping West, which hitherto has stood
As one, in long-lamented widowhood,
Looks like a bride now, or a bed of flowers,   5
Newly refresh'd both by the sun and showers.
War, which before was horrid, now appears
Lovely in you, brave Prince of Cavaliers !

A deal of courage in each bosom springs
By your access, O you the best of Kings!
Ride on with all white omens, so that where
Your standard's up, we fix a conquest there.

82. TO THE REVEREND SHADE OF HIS RELIGIOUS FATHER.

THAT for seven lustres I did never come
To do the rites to thy religious tomb;
That neither hair was cut, or true tears shed
By me o'er thee, as justments to the dead;
Forgive, forgive me; since I did not know
Whether thy bones had here their rest or no.
But now 'tis known, behold, behold, I bring
Unto thy ghost th' effused offering;
And look, what smallage, nightshade, cypress, yew,
Unto the shades have been, or now are due,
Here I devote; and something more than so,
I come to pay a debt of birth I owe.
Thou gav'st me life, but mortal; for that one
Favour I'll make full satisfaction;
For my life mortal, rise from out thy hearse,
And take a life immortal from my verse.

83. DELIGHT IN DISORDER.

A SWEET disorder in the dress
Kindles in clothes a wantonness;
A lawn about the shoulders thrown
Into a fine distraction;
An erring lace, which here and there
Enthrals the crimson stomacher;
A cuff neglectful, and thereby
Ribbands to flow confusedly;

A winning wave, deserving note,
In the tempestuous petticoat;   10
A careless shoe-string, in whose tie .
I see a wild civility;
Do more bewitch me, than when art
Is too precise in every part.

86. TO DEAN-BOURN, A RUDE RIVER IN DEVON, BY
WHICH SOMETIMES HE LIVED.

DEAN-BOURN, farewell; I never look to see
Dean or thy wat'ry incivility;
Thy rocky bottom, that doth tear thy streams
And makes them frantic ev'n to all extremes,
To my content I never should behold,   5
Were thy streams silver, or thy rocks all gold.
Rocky thou art; and rocky we discover
Thy men, and rocky are thy ways all over.
O men, O manners; there, and ever known
To be a rocky generation!   10
A people currish, churlish as the seas,
And rude almost as rudest salvages.
With whom I did, and may re-sojourn when
Rocks turn to rivers, rivers turn to men.

88. TO JULIA.

How rich and pleasing thou, my Julia, art
In each thy dainty and peculiar part!
First, for thy queenship, on thy head is set
Of flowers a sweet commingled coronet;
About thy neck a carcanet is bound,   5
Made of the ruby, pearl, and diamond;
A golden ring, that shines upon thy thumb;
About thy wrist the rich Dardanium;

Between thy breasts, than down of swans more white,
There plays the sapphire with the chrysolite.
No part besides must of thyself be known,
But by the topaz, opal, chalcedon.

89. TO LAURELS.

A FUNERAL stone
Or verse, I covet none;
But only crave
Of you that I may have
A sacred laurel springing from my grave,
Which being seen
Blest with perpetual green,
May grow to be
Not so much call'd a tree
As the eternal monument of me.

90. HIS CAVALIER.

GIVE me that man that dares bestride
The active sea-horse, and with pride
Through that huge field of waters ride:

Who, with his looks, too, can appease
The ruffling winds and raging seas,
In midst of all their outrages:

This, this a virtuous man can do,
Sail against rocks, and split them too;
Ay, and a world of pikes pass through.

97. DUTY TO TYRANTS.

GOOD princes must be pray'd for; for the bad
They must be borne with, and in rev'rence had.
Do they first pill thee, next pluck off thy skin?
Good children kiss the rods that punish sin.

Touch not the tyrant, let the gods alone 5
To strike him dead that but usurps a throne.

106. A COUNTRY LIFE: TO HIS BROTHER, M. THO: HERRICK.

THRICE, and above, bless'd, my soul's half, art thou,
    In thy both last and better vow.
Could'st leave the city, for exchange, to see
    The country's sweet simplicity,
And it to know and practise, with intent 5
    To grow the sooner innocent
By studying to know virtue, and to aim
    More at her nature than her name.
The last is but the least, the first doth tell
    Ways less to live than to live well; 10
And both are known to thee, who now can'st live,
    Led by thy conscience, to give
Justice to soon-pleas'd nature, and to show
    Wisdom and she together go,
And keep one centre; this with that conspires 15
    To teach man to confine desires,
And know that riches have their proper stint
    In the contented mind, not mint;
And can'st instruct that those who have the itch
    Of craving more are never rich. 20
These things thou know'st to th' height, and dost prevent
    That plague, because thou art content
With that Heav'n gave thee with a wary hand
    (More blessed in thy brass than land)
To keep cheap Nature even and upright, 25
    To cool, not cocker appetite.
Thus thou canst tersely live to satisfy
    The belly chiefly, not the eye;

Keeping the barking stomach wisely quiet,
　　Less with a neat than needful diet.　　　　30
But that which most makes sweet thy country life
　　Is the fruition of a wife,
Whom, stars consenting with thy fate, thou hast
　　Got not so beautiful as chaste;
By whose warm side thou dost securely sleep,　　35
　　While love the sentinel doth keep,
With those deeds done by day which ne'er affright
　　Thy silken slumbers in the night.
Nor has the darkness power to usher in
　　Fear to those sheets that know no sin.　　　40
The damask'd meadows and the pebbly streams
　　Sweeten and make soft your dreams;
The purling springs, groves, birds, and well weav'd bowers, 45
　　With fields enamelled with flowers,
Present their shapes, while fantasy discloses
　　Millions of lilies mix'd with roses.
Then dream ye hear the lamb by many a bleat
　　Woo'd to come suck the milky teat,　　.　　50
While Faunus in the vision comes to keep
　　From rav'ning wolves the fleecy sheep,
With thousand such enchanting dreams that meet
　　To make sleep not so sound as sweet;
Nor can these figures so thy rest endear,　　　55
　　As not to rise when Chanticleer
Warns the last watch, but with the dawn dost rise
　　To work, but first to sacrifice;
Making thy peace with Heav'n for some late fault,
　　With holy-meal and spirting salt;　　　　60
Which done, thy painful thumb this sentence tells us,
　　Jove for our labor all things sells us.
Nor are thy daily and devout affairs,
　　Attended with those desp'rate cares

Th' industrious merchant has, who for to find   65
     Gold, runneth to the Western Inde,
And back again, tortur'd with fears, doth fly,
     Untaught to suffer poverty.
But thou at home, bless'd with securest ease,
     Sitt'st, and believ'st that there be seas   70
And wat'ry dangers, while thy whiter hap
     But sees these things within thy map ;
And viewing them with a more safe survey
     Mak'st easy fear unto thee say,
A heart thrice wall'd with oak and brass that man   75
     Had, first durst plough the ocean.
But thou at home, without or tide or gale,
     Canst in thy map securely sail,
Seeing those painted countries, and so guess
     By those fine shades their substances ;   80
And, from thy compass taking small advice,
     Buy'st travel at the lowest price.
Nor are thine ears so deaf but thou canst hear,
     Far more with wonder than with fear,
Fame tell of states, of countries, courts, and kings,   85
     And believe there be such things,
When of these truths thy happier knowledge lies
     More in thine ears than in thine eyes.
And when thou hear'st by too true report,
     Vice rules the most or all at court,   90
Thy pious wishes are, though thou not there,
     Virtue had, and mov'd her sphere.
But thou liv'st fearless ; and thy face ne'er shows
     Fortune when she comes or goes,
But, with thy equal thoughts, prepar'd dost stand   95
     To take her by the either hand ;
Nor car'st which comes the first, the foul or fair.
     A wise man ev'ry way lies square ;

And like a surly oak with storms perplex'd,
    Grows still the stronger, strongly vex'd.   100
Be so, bold spirit; stand centre-like unmov'd;
    And be not only thought but prov'd
To be what I report thee, and inure
    Thyself, if want comes, to endure.
And so thou dost; for thy desires are   105
    Confin'd to live with private Lar,
Nor curious whether appetite be fed
    Or with the first or second bread.
Who keep'st no proud mouth for delicious cates
    (Hunger makes coarse meats delicates)   110
Canst, and unurg'd, forsake that larded fare,
    Which art, not nature makes so rare;
To taste boil'd nettles, coleworts, beets, and eat
    These and sour herbs as dainty meat,
While soft opinion makes thy Genius say,   115
    Content makes all ambrosia.
Nor is it that thou keep'st this stricter size
    So much for want as exercise;
To numb the sense of dearth, which, should sin haste it,
    Thou might'st but only see 't, not taste it.   120
Yet can thy humble roof maintain a quire
    Of singing crickets by thy fire;
And the brisk mouse may feast herself with crumbs,
    Till that the green-ey'd kitling comes;
Then to her cabin, bless'd she can escape   125
    The sudden danger of a rape.
And thus thy little well-kept stock doth prove,
    Wealth cannot make a life, but love.
Nor art thou so close-handed, but can'st spend
    (Counsel concurring with the end)   130
As well as spare; still conning o'er this theme,
    To shun the first and last extreme;

Ordaining that thy small stock find no breach,
 Or to exceed thy tether's reach,
But to live round, and close, and wisely true   135
 To thine own self, and known to few.
Thus let thy rural sanctuary be
 Elisium to thy wife and thee;
There to disport yourselves with golden measure :
 For seldom use commends the pleasure.   140
Live, and live bless'd, thrice happy pair; let breath,
 But lost to one, be th'other's death.
And as there is one love, one faith, one troth,
 Be so one death, one grave to both.
Till when, in such assurance, live ye may,   145
 Nor fear or wish your dying day.

110. UPON FONE, A SCHOOLMASTER. EPIG.

FONE says, those mighty whiskers he does wear
Are twigs of birch and willow growing there;
If so, we'll think, too, when he does condemm
Boys to the lash, that he does whip with them.

111. A LYRIC TO MIRTH.

WHILE the milder fates consent,
Let's enjoy our merriment;
Drink, and dance, and pipe, and play,
Kiss our dollies night and day;
Crown'd with clusters of the vine,   5
Let us sit and quaff our wine;
Call on Bacchus, chant his praise,
Shake the thyrse and bite the bays;
Rouse Anacreon from the dead,
And return him drunk to bed;   10

Sing o'er Horace; for ere long
Death will come and mar the song;
Then shall Wilson and Gotiere
Never sing or play more here.

114. UPON JULIA'S RIBBAND.

As shows the air when with a rainbow grac'd,
So smiles that ribband 'bout my Julia's waist;
Or like—— Nay, 'tis that zonulet of love
Wherein all pleasures of the world are wove.

123. THE TEAR SENT TO HER FROM STAINES.

[This poem and 122 are addressed to Mrs. Dorothy Keneday.]

GLIDE, gentle streams, and bear
Along with you my tear
    To that coy girl,
    Who smiles yet slays
    Me with delays,
And strings my tears as pearl.

See, see, she's yonder set,
Making a carcanet
    Of maiden flowers!
    There, there present
    This orient
And pendent pearl of ours.

Then say I've sent one more
Gem to enrich her store;
    And that is all
    Which I can send,
    Or vainly spend,
For tears no more will fall.

Nor will I seek supply
Of them, the spring's once dry;   20
    But I'll devise,
    Among the rest,
    A way that's best
How I may save mine eyes.

Yet say, should she condemn   25
Me to surrender them;
    Then say, my part
    Must be to weep
    Out them, to keep
A poor, yet loving heart.   30

Say, too, she would have this;
She shall. Then my hope is,
    That when I'm poor,
    And nothing have
    To send or save,   35
I'm sure she'll ask no more.

128. HIS FAREWELL TO SACK.

FAREWELL, thou thing, time past so known, so dear
To me, as blood to life and spirit.   Near,
Nay, thou more near than kindred, friend, man, wife,
Male to the female, soul to body.   Life
To quick action, or the warm soft side   5
Of the resigning, yet resisting bride.
These, and a thousand sweets, could never be
So near or dear as thou wast once to me.   10
O, thou the drink of gods and angels! wine
That scatter'st spirit and lust; whose purest shine,
More radiant than the summer's sunbeams shows,
Each way illustrious, brave, and like to those

Comets we see by night, whose shagg'd portents   15
Foretell the coming of some dire events;
Or some full flame, which with a pride aspires,
Throwing about his wild and active fires.
'Tis thou, above nectar, O divinest soul!
Eternal in thyself, that canst control   20
That which subverts whole Nature, grief and care,
Vexation of the mind, and damn'd despair.
'Tis thou alone, who, with thy mystic fan,
Work'st more than Wisdom, Art, or Nature can,
To rouse the sacred madness, and awake   25
The frost-bound blood and spirits, and to make
Them frantic with thy raptures, flashing through
The soul like lightning, and as active too.
'Tis not Apollo can, or those thrice three
Castalian sisters sing, if wanting thee.   30
Horace, Anacreon, both had lost their fame,
Hadst thou not fill'd them with thy fire and flame.
Phœbean splendor! and thou, Thespian spring!
Of which sweet swans must drink before they sing
Their true-pac'd numbers and their holy lays,   35
Which makes them worthy cedar and the bays.
But why, why longer do I gaze upon
Thee with the eye of admiration?
Since I must leave thee, and enforc'd must say,
To all thy witching beauties, Go, away!   40
But if thy whimp'ring looks do ask me why?
Then know that Nature bids thee go, not I.
'Tis her erroneous self has made a brain
Uncapable of such a sovereign,
As is thy powerful self. Prithee, not smile,   45
Or smile more inly, lest thy looks beguile
My vows denounc'd in zeal, which thus much show thee
That I have sworn but by thy looks to know thee.

Let others drink thee freely, and desire
Thee and their lips espous'd, while I admire 50
And love thee, but not taste thee. Let my muse
Fail of thy former helps, and only use
Her inadult'rate strength ; what's done by me
Hereafter, shall smell of the lamp, not thee.

197. THE WELCOME TO SACK.

So soft streams meet, so springs with gladder smiles
Meet after long divorcement by the isles,
When love, the child of likeness, urgeth on
Their crystal natures to an union ;
So meet stol'n kisses, when the moony nights 5
Call forth fierce lovers to their wish'd delights ;
So kings and queens meet, when desire convinces
All thoughts but such as aim at getting princes,
As I meet thee. Soul of my life and fame !
Eternal lamp of love ! whose radiant flame 10
Outglares the heav'ns' Osiris ; and thy gleams
Outshine the splendor of his midday beams.
Welcome, O welcome, my illustrious spouse ;
Welcome as are the ends unto my vows.
Ay, far more welcome than the happy soil 15
The sea-scourg'd merchant, after all his toil,
Salutes with tears of joy, when fires betray
The smoky chimneys of his Ithaca.
Where hast thou been so long from my embraces,
Poor pitied exile ? Tell me, did thy graces 20
Fly discontented hence, and for a time
Did rather choose to bless another clime ?
Or went'st thou to this end, the more to move me
By thy short absence to desire and love thee ?
Why frowns my sweet ? Why won't my saint confer 25
Favors on me, her fierce idolater ?

Why are those looks, those looks the which have been
Time past so fragrant, sickly now drawn in
Like a dull twilight?   Tell me, and the fault
I'll expiate with sulphur, hair, and salt,   30
And with the crystal humor of the spring,
Purge hence the guilt, and kill this quarrelling.
Wo't thou not smile, or tell me what's amiss?
Have I been cold to hug thee, too remiss,
Too temp'rate in embracing?   Tell me, has desire   35
To thee-ward died i' th' embers, and no fire
Left in this rak'd-up ash-heap, as a mark
To testify the glowing of a spark?
Have I divorc'd thee only to combine
In hot adult'ry with another wine?   -   40
True, I confess I left thee, and appeal
'Twas done by me, more to confirm my zeal,
And double my affection on thee; as do those
Whose love grows more enflam'd by being foes.
But to forsake thee ever, could there be   45
A thought of such like possibility,
When thou thyself dar'st say, thy isles shall lack
Grapes, before Herrick leaves Canary sack?
Thou mak'st me airy, active to be borne,
Like Iphyclus, upon the tops of corn.   50
Thou mak'st me nimble, as the winged hours,
To dance and caper on the heads of flowers,
And ride the sunbeams.   Can there be a thing
Under the heavenly Isis, that can bring
More love unto my life, or can present   55
My genius with a fuller blandishment?
Illustrious idol! could the Egyptians seek
Help from the garlic, onion, and the leek,
And pay no vows to thee? who wast their best
God, and far more transcendent than the rest?   60

Had Cassius, that weak water-drinker, known
Thee in thy vine, or had but tasted one
Small chalice of thy frantic liquor, he
As the wise Cato, had approv'd of thee.
Come, come and kiss me; love and lust commends
Thee and thy beauties; kiss, we will be friends   70
Too strong for fate to break us. Look upon
Me with that full pride of complexion,
As queens meet queens; or come thou unto me,
As Cleopatra came to Anthony,
When her high carriage did at once present   75
To the Triumvir love and wonderment.
Swell up my nerves with spirit; let my blood
Run through my veins like to a hasty flood;
Fill each part full of fire, active to do
What thy commanding soul shall put it to;   80
And till I turn apostate to thy love,
Which here I vow to serve, do not remove
Thy fiërs from me; but Apollo's curse
Blast these-like actions, or a thing that's worse;
When these circumstants shall but live to see   85
The time that I prevaricate from thee,
Call me the Son of Beer, and then confine
Me to the tap, the toast, the turf; let wine
Ne'er shine upon me, may my numbers all
Run to a sudden death and funeral.   90
And last, when thee, dear spouse, I disavow,
Ne'er may prophetic Daphne crown my brow.

178. CORINNA'S GOING A–MAYING.

GET up, get up for shame, the blooming morn
Upon her wings presents the god unshorn.
    See how Aurora throws her fair
    Fresh-quilted colors through the air;

Get up, sweet slug-a-bed, and see   5
　The dew bespangling herb and tree.
Each flower has wept, and bow'd toward the east,
Above an hour since, yet you not dress'd,
　　Nay! not so much as out of bed?
　　When all the birds have matins said,   10
　　And sung their thankful hymns; 'tis sin,
　　Nay, profanation to keep in,
Whenas a thousand virgins on this day   .
Spring, sooner than the lark, to fetch in May.

Rise, and put on your foliage, and be seen   15
To come forth, like the Spring-time, fresh and green,
　　And sweet as Flora.   Take no care
　　For jewels for your gown or hair;
　　Fear not, the leaves will strew
　　Gems in abundance upon you;   20
Besides, the childhood of the day has kept
Against you come, some orient pearls unwept.   .
　　Come, and receive them while the light
　　Hangs on the dew-locks of the night,
　　And Titan on the eastern hill   25
　　Retires himself, or else stands still
Till you come forth.   Wash, dress, be brief in praying;
Few beads are best, when once we go a-Maying.

Come, my Corinna, come; and coming mark
How each field turns a street, each street a park 30
　　Made green, and trimm'd with trees; see how
　　Devotion gives each house a bough
　　Or branch; each porch, each door, ere this,
　　An ark, a tabernacle is,
Made up of white-thorn neatly enterwove,   35
As if here were those cooler shades of love.

Can such delights be in the street
And open fields, and we not see't?
Come, we'll abroad, and let's obey
The proclamation made for May, 40
And sin no more, as we have done, by staying;
But, my Corinna, come, let's go a-Maying.

There's not a budding boy or girl, this day,
But is got up and gone to bring in May.
A deal of youth, ere this, is come 45
Back, and with white-thorn laden home.
Some have despatch'd their cakes and cream
Before that we have left to dream:
And some have wept, and woo'd and plighted troth,
And chose their priest, ere we can cast off sloth; 50
Many a green-gown has been given,
Many a kiss, both odd and even,
Many a glance, too, has been sent
From out the eye, Love's firmament;
Many a jest told of the key's betraying 55
This night, and locks pick'd, yet w'are not a-Maying.

Come, let us go, while we are in our prime,
And take the harmless folly of the time.
We shall grow old apace and die
Before we know our liberty. 60
Our life is short, and our days run
As fast away as does the sun,
And as a vapor, or a drop of rain
Once lost, can ne'er be found again;
So when or you or I are made 65
A fable, song, or fleeting shade,
All love, all liking, all delight
Lies drown'd with us in endless night.

Then while time serves, and we are but decaying,
Come, my Corinna, come, let's go a-Maying.   70

181. A DIALOGUE BETWIXT HORACE AND LYDIA,

Translated Anno 1627, and set by

MR. RO: RAMSEY.

Hor. WHILE, Lydia, I was lov'd of thee,
　　Nor any was preferr'd 'fore me
　　To hug thy whitest neck; than I,
　　The Persian King liv'd not more happily.

Lyd. While thou no other didst affect,   5
　　Nor Chloe was of more respect;
　　Then Lydia, far-famed Lydia,
　　I flourish'd more than Roman Ilia.

Hor. Now Thracian Chloe governs me,
　　Skilful i' th' harp and melody;   10
　　For whose affection, Lydia, I,
　　So fate spares her, am well content to die.

Lyd. My heart now set on fire is
　　By Ornyth's son, young Calais;
　　For whose commutual flames here I,   15
　　To save his life, twice am content to die.

Hor. Say our first loves we should revoke,
　　And sever'd, join in brazen yoke;
　　Admit I Chloe put away,
　　And love again love-cast-off Lydia?   20

Lyd. Though mine be brighter than the star;
　　Thou lighter than the cork by far,
　　Rough as th' Adratic sea, yet I
　　Will live with thee, or else for thee will die.

183. UPON PRIG.

PRIG now drinks water, who before drank beer;
What's now the cause? We know the case is clear;
Look in Prig's purse, the chev'ril there tells you
Prig money wants, either to buy or brew.

186. TO HIS DYING BROTHER, MASTER WILLIAM HERRICK.

LIFE of my life, take not so soon thy flight,
But stay the time till we have bade good night.
Thou hast both wind and tide with thee; thy way
As soon dispatch'd is by the night as day:
Let us not then so rudely henceforth go   5
Till we have wept, kiss'd, sigh'd, shook hands, or so.
There's pain in parting, and a kind of hell
When once true lovers take their last farewell.
What? shall we two our endless leaves take here
Without a sad look, or a solemn tear?   10
He knows not love that hath not this truth proved,
Love is most loth to leave the thing beloved.
Pay• we our vows and go; yet when we part,
Then, even then, I will bequeath my heart
Into thy loving hands; for I'll keep none   15
To warm my breast, when thou my pulse art gone.
No, here I'll last, and walk, a harmless shade,
About this urn, wherein thy dust is laid,
To guard it so as nothing here shall be
Heavy, to hurt those sacred seeds of thee.   20

188. UPON MUCH-MORE. EPIG.

MUCH-MORE provides and hoards up like an ant,
Yet Much-more still complains he is in want.
Let Much-more justly pay his tithes, then try
How both his meal and oil will multiply.

191. TO PANSIES.

AH, cruel Love! must I endure
Thy many scorns, and find no cure?
Say, are thy medicines made to be
Helps to all others but to me?
I'll leave thee, and to Pansies come;
Comforts you'll afford me some:
You can ease my heart, and do
What love could ne'er be brought unto.

192. ON GILLY-FLOWERS BEGOTTEN.

WHAT was't that fell but now
　　From that warm kiss of ours?
Look, look, by love I vow
　　They were two gilly-flowers.

Let's kiss, and kiss again;
　　For if so be our closes
Make gilly-flowers, then
　　I'm sure they'll fashion roses.

194. TO HIS BOOK.

LIKE to a bride, come forth, my book, at last,
With all thy richest jewels overcast;
Say, if there be 'mongst many gems here one
Deserveless of the name of Paragon;

Blush not at all for that, since we have set 5
Some pearls on queens that have been counterfet.

197. THE WELCOME TO SACK.

[Put after 128.]

201. TO LIVE MERRILY, AND TO TRUST TO GOOD VERSES.

Now is the time for mirth,
   Nor cheek or tongue be dumb;
For with the flow'ry earth,
   The golden pomp is come.

The golden pomp is come; 5
   For now each tree does wear,
Made of her pap and gum,
   Rich beads of amber here.

Now reigns the Rose, and now
   Th' Arabian dew besmears 10
My uncontrolled brow,
   And my retorted hairs.

Homer, this health to thee,
   In sack of such a kind
That it would make thee see, 15
   Though thou wert ne'er so blind.

Next, Virgil I'll call forth,
   To pledge this second health
In wine whose each cup's worth
   An Indian commonwealth. 20

A goblet next I'll drink
  To Ovid; and suppose
Made he the pledge, he'd think
  The world had all one nose.

Then this immensive cup   25
  Of aromatic wine,
Catullus, I quaff up
  To that terse muse of thine.

Wild I am now with heat,
  O Bacchus! cool thy rays,   30
Or frantic I shall eat
  Thy thyrse, and bite the bays.

Round, round, the roof does run;
  And being ravish'd thus,
Come, I will drink a tun   35
  To my Propertius.

Now, to Tibullus next,
  This flood I drink to thee;
But stay, I see a text,
  That this presents to me.   40

Behold! Tibullus lies
  Here burnt, whose small return
Of ashes scarce suffice
  To fill a little urn.

Trust to good verses then;   45
  They only will aspire,
When pyramids, as men,
  Are lost i' th' funeral fire,

And when all bodies meet,
 In Lethe to be drown'd;   50
Then only numbers sweet
 With endless life are crown'd.

205. TO VIOLETS.

WELCOME, maids of honor,
  You do bring
  In the spring,
And wait upon her.

She has virgins many,   5
  Fresh and fair;
  Yet you are
More sweet than any.

Y'are the maiden posies,
  And so grac'd,   10
  To be plac'd,
'Fore damask roses.

Yet though thus respected,
  By-and-by
  Ye do lie,   15
Poor girls, neglected.

206. UPON BUNCE. EPIG.

MONEY thou ow'st me : prithee fix a day
For payment promis'd, though thou never pay:
Let it be doomsday; nay, take longer scope;
Pay when th'art honest, let me have some hope.

208. TO THE VIRGINS, TO MAKE MUCH OF TIME.

GATHER ye rosebuds while ye may,
　　Old Time is still a-flying;
And this same flower that smiles to-day,
　　To-morrow will be dying.

The glorious lamp of heaven, the sun,　　　5
　　The higher he's a-getting,
The sooner will his race be run,
　　And nearer he's to setting.

That age is best which is the first,
　　When youth and blood are warmer;　　　10
But being spent, the worse and worst
　　Times still succeed the former.

Then be not coy, but use your time,
　　And while ye may, go marry;
For having lost but once your prime,　　　15
　　You may for ever tarry.

211. HIS POETRY HIS PILLAR.

ONLY a little more
　　I have to write,
　　Then I'll give o'er,
And bid the world good-night.

'Tis but a flying minute　　　5
　　That I must stay,
　　Or linger in it;
And then I must away.

O Time, that cut'st down all,
　　And scarce leav'st here　　　10
　　Memorial
Of any men that were!

How many lie forgot
   In vaults beneath,
   And piecemeal rot   15
Without a fame in death !

Behold this living stone
   I rear for me,
   Ne'er to be thrown
Down, envious Time, by thee.   20

Pillars let some set up,
   If so they please,
   Here is my hope,
And my pyramides.

213. A PASTORAL UPON THE BIRTH OF PRINCE CHARLES,

Presented to the King, and set by

MR. NIC: LANIERE.

The Speakers — *Mirtillo, Amintas,* and *Amarillis.*

Amin. GOOD day, Mirtillo. *Mirt.* And to you no less ;
And all fair signs lead on our shepherdess.
Amar. With all white luck to you. *Mirt.* But say, what
    news
Stirs in our sheep-walk? *Amin.* None, save that my ewes,
My wethers, lambs, and wanton kids are well,   5
Smooth, fair, and fat, none better I can tell :
Or that this day Menalcas keeps a feast
For his sheep-shearers. *Mirt.* True, these are the least.
But, dear Amintas, and sweet Amarillis,
Rest but awhile here by this bank of lilies ;   10
And lend a gentle ear to one report
The country has. *Amin.* From whence? *Amar.* From
    whence? *Mirt.* The Court.

Three days before the shutting in of May
(With whitest wool be ever crown'd that day!)
To all our joy, a sweet-fac'd child was born,   15
More tender than the childhood of the morn.
   Chor. Pan pipe to him, and bleats of lambs and sheep
Let lullaby the pretty Prince asleep.
   Mirt. And that his birth should be more singular,
At noon of day was seen a silver star,   20
Bright as the Wise-men's torch which guided them
To God's sweet babe, when born at Bethlehem;
While golden angels, some have told to me,
Sung out his birth with heav'nly minstrelsy.
   Amin. O rare!   But is't a trespass, if we three   25
Should wend along his Baby-ship to see?
   Mirt. Not so, not so.   *Chor.* But if it chance to prove
At most a fault, 'tis but a fault of love.
   Amar. But, dear Mirtillo, I have heard it told,
Those learned men brought incense, myrrh, and gold,   30
From countries far, with store of spices sweet,
And laid them down for offerings at his feet.
   Mirt. 'Tis true, indeed; and each of us will bring
Unto our smiling and our blooming King,
A neat, though not so great an offering.   35
   Amar. A garland for my gift shall be,
Of flowers ne'er suck'd by th' thieving bee;
And all most sweet, yet all less sweet than he.
   Amin. And I will bear along with you
Leaves dropping down the honied dew,   40
With oaten pipes, as sweet, as new.
   Mirt. And I a sheep-hook will bestow
To have his little king-ship know,
As he is prince, he's shepherd too.
   Chor. Come, let's away, and quickly let's be dress'd,   45
And quickly give. *The swiftest grace is best.*

And when before him we have laid our treasures,
We'll bless the babe, then back to country pleasures.

214. TO THE LARK.

Good speed, for I this day
Betimes my matins say;
   Because I do
   Begin to woo.
   Sweet singing lark,   5
   Be thou the clerk,
   And know thy when
   To say, *Amen.*
   And if I prove
   Blest in my love,   .   10
   Then thou shalt be
   High-priest to me,
   At my return,
   To incense burn;
And so to solemnize   15
Love's and my sacrifice.

216. A MEDITATION FOR HIS MISTRESS.

You are a Tulip seen to-day,
But, dearest, of so short a stay,
That where you grew, scarce man can say.

You are a lovely July-flower,
Yet one rude wind, or ruffling shower,   5
Will force you hence, and in an hour.

You are a sparkling Rose i' th' bud,
Yet lost, ere that chaste flesh and blood
Can show where you or grew or stood.

You are a full-spread, fair-set Vine,
And can with tendrils love entwine,
Yet dried, ere you distil your wine.

You are like Balm, inclosed well
In amber, or some crystal shell,
Yet lost ere you transfuse your smell.

You are a dainty Violet,
Yet wither'd, ere you can be set
Within the virgin's coronet.

You are the Queen all flowers among,
But die you must, fair maid, ere long,
As he, the maker of this song.

218. LYRIC FOR LEGACIES.

GOLD I've none, for use or show,
Neither silver to bestow
At my death; but thus much know,
That each lyric here shall be
Of my love a legacy,
Left to all posterity.
Gentle friends, then do but please
To accept such coins as these,
As my last remembrances.

223. THE FAIRY TEMPLE; OR, OBERON'S CHAPEL.

Dedicated to MR. JOHN MERRIFIELD,
Counsellor-at-Law.

RARE temples thou hast seen, I know,
And rich for in and outward show;
Survey this chapel, built alone
Without or lime, or wood or stone,

Then say, if one th'ast seen more fine   5
Than this, the fairies' once, now thine.

THE TEMPLE.

A way enchas'd with glass and beads
There is, that to the chapel leads,
Whose structure, for his holy rest,
Is here the halcyon's curious nest ;
Into the which who looks, shall see   5
His temple of idolatry,
Where he of godheads has such store,
As Rome's Pantheon had not more.
His house of Rimmon this he calls,
Girt with small bones, instead of walls.   10
First, in a niche, more black than jet,
His idol-cricket there is set ;
Then in a polish'd oval by,
There stands his idol-beetle-fly ;
Next, in an arch, akin to this,   15
His idol-canker seated is ;
Then in a round, is plac'd by these
His golden god, Cantharides.
So that where'er ye look, ye see
No capital, no cornish free,   20
Or frieze, from this fine frippery.
Now, this the fairies would have known,
Theirs is a mix'd religion :
And some have heard the elves it call
Part Pagan, part Papistical.   25
If unto me all tongues were granted,
I could not speak the saints here painted.
Saint Tit, Saint Nit, Saint Is, Saint Itis,
Who 'gainst Mab's state plac'd here right is.

Saint Will o'th' Wisp, of no great bigness,   30
But alias call'd here *Fatuus ignis.*
Saint Frip, Saint Trip, Saint Fill, Saint Filly,
Neither those other saintships will I
Here go about for to recite
Their number, almost infinite;   35
Which, one by one, here set down are
In this most curious calendar.
First, at the entrance to the gate,
A little puppet-priest doth wait,
Who squeaks to all the comers there,   40
Favor your tongues, who enter here.
Pure hands bring hither, without stain.
A second pules, *Hence, hence, profane.*
Hard by, i' th' shell of half a nut,
The holy-water there is put;   45
A little brush of squirrel's hairs,
Compos'd of odd, not even pairs,
Stands in the platter or close by,
To purge the fairy family.
Near to the altar stands the priest,   50
There off'ring up the Holy Grist, .
Ducking in mood and perfect tense,
With (much good do't him) reverence.
The altar is not here four-square,
Nor in a form triangular;   55
Nor made of glass, or wood, or stone,
But of a little transverse bone
Which boys and bruckel'd children call
(Playing for points and pins) cockall.
Whose linen drapery is a thin,   60
Subtile, and ductile codlin's skin;
Which o'er the board is smoothly spread
With little seal-work damasked.

The fringe that circumbinds it, too,
Is spangle-work of trembling dew, 65
Which, gently gleaming, makes a show
Like frost-work glitt'ring on the snow.
Upon this fetuous board doth stand
Something for shew-bread, and at hand
(Just in the middle of the altar) 70
Upon an end, the Fairy-psalter,
Graced with the trout-fly's curious wings,
Which serve for watched ribbonings.
Now, we must know, the elves are led
Right by the Rubric, which they read : 75
And if report of them be true,
They have their text for what they do,
Ay, and their book of canons too.
And, as Sir Thomas Parson tells,
They have their book of Articles ; 80
And if that Fairy knight not lies,
They have their Book of Homilies ;
And other Scriptures, that design
A short, but righteous discipline.
The basin stands the board upon 85
To take the Free Oblation,
A little pin-dust, which they hold
More precious than we prize our gold ;
Which charity they give to many
Poor of the parish, if there's any. 90
Upon the ends of these neat rails,
Hatch'd with the silver-light of snails,
The elves, in formal manner, fix
Two pure and holy candlesticks,
In either which a small tall bent 95
Burns for the altar's ornament.
For sanctity, they have, to these,

Their curious copes and surplices
Of cleanest cobweb, hanging by
In their religious vestery.
They have their ash-pans and their brooms,
To purge the chapel and the rooms ;
Their many mumbling mass-priests here,
And many a dapper chorister.
Their ush'ring vergers here likewise,
Their canons and their chanteries ;
Of cloister-monks they have enow,
Ay, and their abbey-lubbers too.
And if their Legend do not lie,
They much affect the Papacy ;
And since the last is dead, there's hope
Elf Boniface shall next be Pope.
They have their cups and chalices,
Their pardons and indulgences,
Their beads of nits, bells, books, and wax
Candles, forsooth, and other knacks ;
Their holy oil, their fasting spittle,
Their sacred salt here, not a little.
Dry chips, old shoes, rags, grease, and bones,
Beside their fumigations.
Many a trifle, too, and trinket,
And for what use, scarce man would think it.
Next then, upon the chanters' side
An apple's-core is hung up dry'd,
With rattling kernels, which is rung
To call to morn and even-song.
The saint, to which the most he prays
And offers incense nights and days,
The Lady of the Lobster is,
Whose foot-pace he doth stroke and kiss,
And humbly chives of saffron brings,

For his most cheerful offerings.
When, after these, h'as paid his vows,   135
He lowly to the altar bows ;
And then he dons the silkworm's shed,
Like a Turk's turbant on his head,
And reverently departeth thence,
Hid in a cloud of frankincense ;   140
And by the glow-worm's light well guided,
Goes to the feast that's now provided.

293. OBERON'S FEAST.

SHAPCOT ! to thee the fairy state
I with discretion dedicate ;
Because thou prizest things that are
Curious and unfamiliar.
Take first the Feast; these dishes gone,   5
We'll see the Fairy-Court anon.

A little mushroom table spread,
After short prayers they set on bread,
A moon-parch'd grain of purest wheat,
With some small glitt'ring grit, to eat   10
His choice bits with ; then in a trice
They make a feast less great than nice.
But all this while his eye is serv'd,
We must not think his ear was starv'd ;
But that there was in place to stir   15
His spleen, the chirring grasshopper,
The merry cricket, puling fly,
The piping gnat for minstrelsy.
And now, we must imagine first,
The elves present, to quench his thirst,   20

A pure seed-pearl of infant dew,
Brought and besweet'ned in a blue
And pregnant violet ; which done,
His kitling eyes begin to run
Quite through the table, where he spies   25
The horns of papery butterflies,
Of which he eats ; and tastes a little
Of that we call the cuckoo's spittle ;
A little fuzz-ball pudding stands
By, yet not blessed by his hands,   30
That was too coarse ; but then forthwith
He ventures boldly on the pith
Of sug'red rush, and eats the sag
And well bestrutted bee's sweet bag ;
Gladding his palate with some store   35
Of emmets' eggs ; what would he more,
But beards of mice, a newt's stew'd thigh,
A bloated earwig, and a fly ;
With the red-capp'd worm, that's shut
Within the concave of a nut,   40
Brown as his tooth.   A little moth,
Late fat'ned in a piece of cloth ;
With withered cherries, mandrake's ears,
Mole's eyes ; to these the slain stag's tears ;
The unctuous dewlaps of a snail,   45
The broke-heart of a nightingale
O'er-come in music ; with a wine
Ne'er ravish'd from the flattering vine,
But gently press'd from the soft side
Of the most sweet and dainty bride,   50
Brought in a dainty daisy, which
He fully quaffs up to bewitch
His blood to height ; this done, commended
Grace by his priest, the feast is ended.

444. OBERON'S PALACE.

AFTER the feast, my Shapcot, see
The Fairy Court I give to thee ;
Where we'll present our Oberon led
Half-tipsy to the Fairy bed,
Where Mab he finds, who there doth lie   5
Not without mickle majesty.
Which done, and thence remov'd the light,
We'll wish both them and thee good-night.

Full as a bee with thyme, and red
As cherry harvest, now high fed   10
For lust and action ; on he'll go
To lie with Mab, though all say no.
Lust has no ears ; he's sharp as thorn,
And fretful, carries hay in 's horn,
And lightning in his eyes ; and flings   15
Among the elves, if mov'd, the stings
Of peltish wasps ; well know his guard,
Kings, though th' are hated, will be fear'd.
Wine lead him on.   Thus to a grove,
Sometimes devoted unto love,   20
Tinsel'd with twilight, he and they
Led by the shine of snails, a way
Beat with their num'rous feet, which by
Many a neat perplexity,
Many a turn, and man' a cross-   25
Track, they redeem a bank of moss
Spongy and swelling, and far more
Soft then the finest Lemster ore ;
Mildly disparkling, like those fires
Which break from the injewel'd tyres   30

Of curious brides; or like those mites
Of candy'd dew in moony nights.
Upon this convex, all the flowers
Nature begets by th' sun and showers,
Are to a wild digestion brought,   35
As if Love's sampler here was wrought;
Or Citherea's ceston, which
All with temptation doth bewitch.
Sweet airs move here, and more divine
Made by the breath of great-ey'd kine,   40
Who, as they low, empearl with milk
The four-leav'd grass, or moss like silk.
The breath of monkeys, met to mix
With musk-flies, are th' aromatics
Which cense this arch; and here and there,   45
And farther off, and everywhere
Throughout that brave mosaic yard,
Those picks or diamonds in the card;
With peeps of hearts, of club and spade,
Are here most neatly interlaid.   50
Many a counter, many a die,
Half-rotten and without an eye,
Lies hereabouts; and for to pave
The excellency of this cave,
Squirrels' and children's teeth late shed,   55
Are neatly here enchequered,
With brownest toadstones, and the gum
That shines upon the bluer plum,
The nails fallen off by whit-flaws; Art's
Wise hand enchasing here those warts   60
Which we to others (from ourselves)
Sell, and brought hither by the elves.
The tempting mole, stol'n from the neck
Of the shy virgin, seems to deck

The holy entrance; where within 65
The room is hung with the blue skin
Of shifted snake; enfriez'd throughout
With eyes of peacocks' trains, and trout-
flies' curious wings; and these among
Those silver-pence, that cut the tongue 70
Of the red infant, neatly hung.
The glow-worm's eyes, the shining scales
Of silv'ry fish, wheat-straws, the snail's
Soft candle-light, the kitling's eyne,
Corrupted wood, serve here for shine. 75
No glaring light of bold-fac'd day,
Or other over-radiant ray,
Ransacks this room; but what weak beams
Can make reflected from these gems,
And multiply; such is the light, 80
But ever doubtful, day or night.
By this quaint taper-light, he winds
His errors up; and now he finds
His moon-tann'd Mab, as somewhat sick,
And, love knows, tender as a chick. 85
Upon six plump dandillions, high-
Rear'd, lies her elvish majesty,
Whose woolly bubbles seemed to drown
Her Mabship in obedient down;
For either sheet was spread the caul 90
That doth the infant's face enthral,
When it is born, by some enstyl'd
The lucky omen of the child;
And next to these, two blankets o'er-
Cast of the finest gossamore; . 95
And then a rug of carded wool,
Which, sponge-like, drinking in the dull
Light of the moon, seemed to comply,

Cloud-like, the dainty deity.
Thus soft she lies; and over-head   100
A spinner's circle is bespread
With cobweb curtains, from the roof
So neatly sunk, as that no proof
Of any tackling can declare
What gives it hanging in the air.   105

*   *   *   *   *

445. TO HIS PECULIAR FRIEND, MASTER THOMAS SHAPCOTT, LAWYER.

I've paid thee what I promis'd; that's not all;
Besides, I give thee here a verse that shall,
When hence thy circummortal part is gone,
Arch-like, hold up, thy name's inscription.
Brave men can't die, whose candid actions are   5
Writ in the poet's endless calendar:
Whose vellum and whose volume is the sky,
And the pure stars the praising poetry.
                                        Farewell.

224. TO MISTRESS KATHERINE BRADSHAW, THE LOVELY, THAT CROWNED HIM WITH LAUREL.

My Muse in meads has spent her many hours
Sitting, and sorting several sorts of flowers,
To make for others garlands; and to set
On many a head here, many a coronet.
But amongst all encircled here, not one   5
Gave her a day of coronation,
Till you, sweet mistress, came and interwove
A laurel for her, ever young as love.

You first of all crown'd her; she must, of due,
Render for that a crown of life to you.　　　　　10

225. THE PLAUDITE; OR, END OF LIFE.

IF after rude and boist'rous seas,
My wearied pinnace here finds ease;
If so it be I've gain'd the shore,
With safety of a faithful oar;
If having run my barque on ground,　　　　　5
Ye see the aged vessel crown'd;
What's to be done, but on the sands
Ye dance and sing, and now clap hands?
The first act's doubtful, but we say,
It is the last commends the play.　　　　　10

227. TO MUSIC, TO BECALM HIS FEVER.

CHARM me asleep, and melt me so
　　With thy delicious numbers,
That being ravish'd, hence I go
　　Away in easy slumbers.
　　　　Ease my sick head,.　　　　　5
　　　　And make my bed,
　　Thou power that canst sever
　　　　From me this ill,
　　　　And quickly still
　　　　Though thou not kill　　　　　10
　　　　　My fever.

Thou sweetly canst convert the same
　　From a consuming fire
.Into a gentle-licking flame,
　　And make it thus expire.　　　　　15

Then make me weep
My pains asleep,
And give me such reposes,
That I, poor I,
May think, thereby,
I live and die
'Mongst roses.

Fall on me like a silent dew,
Or like those maiden showers
Which, by the peep of day, do strew
A baptime o'er the flowers.
Melt, melt my pains,
With thy soft strains,
That having ease me given,
With full delight,
I leave this light,
And take my flight
For Heaven.

247. THE COMING OF GOOD LUCK.

So Good-luck came, and on my roof did light,
Like noiseless snow, or as the dew of night;
Not all at once, but gently, as the trees
Are by the sunbeams tickel'd by degrees.

250. THE HOCK-CART; OR, HARVEST HOME.

To the Right Honorable MILDMAY,
Earl of Westmorland.

COME, sons of summer, by whose toil,
We are the lords of wine and oil;
By whose tough labors and rough hands,
We rip up first, then reap our lands;

Crown'd with the ears of corn, now come,   5
And, to the pipe, sing Harvest home !
Come forth, my lord, and see the cart
Dress'd up with all the country art.
See, here a maukin, there a sheet,
As spotless pure as it is sweet ;   10
The horses, mares, and frisking fillies,
Clad all in linen white as lilies ;
The harvest swains and wenches bound
For joy, to see the Hock-cart crown'd.
About the cart hear how the rout   15
Of rural younglings raise the shout,
Pressing before, some coming after,
Those with a shout, and these with laughter.
Some bless the cart, some kiss the sheaves,
Some prank them up with oaken leaves ;   20
Some cross the fill-horse, some with great
Devotion stroke the home-borne wheat,
While other rustics, less attent
To prayers than to merriment,
Run after with their breeches rent.   25
Well, on, brave boys, to your lord's hearth,
Glitt'ring with fire, where, for your mirth,
Ye shall see first the large and chief
Foundation of your feast, fat beef ;
With upper stories, mutton, veal,   30
And bacon, which makes full the meal,
With sev'ral dishes standing by,
As, here a custard, there a pie,
And here all-tempting frumenty.
And for to make the merry cheer, ·   35
If smirking wine be wanting here,
There's that which drowns all care, stout beer,
Which freely drink to your lord's health,

Then to the plough, (the commonwealth);
Next to your flails, your fanes, your fats ;
Then to the maids with wheaten hats ;
To the rough sickle, and the crook'd scythe;
Drink, frolic, boys, till all be blithe.
Feed and grow fat, and as ye eat,
Be mindful that the lab'ring neat,
As you, may have their fill of meat ;
And know, besides, ye must revoke
The patient ox unto the yoke,
And all go back unto the plough
And harrow, though they're hang'd up now.
And, you must know, your lord's word's true,
Feed him ye must, whose food fills you.
And that this pleasure is like rain,
Not sent ye for to drown your pain,
But for to make it spring again.

251. THE PERFUME.

To-morrow, Julia, I betimes must rise,
For some small fault to offer sacrifice ;
The altar's ready; fire to consume
The fat ; breathe thou, and there's the rich perfume.

255. TO THE WESTERN WIND.

Sweet western wind, whose luck it is,
    Made rival with the air,
To give Perenna's lip a kiss,
    And fan her wanton hair.

Bring me but one, I'll promise thee,
    Instead of common showers,
Thy wings shall be embalm'd by me,
    And all beset with flowers.

256. UPON THE DEATH OF HIS SPARROW.

An Elegy.

WHY do not all fresh maids appear
To work Love's sampler only here,
Where spring-time smiles throughout the year?
Are not here rosebuds, pinks, all flowers
Nature begets by th' sun and showers, 5
Met in one hearse-cloth, to o'erspread
The body of the under-dead?
Phil, the late dead, the late dead dear,
O! may no eye distil a tear
For you once lost, who weep not here! 10
Had Lesbia, too too kind, but known
This sparrow, she had scorn'd her own,
And for this dead which under-lies,
Wept out her heart, as well as eyes.
But endless peace, sit here, and keep 15
My Phil, the time he has to sleep,
And thousand virgins come and weep,
To make these flow'ry carpets show
Fresh as their blood, and ever grow,
Till passengers shall spend their doom; 20
Not Virgil's gnat had such a tomb.

257. TO PRIMROSES FILL'D WITH MORNING DEW.

WHY do ye weep, sweet babes? Can tears
  Speak grief in you,
  Who were but born
 . Just as the modest morn
  Teem'd her refreshing dew? 5
Alas, you have not known that shower
  That mars a flower,

Nor felt th' unkind
Breath of a blasting wind,
Nor are ye worn with years,
Or warp'd, as we,
Who think it strange to see
Such pretty flowers, like to orphans young,
To speak by tears before ye have a tongue.　.

Speak, whimp'ring younglings, and make known
The reason why
Ye droop and weep.
Is it for want of sleep?
Or childish lullaby?
Or that ye have not seen as yet
The violet?
Or brought a kiss　.
From that sweetheart to this?
No, no, this sorrow shown
By your tears shed
Would have this lecture read,
That things of greatest, so of meanest worth,
Conceiv'd with grief are, and with tears brought forth.

258. HOW ROSES CAME RED.

ROSES at first were white,
Till they could not agree,
Whether my Sapho's breast
Or they more white should be.

But being vanquish'd quite,
A blush their cheeks bespread;
Since which, believe the rest,
The roses first came red.

262. TO THE WILLOW TREE.

THOU art to all lost love the best,
　　The only true plant found,
Wherewith young men and maids distress'd,
　　And left of love, are crown'd.

When once the lover's rose is dead,　　　　　　5
　　Or laid aside forlorn,
Then willow garlands 'bout the head,
　　Bedew'd with tears, are worn.

When with neglect, the lover's bane,
　　Poor maids rewarded be,　　　　　　　　10
For their lost love, their only gain
　　Is but a wreath from thee.

And underneath thy cooling shade,
　　When weary of the light,
The love-spent youth and love-sick maid　　15
　　Come to weep out the night.

267. TO ANTHEA, WHO MAY COMMAND HIM
ANYTHING.

BID me to live, and I will live
　　Thy Protestant to be;
Or bid me love, and I will give
　　A loving heart to thee.

A heart as soft, a heart as kind,　　　　　　5
　　A heart as sound and free,
As in the whole world thou canst find,
　　That heart I'll give to thee.

Bid that heart stay, and it will stay,
   To honor thy decree;
Or bid it languish quite away,
   And 't shall do so for thee.

Bid me to weep, and I will weep,
   While I have eyes to see;
And having none, yet I will keep
   A heart to weep for thee.

Bid me despair, and I'll despair,
   Under that cypress tree;
Or bid me die, and I will dare
   E'en death, to die for thee.

Thou art my life, my love, my heart,
   The very eyes of me;
And hast command of every part,
   To live and die for thee,

269. OBEDIENCE IN SUBJECTS.

THE gods to kings the judgment give to sway;
The subjects' only glory to obey.

273. UPON BROCK. EPIG.

To cleanse his eyes, Tom Brock makes much ado,
But not his mouth, the fouler of the two.
A clammy rheum makes loathsome both his eyes;
His mouth worse furr'd with oaths and blasphemies.

274. TO MEADOWS.

Ye have been fresh and green,
 Ye have been fill'd with flowers;
And ye the walks have been
 Where maids have spent their hours.

You have beheld how they   5
 With wicker arks did come,
To kiss and bear away
 The richer cowslips home.

Y'ave heard them sweetly sing,
 And seen them in a round;   10
Each virgin, like a spring,
 With honeysuckles crown'd.

But now, we see none here
 Whose silv'ry feet did tread
And with dishevell'd hair   15
 Adorn'd this smoother mead.

Like unthrifts, having spent
 Your stock, and needy grown,
Y'are left here to lament
 Your poor estates, alone.   20

275. CROSSES.

Though good things answer many good intents,
Crosses do still bring forth the best events.

278. TO HIS HOUSEHOLD GODS.

Rise, Household gods, and let us go,
But whither, I myself not know.
First, let us dwell on rudest seas;
Next, with severest salvages;

Last, let us make our best abode,
Where human foot as yet ne'er trod;
Search worlds of ice, and rather there
Dwell, than in loathed Devonshire.

279. TO THE NIGHTINGALE AND ROBIN REDBREAST.

WHEN I departed am, ring thou my knell,
Thou pitiful and pretty Philomel;
And when I'm laid out for a corse, then be
Thou sexton, Redbreast, for to cover me.

280. TO THE YEW AND CYPRESS TO GRACE HIS FUNERAL.

BOTH you two have
Relation to the grave;
And where
The fun'ral-trump sounds, you are there.

I shall be made
Ere long a fleeting shade;
Pray come,
And do some honor to my tomb.

Do not deny
My last request, for I
Will be
Thankful to you, or friends for me.

283. A NUPTIAL SONG; OR, EPITHALAMIE ON SIR CLIPSEBY CREW AND HIS LADY.

WHAT'S that we see from far? The spring of day
Bloom'd from the east, or fair injewel'd May
Blown out of April; or some new
Star fill'd with glory to our view,

Reaching at heaven, 5
To add a nobler planet to the seven?
Say, or do we not descry
Some goddess in a cloud of tiffany
To move, or rather the
Emergent Venus from the sea? 10

'Tis she! 'tis she! or else some more divine
Enlight'ned substance; mark how from the shrine
Of holy saints she paces on,
Treading upon vermilion
And amber; spice- 15
ing the chaf'd air with fumes of Paradise.
Then come on, come on, and yield
A savor like unto a blessed field
When the bedabbled morn
Washes the golden ears of corn. 20

See where she comes, and smell how all the street
Breathes vineyards and pomegranates; O how sweet!
As a fir'd altar, is each stone,
Perspiring pounded cinnamon.
The phœnix' nest, 25
Built up of odors, burneth in her breast.
Who therein would not consume
His soul to ash-heaps in that rich perfume?
Bestroking fate the while
He burns to embers on the pile. 30

Hymen, O Hymen! tread the sacred ground;
Show thy white feet, and head with marjoram crown'd:
Mount up thy flames, and let thy torch
Display the bridegroom in the porch,
In his desires 35
More tow'ring, more disparkling than thy fires;

Show her how his eyes do turn
And roll about, and in their motions burn
    Their balls to cinders; haste,
    Or else to ashes he will waste.   40

Glide by the banks of virgins then, and pass
The showers of roses, lucky four-leav'd grass;
    The while the cloud of younglings sing,
    And drown ye with a flow'ry spring;
        While some repeat   45
Your praise, and bless you, sprinkling you with wheat;
    While that others do divine,
Blest is the bride, on whom the sun doth shine;
      And thousands gladly wish
    You multiply, as doth a fish.   50

And beauteous bride, we do confess y'are wise,
In dealing forth these bashful jealousies:
    In Love's name do so, and a price
    Set on your self, by being nice.
        But yet take heed: 55
What now you seem, be not the same indeed,
    And turn apostatë; Love will
Part of the way be met, or sit stone still.
      On then, and though you slow-
    ly go, yet, howsoever, go.   60

And now y'are enter'd, see the coddled cook
Runs from his torrid zone, to pry and look,
    And bless his dainty mistress; see,
    The aged point out, This is she
        Who now must sway   65
The house (Love shield her) with her Yea and Nay;
    And the smirk butler thinks it
Sin, in's nap'ry, not to express his wit;

Each striving to devise
Some gin, wherewith to catch your eyes.　　　　70

By the bride's eyes, and by the teeming life
Of her green hopes, we charge ye, that no strife,
　　Farther than gentleness, gets place
　　Among ye, striving for her lace.
　　　　　O do not fall　　　　85
Foul in these noble pastimes, lest ye call
　　Discord in, and so divide
The youthful bridegroom and the fragrant bride ;
　　　Which Love forefend ; but spoken
　　Be't to your praise, no peace was broken.　　90

And to enchant ye more, see everywhere
About the roof a siren in a sphere,
　　As we think, singing to the din
　　Of many a warbling cherubin.
　　　　　O mark ye how　　　105
The soul of Nature melts in numbers ; now
　　See, a thousand Cupids fly,
To light their tapers at the bride's bright eye.
　　　To bed, or her they'll tire,
　　Were she an element of fire.　　　110

All now is hushed in silence ; midwife moon,
With all her owl-ey'd issue, begs a boon
　　Which you must grant ; that's entrance ; with
　　Which extract all we can call pith
　　　　　And quintessence　　　155
Of planetary bodies ; so commence
　　All fair constellations
Looking upon ye, that, two nations
　　　Springing from two such fires,
　　May blaze the virtue of their sires.　　　160

288. DEVOTION MAKES THE DEITY.

Who forms a godhead out of gold or stone,
Makes not a god; but he that prays to one.

293. OBERON'S FEAST.

[Placed after 223.]

299. THE BELLMAN.

From noise of scare-fires rest ye free,
From murders benedicite,
From all mischances that may fright
Your pleasing slumbers in the night
Mercy secure ye all, and keep
The goblin from ye, while ye sleep.
Past one o'clock, and almost two,
My masters all, Good day to you.

302. UPON PRUDENCE BALDWIN, HER SICKNESS.

Prue, my dearest maid, is sick,
Almost to be lunatic:
Æsculapius, come and bring
Means for her recovering,
And a gallant cock shall be
Offer'd up by her to thee.

306. ON HIMSELF.

Here down my wearied limbs I'll lay;
My pilgrim's staff, my weed of grey,
My palmer's hat, my scallop's shell,
My cross, my cord, and all farewell.

For having now my journey done,   5
Just at the setting of the sun,
Here have I found a chamber fit,
God and good friends be thank'd for it,
Where if I can a lodger be
A little while from tramplers free;   10
At my uprising next, I shall,
If not requite, yet thank ye all.
Meanwhile, the Holy-rood hence fright
The fouler fiend and evil sprite,
From scaring you or yours this night.   15

310. UPON A CHILD THAT DIED.

HERE she lies, a pretty bud,
Lately made of flesh and blood;
Who, as soon fell fast asleep,
As her little eyes did peep.
Give her strewings; but not stir   5
The earth, that lightly covers her.

313. THE ENTERTAINMENT; OR, PORCH-VERSE, at the Marriage of MR. HEN. NORTHLY, and the most witty MRS. LETTICE YARD.

WELCOME! but yet no entrance, till we bless
First you, then you, and both for white success.
Profane no porch, young man and maid, for fear
Ye wrong the Threshold-god that keeps peace here:
Please him, and then all good-luck will betide   5
You, the brisk bridegroom, you, the dainty bride.
Do all things sweetly, and in comely wise;
Put on your garlands first, then sacrifice;

That done, when both of you have seemly fed,
We'll call on night to bring ye both to bed ;
Where being laid, all fair signs looking on,
Fish-like, increase then to a million ;
And millions of spring-times may ye have,
Which spent, one death bring to ye both one grave.

314. THE GOOD-NIGHT, OR BLESSING.

BLESSINGS, in abundance come
To the bride and to her groom ;
Pleasures many here attend ye,
And ere long a boy Love send ye,
Curl'd and comely, and so trim,
Maids, in time, may ravish him.
Thus a dew of graces fall
On ye both.   Good-night to all.

316. TO DAFFODILS.

FAIR Daffodils, we weep to see
You haste away so soon ;
As yet the early rising sun
Has not attain'd his noon.
Stay, stay,
Until the hasting day
Has run
But to the even-song ;
And, having pray'd together, we
Will go with you along.

We have short time to stay, as you,
We have as short a spring ;
As quick a growth to meet decay,
As you, or anything.

We die 15
As your hours do, and dry
Away,
Like to the summer's rain;
Or as the pearls of morning's dew,
Ne'er to be found again. 20

319. A NEW YEAR'S GIFT SENT TO SIR SIMEON
STEWARD.

No news of navies burnt at seas;
No noise of late-spawn'd Tityries,
No closet plot or open vent,
That frights men with a Parliament;
No new device or late found trick, 5
To read by th' stars the kingdom's sick;
No gin to catch the State, or wring
The free-born nosthril of the King,
We send to you; but here a jolly
Verse crowned with ivy and with holly; 10
That tells of winter's tales and mirth,
That milk-maids make about the hearth;
Of Christmas sports, the wassail-bowl,
That tost up after Fox-i'-th'-hole;
Of Blind-man-buff, and of the care 15
That young men have to shoe the mare;
Of Twelf-tide cakes, of peas and beans,
Wherewith ye make those merry scenes,
Whenas ye choose your king and queen,
And cry out, *Hey for our town green.* 20
Of ash-heaps, in the which ye use
Husbands and wives by streaks to choose;
Of crackling laurel, which fore-sounds
A plenteous harvest to your grounds;

Of these, and such like things, for shift,   25
We send instead of New-year's gift:
Read then, and when your faces shine
With buxom meat and cap'ring wine,
Remember us in cups full crown'd,
And let our city-health go round,   30
Quite through the young maids and the men,
To the ninth number, if not ten;
Until the fired chestnuts leap
For joy to see the fruits ye reap
From the plump chalice and the cup   35
That tempts till it be tossed up.
Then as ye sit about your embers,
Call not to mind those fled Decembers;
But think on these that are t' appear
As daughters to the instant year;   40
Sit crown'd with rose-buds, and carouse,
Till Liber Pater twirls the house
About your ears, and lay upon
The year your cares, that's fled and gone.
And let the russet swains the plough   45
And harrow hang up resting now;
And to the bagpipe all address,   ·
Till sleep takes place of weariness.
And thus, throughout, with Christmas plays
Frolic the full twelve holy-days.   50

323. THE CHRISTIAN MILITANT.

A MAN prepar'd against all ills to come,
That dares to dead the fire of martyrdom;
That sleeps at home, and sailing there at ease,
Fears not the fierce sedition of the seas;

That's counter-proof against the farm's mishaps,   5
Undreadful, too, of courtly thunderclaps;
That wears one face, like heaven, and never shows
A change, when fortune either comes or goes;
That keeps his own strong guard, in the despite
Of what can hurt by day, or harm by night;   10
That takes and re-delivers every stroke
Of chance, as made up all of rock and oak;
That sighs at others' death, smiles at his own
Most dire and horrid crucifixion:
Who for true glory suffers thus, we grant   15
Him to be here our Christian militant.

324. A SHORT HYMN TO LAR.

THOUGH I cannot give thee fires
Glitt'ring to my free desires;
These accept, and I'll be free,
Offering poppy unto thee.

325. ANOTHER TO NEPTUNE.

MIGHTY Neptune, may it please
Thee, the rector of the seas,
That my barque may safely run
Through thy wat'ry region,
And a tunny-fish shall be   5
Offer'd up with thanks to thee.

327. HIS EMBALMING: TO JULIA.

FOR my embalming, Julia, do but this,
Give thou my lips but their supremest kiss;
Or else transfuse thy breath into the chest
Where my small reliques must for ever rest;

That breath the balm, the myrrh, the nard shall be,　　5
To give an incorruption unto me.

333. TO LAR.

No more shall I, since I am driven hence,
Devote to thee my grains of frankincense;
No more shall I from mantle-trees hang down,
To honor thee, my little parsley crown ;
No more shall I, I fear me, to thee bring　　5
My chives of garlic for an offering ;
No more shall I, from henceforth, hear a quire
Of merry crickets by my country fire.
Go where I will, thou lucky Lar stay here,
Warm by a glitt'ring chimney all the year.　　10

334. THE DEPARTURE OF THE GOOD DEMON.

WHAT can I do in poetry,
Now the good spirit's gone from me?
Why nothing now, but lonely sit,
And over-read what I have writ.

336. HIS AGE.

Dedicated to his Peculiar Friend, M. JOHN WICKES,
Under the name of Posthumus.

AH Posthumus! our years hence fly,
And leave no sound ; nor piety,
　　　Or prayers, or vow
Can keep the wrinkle from the brow;
　　　But we must on,　　5
As fate does lead or draw us ; none,
None, Posthumus, could e'er decline
The doom of cruel Proserpine.

The pleasing wife, the house, the ground
Must all be left, no one plant found   10
     To follow thee,
Save only the curs'd cypress tree ;
     A merry mind
Looks forward, scorns what's left behind ;
Let's live, my Wickes, then, while we may,   15
And here enjoy our holiday.

W'ave seen the past-best times, and these
Will ne'er return ; we see the seas,
     And moons to wane,
But they fill up their ebbs again ;   20
     But vanish'd man,
Like to a lily lost, ne'er can,
Ne'er can repullulate, or bring
His days to see a second spring.

But on we must, and thither tend,   25
Where Ancus and rich Tullus blend
     Their sacred seed ;
Thus has infernal Jove decreed ;
     We must be made   .
Ere long a song, ere long a shade.   30
Why then, since life to us is short,
Let's make it full up by our sport.

Crown we our heads with roses, then,
And 'noint with Tyrian balm ; for when
     We two are dead,   35
The world with us is buried.
     Then live we free
As is the air, and let us be
Our own fair wind, and mark each one
Day with the white and lucky stone.   40

We are not poor, although we have
No roofs of cedar, nor our brave
   Baiæ, nor keep
Account of such a flock of sheep,
   Nor bullocks fed   45
To lard the shambles, barbels bred
To kiss our hands; nor do we wish
For Pollio's lampreys in our dish.

If we can meet, and so confer,
Both by a shining salt-cellar,   50
   And have our roof,
Although not arch'd, yet weather-proof,
   And ceiling free
From that cheap candle-baudery;
We'll eat our bean with that full mirth, 55
As we were lords of all the earth.

Well, then, on what seas we are toss'd,
Our comfort is, we can't be lost.
   Let the winds drive
Our bark, yet she will keep alive   60
   Amidst the deeps;
'Tis constancy, my Wickes, which keeps
The pinnace up; which though she errs
I' th' seas, she saves her passengers.

Say, we must part; sweet mercy bless 65
Us both i' th' sea, camp, wilderness!
   Can we so far
Stray to become less circular
   Than we are now?
No, no, that self-same heart, that vow 70
Which made us one, shall ne'er undo,
Or ravel so, to make us two.

Live in thy peace; as for myself,
When I am bruised on the shelf
   Of time, and show   75
My locks behung with frost and snow;
   When with the rheum,
The cough, the ptisic, I consume
Unto an almost nothing; then,
The ages fled, I'll call again,   80

And with a tear compare these last
Lame and bad times with those are past,
   While Baucis by,
My old lean wife, shall kiss it dry;
   And so we'll sit   85
By th' fire, foretelling snow and slit,
And weather by our achës, grown
Now old enough to be our own

True calendars, as puss's ear
Wash'd o'er 's to tell what change is near; 90
   Then, to assuage
The gripings of the chine by age,
   I'll call my young
Iülus to sing such a song
I made upon my Julia's breast,   95
And of her blush at such a feast.

Then shall he read that flow'r of mine
Enclos'd within a crystal shrine;
   A primrose next.
A piece then of a higher text.   100

  *   *   *   *

Thus frantic crazy man, God wot,
I'll call to mind things half forgot;

❋

And oft between　　　　　　　115
Repeat the times that I have seen ;
　　　Thus ripe with tears,
And twisting my Iülus' hairs,
Doting, I'll weep and say, *In truth,*
Baucis, these were my sins of youth.　　120

Then next I'll cause my hopeful lad,
If a wild apple can be had
　　　To crown the hearth,
Lar thus conspiring with our mirth,
　　　Then to infuse　　　　　　125
Our browner ale into the cruse ;
Which, sweetly spic'd, we'll first carouse
Unto the genius of the house.

Then the next health to friends of mine,
Loving the brave Burgundian wine,　　130
　　　High sons of pith,
Whose fortunes I have frolick'd with ;
　　　Such as could well
Bear up the magic bough and spell ;
And dancing 'bout the mystic Thyrse,　　135
Give up the just applause to verse.

To those, and then again to thee,
We'll drink, my Wickes, until we be
　　　Plump as the cherry,
Though not so fresh, yet full as merry　　140
　　　As the cricket,
The untam'd heifer, or the pricket,
Until our tongues shall tell our ears
W'are younger by a score of years.

Thus, till we see the fire less shine   145
From th' embers than the kitling's eyne,
      We'll still sit up,
Sphering about the wassail cup
      To all those times
Which gave me honor for my rhymes.   152
The coal once spent, we'll then to bed,
Far more than night-bewearied.

337. A SHORT HYMN TO VENUS.

GODDESS, I do love a girl
Ruby-lipp'd and tooth'd with pearl;
If so be I may but prove
Lucky in this maid I love,
I will promise there shall be   5
Myrtles offer'd up to thee.

345. THE POWER IN THE PEOPLE.

LET kings command, and do the best they may,
The saucy subjects still will bear the sway.

359. TO THE RIGHT HONORABLE PHILIP, EARL OF PEMBROKE AND MONTGOMERY.

How dull and dead are books, that cannot show
A Prince of Pembroke, and that Pembroke you!
You, who are high born, and a lord no less
Free by your fate than fortune's mightiness,
Who hug our poems, honor'd sir, and then   5
The paper gild, and laureate the pen.
Nor suffer you the poets to sit cold,
But warm their wits, and turn their lines to gold.

Others there be, who righteously will swear
Those smooth-pac'd numbers amble everywhere,   10
And these brave measures go a stately trot;
Love those like these; regard, reward them not.
But you, my lord, are one whose hand along
Goes with your mouth, or does outrun your tongue,
Paying before you praise, and cock'ring wit,   15
Give both the gold and garland unto it.

360. A HYMN TO JUNO.

STATELY goddess, do thou please,
Who art chief at marriages,
But to dress the bridal bed,
When my love and I shall wed;
And a peacock proud shall be   5
Offer'd up by us to thee.

366. UPON HIMSELF.

THOU shalt not all die; for while Love's fire shines
Upon his altar, men shall read thy lines;
And learn'd musicians shall, to honor Herrick's
Fame, and his name, both set and sing his lyrics.

367. UPON WRINKLES.

WRINKLES no more are, or no less
Than beauty turn'd to sowerness.

371. HIS LACHRIMÆ; OR, MIRTH TURN'D TO MOURNING.

CALL me no more,
As heretofore,

The music of a feast;
  Since now, alas!
  The mirth that was   5
In me, is dead or ceas'd.

  Before I went
  To banishment,
Into the loathed West,
  I could rehearse   10
  A lyric verse,
And speak it with the best.

  But time, Ai me!
  Has laid, I see,
My organ fast asleep;   15
  And turn'd my voice
  Into the noise
Of those that sit and weep.

375. TO THE MOST FAIR AND LOVELY MISTRESS .
      ANNE SOAME, NOW LADY ABDIE.

So smell those odors that do rise
From out the wealthy spiceries;
So smells the flow'r of blooming clove,
Or roses smother'd in the stove;
So smells the air of spiced wine,   5
Or essences of jessamine;
So smells the breath about the hives,
When well the work of honey thrives,
And all the busy factors come
Laden with wax and honey home;   10
So smell those neat and woven bowers,
All over-arch'd with orange flowers,

And almond blossoms, that do mix
To make rich these aromatics;
So smell those bracelets, and those bands 15
Of amber chaf'd between the hands,
When thus enkindled, they transpire
A noble perfume from the fire.
The wine of cherries, and to these
The cooling breath of respasses, 20
The smell of morning's milk and cream,
Butter of cowslips mix'd with them,
Of roasted warden, or bak'd pear,
These are not to be reckon'd here;
Whenas the meanest part of her 25
Smells like the maiden-pomander.
Thus sweet she smells, or what can be
More lik'd by her, or lov'd by me.

386. A VOW TO MARS.

STORE of courage to me grant,
Now I'm turn'd a combatant;
Help me, so that I my shield,
Fighting, lose not in the field.
That's the greatest shame of all 5
That in warfare can befall.
Do but this, and there shall be
Offer'd up à wolf to thee.

387. TO HIS MAID PREW.

THESE summer birds did with thy master stay
The times of warmth, but then they flew away,
Leaving their poet, being now grown old,
Expos'd to all the coming winter's cold.

But thou, kind Prew, did'st with my fates abide   5
As well the winter's as the summer's tide ;
For which thy love, live with thy master here,
Not one, but all the seasons of the year.

391.   HOW PANSIES, or HEARTEASE, CAME FIRST.

FROLIC virgins once these were,
Over-loving, living here ;
Being here their ends deny'd,
Ran for sweethearts mad, and died.
Love, in pity of their tears,   5
And their loss in blooming years,
For their restless here-spent hours
Gave them heartsease turned to flow'rs.

393.   LAR'S PORTION AND THE POET'S PART.

AT my homely country-seat,
I have there a little wheat,
Which I work to meal, and make
Therewithal a holy-cake ;
Part of which I give to Lar,   5
Part is my peculiar.

413.   THE MAD MAID'S SONG.

GOOD morrow to the day so fair ;   .
Good morning, sir, to you ;
Good morrow to mine own torn hair,
Bedabbled with the dew.

Good morning to this primrose too ;   5
Good morrow to each maid
That will with flowers the tomb bestrew
Wherein my love is laid.

Ah! woe is me, woe, woe is me,
    Alack, and well-a-day!   10
For pity, sir, find out that bee
    Which bore my love away.

I'll seek him in your bonnet brave;
    I'll seek him in your eyes;
Nay, now I think th' ave made his grave   15
    I'th' bed of strawberries.

I'll seek him there; I know, ere this,
    The cold, cold earth doth shake him;
But I will go, or send a kiss
    By you, sir, to awake him.   20

Pray hurt him not; though he be dead,
    He knows well who do love him; ·
And who with green turfs rear his head,
    And who do rudely move him.

He's soft and tender, pray take heed: 25
    With bands of cowslips bind him,
And bring him home; but 'tis decreed,
    That I shall never find him.

420. UPON BRIDGET. EPIG.

OF four teeth only Bridget was possess'd;
Two she spat out, a cough forc'd out the rest.

421. TO SYCAMORES.

I'M sick of love; O let me lie
Under your shades, to sleep or die!
Either is welcome; so I have
Or here my bed, or here my grave.

Why do you sigh and sob, and keep   5
Time with the tears that I do weep?
Say, have ye sense, or do you prove
What crucifixions are in love?
I know ye do; and that's the why
You sigh for love as well as I.   10

436. UPON PARSON BEANS.

OLD Parson Beans hunts six days of the week,
And on the seventh he has his notes to seek;
Six days he hollows so much breath away,
That on the seventh he can nor preach or pray.

439. POLICY IN PRINCES.

THAT Princes may possess a surer seat,
'Tis fit they make no One with them too great.

442. TO DAISIES, NOT TO SHUT SO SOON.

SHUT not so soon; the dull-ey'd night
     Has not as yet begun
To make a seizure on the light,
     Or to seal up the sun.

No marigolds yet closed are,   5
     No shadows great appear;
Nor doth the early shepherd's star
     Shine like a spangle here.

Stay but till my Julia close
     Her life-begetting eye;   10
And let the whole world then dispose
     Itself to live or die.

443. TO THE LITTLE SPINNERS.

YE pretty huswives, would ye know
The work that I would put ye to?
This, this it should be, for to spin
A lawn for me, so fine and thin
As it might serve me for my skin.
For cruel love has me so whipp'd,
That of my skin I all am stripp'd,
And shall despair that any art
Can ease the rawness or the smart,
Unless you skin again each part.
Which mercy, if you will but do,
I call all maids to witness to
What here I promise, that no broom
Shall now, or ever after, come
To wrong a Spinner or her loom.

444. OBERON'S PALACE.

[Placed after 223.]

446. TO JULIA IN THE TEMPLE.

BESIDES us two, i' th' Temple here's not one
To make up now a congregation.
Let's to the altar of perfumes then go,
And say short prayers: and when we have done so,
Then we shall see, how in a little space
Saints will come in to fill each pew and place.

447. TO ŒNONE.

WHAT Conscience, say, is it in thee
    When I a heart had one,
To take away that heart from me,
    And to retain thy own?

For shame or pity, now incline 5
   To play a loving part;
Either to send me kindly thine,
   Or give me back my heart.

Covet not both; but if thou dost
   Resolve to part with neither, 10
Why! yet to show that thou art just,
   Take me and mine together.

451. TO GROVES.

YE silent shades, whose each tree here
Some relique of a saint doth wear,
Who for some sweetheart's sake did prove
The fire and martyrdom of love:
Here is the legend of those saints 5
That died for love, and their complaints;
Their wounded hearts and names we find
Encarv'd upon the leaves and rind.
Give way, give way to me, who come
Scorch'd with the self-same martyrdom; 10
And have deserv'd as much, Love knows,
As to be canoniz'd 'mongst those
Whose deeds and deaths here written are
Within your greeny calendar.
By all those virgins' fillets hung 15
Upon your boughs, and requiems sung
For saints and souls departed hence,
Here honor'd still with frankincense;
By all those tears that have been shed
As a drink-offering to the dead; 20
By all those true love-knots that be
With mottoes carv'd on every tree;
By sweet St. Phillis, pity me!

By dear St. Iphis and the rest
Of all those other saints now blest.
Me, me forsaken, here admit
Among your myrtles to be writ;
That my poor name may have the glory
To live rememb'red in your story.

452. AN EPITAPH UPON A VIRGIN.

HERE a solemn fast we keep,
While all beauty lies asleep,
Hush'd be all things, no noise here
But the toning of a tear;
Or a sigh of such as bring
Cowslips for her covering.

462. THE PLUNDER.

I AM of all bereft,
Save but some few beans left,
Whereof, at last, to make
For me and mine a cake;
Which eaten, they and I
Will say our grace, and die.

469. TO BLOSSOMS.

FAIR pledges of a fruitful tree,
　　Why do ye fall so fast?
　　Your date is not so past,
But you may stay yet here a while,
　　To blush and gently smile,
　　　　And go at last.

What, were ye born to be
  An hour or half's delight,
  And so to bid good-night?
'Twas pity Nature brought ye forth, 10
  Merely to show your worth,
    And lose you quite.

But you are lovely leaves, where we
  May read how soon things have
  Their end, though ne'er so brave; 15
And after they have shown their pride
  Like you a while, they glide
    Into the grave.

475. THE OLD WIVES' PRAYER.

HOLY-ROOD, come forth and shield
Us i'th' city and the field:
Safely guard us, now and aye,
From the blast that burns by day,
And those sounds that us affright 5
In the dead of dampish night:
Drive all hurtful fiends us fro,
By the time the cocks first crow.

477. UPON HIS DEPARTURE HENCE.

  THUS I
  Pass by,
  And die,
  As one
  Unknown 5
  And gone:
  I'm made
  A shade,

And laid
I'th' grave,
There have
My cave :
Where tell
I dwell,
Farewell.

478. THE WASSAIL.

GIVE way, give way, ye gates, and win
An easy blessing to your bin
And basket, by our ent'ring in.

May both with manchet stand replete,
Your larders, too, so hung with meat,
That though a thousand, thousand eat,

Yet ere twelve moons shall whirl about
Their silv'ry spheres, there's none may doubt
But more's sent in than was serv'd out.

Next, may your dairies prosper so
As that your pans no ebb may know;
But if they do, the more to flow

Like to a solemn sober stream,
Bank'd all with lilies, and the cream
Of sweetest cowslips filling them.

Then may your plants be press'd with fruit,
Nor bee or hive you have be mute,
But sweetly sounding like a lute.

Next may your duck and teeming hen
Both to the cock's tread say Amen,
And for their two eggs render ten.

Last, may your harrows, shares, and ploughs,
Your stacks, your stocks, your sweetest mows,
All prosper by our virgin-vows.

Alas! we bless, but see none here,   25
That brings us either ale or beer;
In a dry house all things are near.

Let's leave a longer time to wait,
Where rust and cobwebs bind the gate;
And all live here with needy fate;   30

Where chimneys do for ever weep
For want of warmth, and stomachs keep
With noise the servants' eyes from sleep.

It is in vain to sing, or stay
Our free feet here, but we'll away;   35
Yet to the Lares this we'll say:

The time will come when you'll be sad;
And reckon this for fortune bad,
T'ave lost the good ye might have had.

486. UPON JULIA'S HAIR FILL'D WITH DEW.

DEW sat on Julia's hair,
    And spangled too,
Like leaves that laden are
    With trembling dew;
Or glitter'd to my sight   5
    As when the beams
Have their reflected light
    Danc'd by the streams.

488. LOSS FROM THE LEAST.

GREAT men by small means oft are overthrown;
He's lord of thy life who contemns his own.

490. SHAME NO STATIST.

SHAME is a bad attendant to a state;
He rents his crown that fears the people's hate.

499. UPON A FLY.

A GOLDEN fly one show'd to me,
Clos'd in a box of ivory,
Where both seem'd proud — the fly to have
His burial in an ivory grave;
The ivory took state to hold   5
A corpse as bright as burnish'd gold.
One fate had both; both equal grace,
The buried and the burying-place.
Not Virgil's gnat, to whom the Spring
All flowers sent to 'is burying;   10
Not Martial's bee, which in a bead
Of amber quick was buried;
Nor that fine worm that does inter
Herself i' th' silken sepulchre;
Nor my rare Phil, that lately was   15
With lilies tomb'd up in a glass,
More honour had than this same fly,
Dead, and clos'd up in ivory.

503. UPON PARRAT.

PARRAT protests 'tis he, and only he,
Can teach a man the *Art of memory;*
Believe him not, for he forgot it quite,
Being drunk, who 'twas that can'd his ribs last night.

517. HIS WINDING-SHEET.

COME thou, who art the wine and wit
  Of all I've writ;
The grace, the glory, and the best
  Piece of the rest;
Thou art of what I did intend   5
  The all and end;
And what was made, was made to meet
  Thee, thee, my sheet;
Come then, and be to my chaste side
  Both bed and bride.   10
We two, as reliques left, will have
  One rest, one grave;
And, hugging close, we will not fear
  Lust ent'ring here,
Where all desires are dead or cold,   15
  As is the mould;
And all affections are forgot,
  Or trouble not.
Here, here the slaves and pris'ners be
  From shackles free,   20
And weeping widows, long oppress'd,
  Do here find rest.
The wronged client ends his laws
  Here, and his cause;
Here those long suits of Chancery lie 25
  Quiet, or die,
And all Star Chamber bills do cease,
  Or hold their peace.
Here needs no Court for our Request,
  Where all are best,   30
All wise, all equal, and all just
  Alike i'th' dust.

Nor need we here to fear the frown
 Of court or crown,
Where Fortune bears no sway o'er things, 35
 There all are kings.
In this securer place we'll keep,
 As lull'd asleep;
Or for a little time we'll lie,
 As robes laid by, 40
To be another day re-worn,
 Turn'd, but not torn;
Or like old testaments ingross'd,
 Lock'd up, not lost;
And for a while lie here conceal'd, 45
 · To be reveal'd
Next, at that great Platonic Year,
 And then meet here.

523. TO PHILLIS TO LOVE, AND LIVE WITH HIM.

LIVE, live with me, and thou shalt see
The pleasures I'll prepare for thee.
· What sweets the country can afford
Shall bless thy bed, and bless thy board.
The soft sweet moss shall be thy bed, 5
With crawling woodbine overspread;
By which the silver-shedding streams
Shall gently melt thee into dreams.
Thy clothing next shall be a gown
Made of the fleece's purest down; 10
The tongues of kids shall be thy meat,
Their milk thy drink, and thou shalt eat
The paste of filberts for thy bread,
With cream of cowslips buttered.

Thy feasting-tables shall be hills   15
With daisies spread, and daffodils;
Where thou shalt sit, and redbreast by
For meat shall give thee melody.
I'll give thee chains and carcanets
Of primroses and violets.   20
A bag and bottle thou shalt have,
That richly wrought, and this as brave;
So that as either shall express
The wearer's no mean shepherdess.
At shearing-time and yearly wakes,   25
When Themilis his pastime makes,
There thou shalt be, and be the wit,
Nay, more, the feast, and grace of it.
On holy days, when virgins meet
To dance the heyes with nimble feet,   30
Thou shalt come forth, and then appear
The Queen of Roses for that year;
And having danc'd, 'bove all the best,
Carry the garland from the rest.
In wicker baskets maids shall bring   35
To thee, my dearest shepharling,
The blushing apple, bashful pear,
And shame-fac'd plum, all simp'ring there.
Walk in the groves, and thou shalt find
The name of Phillis in the rind   40
Of every straight and smooth-skin tree;
Where, kissing that, I'll twice kiss thee.
To thee a sheep-hook I will send,
Beprank'd with ribands, to this end,
This, this alluring hook might be   45
Less for to catch a sheep than me.
Thou shalt have possets, wassails fine,
Not made of ale, but spiced wine;

To make thy maids and self free mirth,
All sitting near the glitt'ring hearth.
Thou sha't have ribbands, roses, rings,
Gloves, garters, stockings, shoes, and strings
Of winning colors, that shall move
Others to lust, but me to love.
These, nay, and more, thine own shall be,
If thou wilt love and live with me.

525. UPON MISTRESS SUSANNA SOUTHWELL HER CHEEKS.

RARE are thy cheeks, Susanna, which do show
Ripe cherries smiling, while that others blow.

526. UPON HER EYES.

CLEAR are her eyes,
Like purest skies ;
Discovering from thence
A baby there
That turns each sphere,
Like an Intelligence.

527. UPON HER FEET.

HER pretty feet
Like snails did creep
A little out, and then,
As if they started at bo-peep,
Did soon draw in again.

532. A VOW TO MINERVA.

GODDESS, I begin an art;
Come thou in with thy best part,
For to make the texture lie
Each way smooth and civilly;
And a broad-fac'd owl shall be   . 5
Offer'd up with vows to thee.

538. ILL GOVERNMENT.

PREPOSTEROUS is that government, and rude,
When kings obey the wilder multitude.

541. TO JULIA, THE FLAMINICA DIALIS, OR QUEEN-PRIEST.

THOU know'st, my Julia, that it is thy turn
This morning's incense to prepare and burn.
The chaplet and inarculum here be,
With the white vestures, all attending thee.
This day the Queen-Priest thou art made, t'appease   5
Love for our very many trespasses.
One chief transgression is, among the rest,
Because with flowers her temple was not dress'd;
The next, because her altars did not shine
With daily fires; the last, neglect of wine: 10
For which, her wrath is gone forth to consume
Us all, unless preserv'd by thy perfume.
Take then thy censer; put in fire, and thus,
O pious Priestess! make a peace for us.
For our neglect, Love did our death decree;   15
That we escape, redemption comes by thee.

546. AN ODE TO SIR CLIPSEBY CREW.

HERE we securely live, and eat
          The cream of meat;
      And keep eternal fires,
By which we sit, and do divine
          As wine   5
      And rage inspires.

If full, we charm; then call upon
          Anacreon
      To grace the frantic thyrse:
And having drunk, we raise a shout   10
          Throughout,
      To praise his verse.

Then cause we Horace to be read,
          Which sung or said,
      A goblet, to the brim,   15
Of lyric wine, both swell'd and crown'd,
          Around
      We quaff to him.

Thus, thus we live, and spend the hours
          In wine and flowers;   20
      And make the frolic year,
The month, the week, the instant day,
          To stay
      The longer here.

Come then, brave knight, and see the cell   25
          Wherein I dwell,
      And my enchantments too;
Which love and noble freedom is,
          And this
      Shall fetter you.   30

Take horse, and come ; or be so kind
    To send your mind,
  Though but in numbers few,
And I shall think I have the heart,
     Or part,   35
  Of Clipseby Crew.

547. TO HIS WORTHY KINSMAN, MR. STEPHEN SOAME.

Nor is my number full, till I inscribe
Thee, sprightly Soame, one of my righteous tribe :
A tribe of one lip-leaven, and of one
Civil behavior and religion :
A stock of saints, where every one doth wear   5
A stole of white, and canonized here ;
Among which holies be thou ever known,
Brave kinsman, mark'd out with the whiter stone ;
Which seals thy glory, since I do prefer
Thee here in my eternal calendar.   10

548. TO HIS TOMB-MAKER.

Go I must ; when I am gone,
Write but this upon my stone :
Chaste I liv'd, without a wife,
That's the story of my life.
Strewings need none, every flower   5
Is in this word, bachelor.

549. GREAT SPIRITS SUPERVIVE.

Our mortal parts may wrapp'd in cere-cloths lie ;
Great spirits never with their bodies die.

554. HIS CONTENT IN THE COUNTRY.

HERE, here I live with what my board
Can with the smallest cost afford;
Though ne'er so mean the viands be,
They well content my Prew and me:
Or pea or bean, or wort or beet,   5
Whatever comes, content makes sweet.
Here we rejoice because no rent
We pay for our poor tenement,
Wherein we rest, and never fear
The landlord or the usurer.   10
The quarter-day does ne'er affright
Our peaceful slumbers in the night;
We eat our own, and batten more
Because we feed on no man's score;
But pity those whose flanks grow great 15
Swell'd with the lard of others' meat.
We bless our fortunes when we see
Our own beloved privacy;
And like our living, where w'are known
To very few, or else to none.   20

556. ON HIMSELF.

SOME parts may perish, die thou canst not all;
The most of thee shall scape the funeral.

577. THE APPARITION OF HIS MISTRESS CALLING HIM TO ELYSIUM.

Desunt nonnulla ——

COME then, and like two doves with silv'ry wings,
Let our souls fly to th' shades, where ever springs

Sit smiling in the meads; where balm and oil,
Roses and cassia, crown the untill'd soil;
Where no disease reigns, or infection comes 5
To blast the air, but amber-greece and gums.
This, that, and ev'ry thicket doth transpire
More sweet than storax from the hallowed fire;
Where ev'ry tree a wealthy issue bears
Of fragrant apples, blushing plums, or pears, 10
And all the shrubs, with sparkling spangles, shew
Like morning sunshine, tinselling the dew.
Here in green meadows sits eternal May,
Purfling the margents, while perpetual day
So double gilds the air, as that no night 15
Can ever rust th' enamel of the light;
Here naked younglings, handsome striplings, run
Their goals for virgins' kisses; which when done,
Then unto dancing forth the learned round
Commix'd they meet, with endless roses crown'd. 20
And here we'll sit on primrose-banks, and see
Love's chorus led by Cupid; and we'll be
Two loving followers too unto the grove
Where poets sing the stories of our love:
There thou shalt hear divine Musæus sing 25
Of Hero and Leander; then I'll bring
Thee to the stand, where honour'd Homer reads
His Odysseys and his high Iliads;
About whose throne the crowd of poets throng
To hear the incantation of his tongue: 30
To Linus, then to Pindar; and that done,
I'll bring thee, Herrick, to Anacreon,
Quaffing his full-crown'd bowls of burning wine,
And in his raptures speaking lines of thine,
Like to his subject; and as his frantic 35
Looks show him truly Bacchanalian like,

Besmear'd with grapes, welcome he shall thee thither,
Where both may rage, both drink and dance together.
Then stately Virgil, witty Ovid, by
Whom fair Corinna sits, and doth comply   40
With ivory wrists his laureate head, and steeps
His eye in dew of kisses while he sleeps;
Then soft Catullus, sharp-fang'd Martial,
And towering Lucan, Horace, Juvenal,
And snaky Persius; these, and those whom rage   45
Dropp'd from the jars of heaven, fill'd t' engage
All times unto their frenzies; thou shalt there
Behold them in a spacious theatre.
Among which glories, crown'd with sacred bays
And flatt'ring ivy, two recite their plays,   50
Beaumont and Fletcher, swans, to whom all ears
Listen, while they, like sirens in their spheres,
Sing their Evadne: and still more for thee
There yet remains to know than thou canst see
By glimm'ring of a fancy; do but come,   55
And there I'll show thee that capacious room
In which thy father, Jonson, now is plac'd,
As in a globe of radiant fire and grac'd
To be in that orb crown'd, that doth include
Those prophets of the former magnitude,   60
And he one chief.   But hark, I hear the cock,
The bellman of the night, proclaim the clock
Of late struck one; and now I see the prime
Of daybreak from the pregnant east, 'tis time
I vanish; more I had to say,   65
But night determines here.   Away!

579. UPON URLES. EPIG.

URLES had the gout so, that he could not stand
Then from his feet it shifted to his hand;
When 'twas in 's feet his charity was small;
Now 'tis in 's hand, he gives no alms at all.

582. THE PRIMROSE.

ASK me why I send you here
This sweet Infanta of the year;
   Ask me why I send to you
This Primrose, thus bepearl'd with dew:
   I will whisper to your ears,   5
The sweets of love are mix'd with tears.

   Ask me why this flower does show
So yellow-green, and sickly too;
   Ask me why the stalk is weak,
And bending, yet it does not break: 10
   I will answer, these discover
What fainting hopes are in a lover.

586. TO JULIA.

THE saints-bell calls; and Julia, I must read
The proper lessons for the saints now dead;
To grace which service, Julia, there shall be
One holy collect said or sung for thee.
Dead when thou art, dear Julia, thou shalt have   5
A trental sung by virgins o'er thy grave;
Meantime we two will sing the dirge of these,
Who, dead, deserve our best remembrances.

598. UPON THE TROUBLESOME TIMES.

O TIMES most bad!
Without the scope
Of hope
Of better to be had!

Where shall I go,   5
Or whither run
To shun
This public overthrow?

No places are,
(This I am sure)   10
Secure
In this our wasting war.

Some storms w'ave past;
Yet we must all
Down fall,   15
And perish at the last.

'603. SHIPWRACK.

He who has suffer'd shipwrack, fears to sail
Upon the seas, though with a gentle gale.

605. TO HIS BOOK.

Be bold, my book, nor be abash'd, or fear
The cutting thumb-nail, or the brow severe;
But by the Muses swear, all here is good,
If but well read; or, ill read, understood.

606. HIS PRAYER TO BEN JONSON.

WHEN I a verse shall make,
    Know I have pray'd thee,
For old religion's sake,
    Saint Ben, to aid me.

Make the way smooth for me,
    When I, thy Herrick,
Honoring thee, on my knee
    Offer my Lyric.

Candles I'll give to thee,
    And a new altar;
And thou, Saint Ben, shalt be
    Writ in my psalter.

607. POVERTY AND RICHES.

GIVE want her welcome, if she comes; we find
Riches to be but burthens to the mind.

608. AGAIN.

WHO with a little cannot be content
Endures an everlasting punishment.

610. LAWS.

WHEN laws full power have to sway, we see
Little or no part there of tyranny.

618. TO THE MAIDS TO WALK ABROAD.

COME, sit we under yonder tree,
Where merry as the maids we'll be;

And as on primroses we sit,
We'll venture, if we can, at wit,
If not, at draw-gloves we will play,   5
So spend some minutes of the day;
Or else spin out the thread of sands,
Playing at questions and commands,
Or tell what strange tricks love can do
By quickly making one of two.   10
Thus we will sit and talk, but tell
No cruel truths of Philomel,
Or Phillis, whom hard fate forc'd on
To kill herself for Demophon.
But fables we'll relate — how Jove   15
Put on all shapes to get a love,
As now a satyr, then a swan,
A bull but then, and now a man.
Next, we will act how young men woo,
And sigh and kiss as lovers do;   20
And talk of brides, and who shall make
That wedding-smock, this bridal cake,
That dress, this sprig, that leaf, this vine,
That smooth and silken columbine.
This done, we'll draw lots who shall buy   25
And gild the bays and rosemary;
What posies for our wedding rings,
What gloves we'll give, and ribanings;
And smiling at ourselves, decree ·
Who then the joining priest shall be;   30
What short sweet prayers shall be said,
And how the posset shall be made
With cream of lilies, not of kine,
And maiden's-blush for spiced wine.
Thus having talk'd, we'll next commend   35
A kiss to each, and so we'll end.

619. HIS OWN EPITAPH.

As wearied pilgrims, once possess'd
Of long'd-for lodging, go to rest;
So I, now having rid my way, .
Fix here my button'd staff and stay.
Youth, I confess, hath me misled, 5
But age hath brought me right to bed.

621. THE NIGHT-PIECE, TO JULIA.

HER eyes the glow-worm lend thee,
The shooting stars attend thee;
   And the elves also,
   Whose little eyes glow
Like the sparks of fire, befriend thee. 5

No Will-o'-th'-Wisp mislight thee,
Nor snake or slow-worm bite thee;
   But on, on thy way,
   Not making a stay,
Since ghost there's none to affright thee. 10

Let not the dark thee cumber;
What though the moon does slumber?
   The stars of the night
   Will lend thee their light,
Like tapers clear without number. 15

Then, Julia, let me woo thee,
Thus, thus to come unto me;
   And when I shall meet
   Thy silv'ry feet,
My soul I'll pour into thee. 20

625. GLORY.

I MAKE no haste to have my numbers read;
Seldom comes glory till a man be dead.

626. POETS.

WANTONS we are; and though our words be such,
Our lives do differ from our lines by much.

629. HIS CHARGE TO JULIA AT HIS DEATH.

DEAREST of thousands, now the time draws near
That with my lines my life must full-stop here.
Cut off thy hairs, and let thy tears be shed
Over my turf, when I am buried.
Then for effusions, let none wanting be,   5
Or other rites that do belong to me;
As love shall help thee, when thou dost go hence
Unto thy everlasting residence.

636. TO HIS LOVELY MISTRESSES.

ONE night i' th' year, my dearest beauties, come
And bring those due drink-offerings to my tomb;
When thence ye see my reverend ghost to rise,
And there to lick th' effused sacrifice,
Though paleness be the livery that I wear,   5
Look ye not wan or colorless for fear;
Trust me, I will not hurt ye, or once show
The least grim look, or cast a frown on you;
Nor shall the tapers, when I'm there, burn blue.
This I may do, perhaps, as I glide by,   10
Cast on my girls a glance, and loving eye;

Or fold mine arms, and sigh, because I've lost
The world so soon, and in it you the most:
Than these, no fears more on your fancies fall,
Though then I smile, and speak no words at all.   15

645. THE HAG.

THE hag is astride
This night for to ride,
The devil and she together;
Through thick and through thin,
Now out and then in,   5
Though ne'er so foul be the weather.

A thorn or a burr
She takes for a spur;
With a lash of a bramble she rides now,
Through brakes and through briars,   10
O'er ditches and mires,
She follows the spirit that guides now.

No beast for his food
Dares now range the wood,
But hush'd in his lair he lies lurking;   15
While mischiefs by these,
On land and on seas,
At noon of night are a-working.

The storm will arise
And trouble the skies   20
This night; and, more for the wonder,
The ghost from the tomb
Affrighted shall come,
Call'd out by the clap of the thunder.

653. TO SILVIA.

I AM holy while I stand
Circumcross'd by thy pure hand;
But when that is gone, again
I, as others, am profane.

654. TO HIS CLOSET GODS.

WHEN I go hence, ye closet gods, I fear
Never again to have ingression here ;
Where I have had whatever things could be
Pleasant and precious to my muse and me.
Besides rare sweets, I had a book which none　　　5
Could read the intext but myself alone ;
About the cover of this book there went
A curious-comely, clean compartiement ;
And in the midst, to grace it more, was set
A blushing pretty-peeping rubelet ;　　　　　10
But now 'tis clos'd, and being shut and seal'd,
Be it, O be it never more reveal'd !
Keep here still, closet gods, 'fore whom I've set
Oblations oft of sweetest marmelet.

662. TO MOMUS.

WHO read'st this book that I have writ,
And canst not mend, but carp at it ;
By all the Muses, thou shalt be
Anathema to it and me.

664. THE COUNTRY LIFE.

To the Honoured MR. END. PORTER, Groom of the Bedchamber
to His Majesty.

SWEET country life, to such unknown
Whose lives are others', not their own,
But, serving courts and cities, be
Less happy, less enjoying thee.
Thou never plough'st the ocean's foam   5
To seek and bring rough pepper home ;
Nor to the Eastern Ind dost rove
To bring from thence the scorched clove ;
Nor, with the loss of thy lov'd rest,
Bring'st home the ingot from the West :   10
No, thy ambition's masterpiece
Flies no thought higher than a fleece ;
Or how to pay thy hinds, and clear
All scores, and so to end the year :
But walk'st about thine own dear bounds,   15
Not envying others' larger grounds,
For well thou know'st, *'tis not th' extent*
Of land makes life, but sweet content.
When now the cock, the ploughman's horn,
Calls forth the lily-wristed morn,   20
Then to thy corn-fields thou dost go.
Which, though well soil'd, yet thou dost know
That the best compost for the lands
Is the wise master's feet and hands.
There at the plough thou find'st thy team,   25
With a hind whistling there to them,
And cheer'st them up by singing how
The kingdom's portion is the plough.
This done, then to th' enamell'd meads
Thou go'st, and as thy foot there treads,   30

Thou seest a present godlike power
Imprinted in each herb and flower,
And smell'st the breath of great-eyed kine,
Sweet as the blossoms of the vine.
Here thou behold'st thy large sleek neat　　　　35
Unto the dewlaps up in meat;
And as thou look'st, the wanton steer,
The heifer, cow, and ox draw near,
To make a pleasing pastime there.
These seen, thou goest to view thy flocks　　　　40
Of sheep, safe from the wolf and fox,
And find'st their bellies there as full
Of short sweet grass as backs with wool,
And leav'st them, as they feed and fill,
A shepherd piping on a hill.　　　　45
For sports, for pageantry, and plays,
Thou hast thy eves and holydays,
On which the young men and maids meet
To exercise their dancing feet,
Tripping the comely country round,　　　　50
With daffodils and daisies crown'd.
Thy wakes, thy quintels, here thou hast,
Thy Maypoles too with garlands grac'd,
Thy morris-dance, thy Whitsun-ale,　　．
Thy shearing-feast, which never fail,　　　　55
Thy harvest home, thy wassail bowl,
That's toss'd up after fox-i'-th'-hole,
Thy mummeries, thy Twelf-tide kings
And queens, thy Christmas revellings,
Thy nut-brown mirth, thy russet wit,　　　　60
And no man pays too dear for it.
To these thou hast thy times to go
And trace the hare i' th' treacherous snow;
Thy witty wiles to draw, and get

The lark into the trammel net;   65
Thou hast thy cockrood and thy glade
To take the precious pheasant made;
Thy lime-twigs, snares, and pitfalls then,
To catch the pilf'ring birds, not men.
O happy life! if that their good   70
The husbandmen but understood,
Who all the day themselves do please,
And younglings, with such sports as these,
And, lying down, have nought t' affright
Sweet sleep, that makes more short the night.   75

Cætera desunt ——

696. BITING OF BEGGARS.

WHO, railing, drives the lazar from his door,
Instead of alms, sets dogs upon the poor.

697. THE MAYPOLE.

THE Maypole is up,
Now give me the cup,
I'll drink to the garlands around it;
But first unto those
Whose hands did compose   5
The glory of flowers that crown'd it.

A health to my girls
Whose husbands may earls
Or lords be, granting my wishes;
And when that ye wed   10
To the bridal bed,
Then multiply all, like to fishes.

704. MEAN THINGS OVERCOME MIGHTY.

By the weak'st means things mighty are o'erthrown
He's lord of thy life, who contemns his own.

706. UPON SMEATON.

How could Luke Smeaton wear a shoe or boot,
Who two and thirty corns had on a foot?

708. HOW ROSES CAME RED.

'Tis said, as Cupid danc'd among
The gods, he down the nectar flung,
Which, on the white rose being shed,
Made it for ever after red.

709. KINGS.

Men are not born kings, but are men renown'd,
Chose first, confirm'd next, and at last are crown'd.

714. LAXARE FIBULAM.

To loose the button is no less
Than to cast off all bashfulness.

716. NOT EVERY DAY FIT FOR VERSE.

'Tis not ev'ry day that I
Fitted am to prophesy;
No, but when the spirit fills
The fantastic pannicles,
Full of fier, then I write
As the godhead doth indite.

Thus inrag'd, my lines are hurl'd,
Like the Sybil's, through the world.
Look how next the holy fire
Either slakes, or doth retire;   10
So the fancy cools, till when
That brave spirit comes again.

719. TRUE SAFETY.

'TIS not the walls or purple that defends
A prince from foes, but 'tis his fort of friends.

725. TO THE GENIUS OF HIS HOUSE.

COMMAND the roof, great Genius, and from thence
Into this house pour down thy influence,
That through each room a golden pipe may run
Of living water by thy benison;
Fulfil the larders, and with strength'ning bread   5
Be evermore these bins replenished.
Next, like a bishop consecrate my ground,
That lucky fairies here may dance their round;
And after that lay down some silver pence,
The master's charge and care to recompense;   10
Charm then the chambers, make the beds for ease
More than for peevish pining sicknesses;
Fix the foundation fast, and let the roof
Grow old with time, but yet keep weather-proof.

726. HIS GRANGE, OR PRIVATE WEALTH.

THOUGH clock,
To tell how night draws hence, I've none,
A cock
I have to sing how day draws on:

I have
A maid, my Prew, by good luck sent,
To save
That little Fates me gave or lent:
A hen
I keep, which, creeking day by day,
Tells when
She goes her long white egg to lay:
A goose
I have, which, with a jealous ear,
Lets loose
Her tongue to tell what danger's near:
A lamb
I keep, tame, with my morsels fed,
Whose dam
An orphan left him, lately dead:
A cat
I keep, that plays about my house,
Grown fat
With eating many a miching mouse:
To these
A Tracy I do keep, whereby
I please
The more my rural privacy:
Which are
But toys, to give my heart some ease.
Where care
None is, slight things do lightly please.

732. CHARON AND PHILOMEL: A DIALOGUE SUNG.

Ph. CHARON! O gentle Charon! let me woo thee,
　By tears and pity now to come unto me.
Ch. What voice so sweet and charming do I hear?
　Say, what thou art. *Ph.* I prithee first draw near.

Ch. A sound I hear, but nothing yet can see,   5
   Speak where thou art. *Ph.* O Charon, pity me!
   I am a bird, and though no name I tell,
   My warbling note will say I'm Philomel.
Ch. What's that to me? I waft nor fish or fowls,
   Nor beasts, fond thing, but only human souls.   10
Ph. Alas, for me! *Ch.* Shame on thy witching note,
   That made me thus hoist sail, and bring my boat:
   But I'll return; what mischief brought thee hither?
Ph. A deal of love, and much, much grief together.
Ch. What's thy request? *Ph.* That since she's now beneath 15
   Who fed my life, I'll follow her in death.
Ch. And is that all? I'm gone. *Ph.* By love, I pray thee.
Ch. Talk not of love; all pray, but few souls pay me.
Ph. I'll give thee vows and tears. *Ch.* Can tears pay scores
   For mending sails, for patching boat and oars?   20
Ph. I'll beg a penny, or I'll sing so long
   Till thou shalt say I've paid thee with a song.
Ch. Why, then begin, and all the while we make
   Our slothful passage o'er the Stygian lake,
   Thou and I'll sing to make these dull shades merry, 25
   Who else with tears would doubtless drown my ferry.

753. OUR OWN SINS UNSEEN.

OTHER men's sins we ever bear in mind;
None sees the fardel of his faults behind.

763. THE WAKE.

COME, Anthea, let us two
Go to feast, as others do:
Tarts and custards, creams and cakes,
Are the junkets still at wakes;

Unto which the tribes resort,
Where the business is the sport.
Morris-dancers thou shalt see,
Marian, too, in pageantry;
And a mimic to devise
Many grinning properties.
Players there will be, and those
Base in action as in clothes;
Yet with strutting they will please
The incurious villages.
Near the dying of the day
There will be a cudgel-play,
Where a coxcomb will be broke,
Ere a good word can be spoke:
But the anger ends all here,
Drench'd in ale or drown'd in beer.
Happy rustics, best content
With the cheapest merriment,
And possess no other fear
Than to want the wake next year.

781. UPON JULIA'S CLOTHES

WHENAS in silks my Julia goes,
Then, then, methinks, how sweetly flows
That liquefaction of her clothes.

Next, when I cast mine eyes, and see
That brave vibration, each way free
O, how that glittering taketh me!

784. UPON PREW, HIS MAID.

In this little urn is laid
Prewdence Baldwin, once my maid,
From whose happy spark here let
Spring the purple violet.

786. CEREMONIES FOR CHRISTMAS.

Come, bring with a noise,
   My merry merry boys,
The Christmas log to the firing,
   While my good dame, she
   Bids ye all be free,   5
And drink to your hearts' desiring.

   With the last year's brand
   Light the new block, and
For good success in his spending,
   On your psalt'ries play,   10
   That sweet luck may
Come while the log is a-teending.

   Drink now the strong beer,
   Cut the white loaf here,
The while the meat is a-shredding;   15
   For the rare mince-pie,
   And the plums stand by,
To fill the paste that's a-kneading.

787. CHRISTMAS EVE: ANOTHER CEREMONY.

Come, guard this night the Christmas-pie,
That the thief, though ne'er so sly,
With his flesh-hooks, don't come nigh
         To catch it

From him who all alone sits there,   5
Having his eyes still in his ear,
And a deal of nightly fear,
                          To watch it.

788. ANOTHER TO THE MAIDS.

WASH your hands, or else the fire
Will not teend to your desire ;
Unwash'd hands, ye maidens, know,
Dead the fire, though ye blow.

789. ANOTHER.

WASSAIL the trees, that they may bear
You many a plum and many a pear ;
For more or less fruits they will bring
As you do give them wassailing.

813. THE MAIDEN-BLUSH.

So look the mornings, when the sun
Paints them with fresh vermilion ;
So cherries blush, and Kathern pears,
And apricocks in youthful years ;
So corals look more lovely red,   5
And rubies lately polished ;
So purest diaper doth shine,
Stain'd by the beams of claret wine ;
As Julia looks when she doth dress
Her either cheek with bashfulness.   10

819. THE AMBER BEAD.

I saw a fly within a bead
Of amber cleanly buried;
The urn was little, but the room
More rich than Cleopatra's tomb.

827. COUNSEL.

'Twas Cæsar's saying: *Kings no less conquerors are*
By their wise counsel, than they be by war.

832. HIS LOSS.

All has been plundered from me but my wit;
Fortune herself can lay no claim to it.

840. UPON A MAID.

Here she lies, in bed of spice,
Fair as Eve in Paradise;
For her beauty, it was such
Poets could not praise too much.
Virgins, come, and in a ring
Her supremest requiem sing;
Then depart, but see ye tread
Lightly, lightly o'er the dead.

841. UPON LOVE.

Love is a circle, and an endless sphere;
From good to good revolving, here and there.

846. TO HIS BOOK.

Make haste away, and let one be
A friendly patron unto thee,
Lest rapt from hence, I see thee lie
Torn for the use of pastery;
Or see thy injur'd leaves serve well
To make loose gowns for mackerel;
Or see the grocers, in a trice,
Make hoods of thee to serve out spice.

849. SOCIETY.

Two things do make society to stand;
The first commerce is, and the next command.

851. SATISFACTION FOR SUFFERINGS.

For all our works a recompense is sure;
'Tis sweet to think on what was hard t' endure.

853. TO M. HENRY LAWES, THE EXCELLENT COMPOSER OF HIS LYRICS.

Touch but thy lyre, my Harry, and I hear
From thee some raptures of the rare Gotire;
Then, if thy voice commingle with the string,
I hear in thee the rare Laniere to sing,
Or curious Wilson. Tell me, canst thou be
Less than Apollo, that usurp'st such three?
Three unto whom the whole world give applause;
Yet their three praises praise but one; that's Lawes.

855. THE BEDMAN, OR GRAVEMAKER.

THOU hast made many houses for the dead;
When my lot calls me to be buried,
For love or pity, prithee let there be
I' th' churchyard made one tenement for me.

856. TO ANTHEA.

ANTHEA, I am going hence
With some small stock of innocence;
But yet those blessed gates I see
Withstanding entrance unto me.
To pray for me do thou begin,   5
The porter then will let me in.

870. TO HIS BOOK.

TAKE mine advice, and go not near
Those faces, sour as vinegar;
For these, and Nobler numbers can
Ne'er please the supercilious man.

872. THE SACRIFICE, BY WAY OF DISCOURSE BETWIXT HIMSELF AND JULIA.

Herr. COME and let 's in solemn wise
    Both address to sacrifice;
    Old Religion first commands
    That we wash our hearts and hands.
    Is the beast exempt from stain,   5
    Altar clean, no fire profane?
    Are the garlands, is the nard
    Ready here?

Jul.   All well prepar'd,
   With the wine that must be shed,
   'Twixt the horns, upon the head   10
   Of the holy beast we bring
   For our trespass-offering.

Herr. All is well : now, next to these,
   Put we on pure surplices ;
   And with chaplets crown'd, we'll roast   15
   With perfumes the holocaust ;
   And, while we the gods invoke,
   Read acceptance by the smoke.

876. AN HYMN TO CUPID.

   THOU, thou that bear'st the sway,
   With whom the sea-nymphs play,
   And Venus, every way ;
   When I embrace thy knee,
   And make short pray'rs to thee,   5
   In love, then prosper me.
   This day I go to woo ;
   Instruct me how to do
   This work thou put'st me to.
   From shame my face keep free,   10
   From scorn I beg of thee,
   Love, to deliver me !
   So shall I sing thy praise,
   And to thee altars raise,
   Unto the end of days.   15

883. UPON JULIA'S HAIR BUNDLED UP IN A
GOLDEN NET.

TELL me, what needs those rich deceits,
These golden toils and trammel-nets,
To take thine hairs, when they are known
Already tame, and all thine own?
'Tis I am wild, and more than hairs   5
Deserve these mashes and those snares.
Set free thy tresses, let them flow
As airs do breathe or winds do blow;
And let such curious networks be
Less set for them than spread for me.   10

890. CHARMS.

BRING the holy crust of bread,
Lay it underneath the head;
'Tis a certain charm to keep
Hags away while children sleep.

891. ANOTHER.

LET the superstitious wife
Near the child's heart lay a knife,
Point be up and haft be down;
While she gossips in the town,
This, 'mongst other mystic charms,   5
Keeps the sleeping child from harms.

893. ANOTHER CHARM FOR STABLES.

HANG up hooks and shears to scare
Hence the hag that rides the mare,

Till they be all over wet
With the mire and the sweat ;
This observ'd, the manes shall be   5
Of your horses all knot-free.

894. CEREMONIES FOR CANDLEMAS EVE.

Down with the rosemary and bays,
    Down with the mistletoe ;
Instead of holly, now upraise
    The greener box, for show.

The holly hitherto did sway ;   5
    Let box now domineer
Until the dancing Easter Day
    Or Easter's eve appear. ᐟ

Then youthful box, which now hath grace
    Your houses to renew,   10
Grown old, surrender must his place
    Unto the crisped yew.

When yew is out, then birch comes in,
    And many flowers beside,
Both of a fresh and fragrant kin,   15
    To honor Whitsuntide.

Green rushes then, and sweetest bents,
    With cooler oaken boughs,
Come in for comely ornaments,
    To re-adorn the house.   20
Thus times do shift, each thing his turn does hold ;
New things succeed as former things grow old.

895. THE CEREMONIES FOR CANDLEMAS DAY.

KINDLE the Christmas brand, and then
  Till sunset let it burn ;
Which quench'd, then lay it up again
  Till Christmas next return.

Part must be kept, wherewith to teend   5
  The Christmas log next year ;
And where 'tis safely kept, the Fiend
  Can do no mischief there.

896. UPON CANDLEMAS DAY.

END now the white-loaf and the pie,
And let all sports with Christmas die.

908. TO A FRIEND.

LOOK in my book, and herein see
Life endless sign'd to thee and me :
We o'er the tombs and fates shall fly,
While other generations die.

912. UPON BEN JONSON.

HERE lies Jonson with the rest
Of the poets, but the best.
Reader, wouldst thou more have known?
Ask his story, not this stone ;
That will speak what this can't tell   5
Of his glory.   So farewell.

913. AN ODE FOR HIM.

AH, Ben !
Say how or when
Shall we, thy guests,
Meet at those lyric feasts
    Made at the Sun,   5
The Dog, the Triple Tun,
Where we such clusters had
As made us nobly wild, not mad,
And yet each verse of thine
Outdid the meat, outdid the frolic wine?   10

My Ben !
Or come again,
Or send to us
Thy wit's great overplus ;
    But teach us yet   15
    Wisely to husband it,
Lest we that talent spend,
And having once brought to an end
That precious stock, the store
Of such a wit the world should have no more.   20

923. PRESENT GOVERNMENT GRIEVOUS.

MEN are suspicious, prone to discontent ;
Subjects still loathe the present government.

929. THE PRESENT TIME BEST PLEASETH.

PRAISE they that will time past, I joy to see
Myself now live ; this age best pleaseth me.

956. ON HIMSELF.

Lost to the world, lost to myself, alone
Here now I rest under this marble stone,
In depth of silence, heard and seen of none.

959. TO JULIA.

Offer thy gift; but first the law commands
Thee, Julia, first to sanctify thy hands:
Do that, my Julia, which the rites require,
Then boldly give thine incense to the fire.

962. TO HIS BOOK.

If hap it must that I must see thee lie
Absyrtus-like, all torn confusedly,
With solemn ·tears and with much grief of heart
I'll re-collect thee, weeping, part by part,
And having wash'd thee, close thee in a chest   5
With spice; that done, I'll leave thee to thy rest.

969. UPON HIS SPANIEL TRACY.

Now thou art dead, no eye shall ever see,
For shape and service, spaniel like to thee;
This shall my love do, give thy sad death one
Tear, that deserves of me a million.

973. STRENGTH TO SUPPORT SOVEREIGNTY.

Let kings and rulers learn this line from me;
Where power is weak, unsafe is majesty.

976. TO JULIA.

HOLY waters hither bring
For the sacred sprinkling ;
Baptise me and thee, and so
Let us to the altar go ;
And, ere we our rites commence,
Wash our hands in innocence ;
Then I'll be the *Rex Sacrorum*,
Thou the Queen of Peace and Quorum.

982. CEREMONY UPON CANDLEMAS EVE.

DOWN with the rosemary, and so
Down with the bays and mistletoe ;
Down with the holly, ivy, all
Wherewith ye dress'd the Christmas hall,
That so the superstitious find
No one least branch there left behind ;
For look, how many leaves there be
Neglected there, maids, trust to me,
So many goblins you shall see.

985. TO HIS KINSMAN, MR. THO: HERRICK, WHO DESIRED TO BE IN HIS BOOK.

WELCOME to this my College, and though late
Th'ast got a place here, standing candidate,
It matters not, since thou art chosen one
Here of my great and good foundation.

986. A BUCOLIC BETWIXT TWO: LACON AND
THYRSIS.

Lacon. FOR a kiss or two, confess
　　What doth cause this pensiveness,
　　Thou most lovely neatherdess?
　　Why so lonely on the hill?
　　Why thy pipe by thee so still,　　　　　　5
　　That erewhile was heard so shrill?
　　Tell me, do thy kine now fail
　　To fulfil the milking-pail?
　　Say, what is 't that thou dost ail?

Thyr. None of these; but out, alas!　　　10
　　A mischance is come to pass,
　　And I'll tell thee what it was;
　　See, mine eyes, are weeping ripe.

Lacon. Tell, and I'll lay down my pipe.

Thyr. I have lost my lovely steer,　　　15
　　That to me was far more dear
　　Than these kine which I milk here:
　　Broad of forehead, large of eye,
　　Parti-colored like a pie,
　　Smooth in each limb as a die,　　　　　20
　　Clear of hoof, and clear of horn,
　　Sharply pointed as a thorn;
　　With a neck by yoke unworn,
　　From the which hung down by strings,
　　Balls of cowslips, daisy rings,　　　　　25
　　Enterplac'd with ribbanings;
　　Faultless every way for shape;
　　Not a straw could him escape;
　　Ever gamesome as an ape,

But yet harmless as a sheep.   30
Pardon, Lacon, if I weep ;
Tears will spring where woes are deep.
Now, ai me ! ai me ! Last night
Came a mad dog, and did bite,
Aye, and kill'd my dear delight.   35

Lacon. Alack, for grief !

Thyr. But I'll be brief.
Hence I must, for time doth call
Me and my sad playmates all,
To his ev'ning funeral.   40
Live long, Lacon ; so adieu !

Lacon. Mournful maid, farewell to you ;
Earth afford ye flowers to strew !

1021. ON HIS BOOK.

THE bound, almost, now of my book I see,
But yet no end of those therein or me ;
Here we begin new life, while thousands quite
Are lost, and theirs, in everlasting night.

1028. SAINT DISTAFF'S DAY ; OR, THE MORROW AFTER TWELFTH DAY.

PARTLY work and partly play
Ye must on St. Distaff's day ;
From the plough soon free your team,
Then come home and fodder them ;

If the maids a-spinning go,   5
Burn the flax and fire the tow;
Bring in pails of water then,
Let the maids bewash the men;
Give St. Distaff all the right,
Then bid Christmas sport good-night,   10
And next morrow every one
To his own vocation.

1030. HIS TEARS TO THAMESIS.

I SEND, I send here my supremest kiss,
To thee, my silver-footed Thamesis;
No more shall I reiterate thy Strand,
Whereon so many stately structures stand,
Nor in the summer's sweeter evenings go,   5
To bathe in thee, as thousand others do;
No more shall I along thy crystal glide
In barge with boughs and rushes beautify'd,
With soft-smooth virgins, for our chaste disport,
To Richmond, Kingston, and to Hampton Court;   10
Never again shall I with finny oar
Put from or draw unto the faithful shore;
And landing here, or safely landing there,
Make way to my beloved Westminster,
Or to the golden Cheapside, where the earth   15
Of Julia Herrick gave to me my birth.
May all clean nymphs and curious water dames
With swan-like state float up and down thy streams;
No drought upon thy wanton waters fall,
To make them lean and languishing at all;   20
No ruffling winds come hither to disease
Thy pure and silver-wristed Naiades.

Keep up your state, ye streams, and as ye spring,
Never make sick your banks by surfeiting;
Grow young with tides, and though I see ye never,   25
Receive this vow; so fare-ye-well for ever.

1032. PEACE NOT PERMANENT.

GREAT cities seldom rest; if there be none
T' invade from far, they'll find worse foes at home.

1035. STUDIES TO BE SUPPORTED.

STUDIES themselves will languish and decay
When either price or praise is ta'en away.

1037. TWELFTH NIGHT; OR, KING AND QUEEN.

Now, now the mirth comes
With the cake full of plums,
Where Bean's the King of the sport here;
Beside, we must know
The Pea also   5
Must revel as Queen in the court here.

Begin then to choose,
This night, as ye use,
Who shall for the present delight here;
Be a King by the lot,   10
And who shall not
Be Twelve-day Queen for the night here.

Which known, let us make
Joy-sops with the cake,
And let not a man then be seen here   15

Who unurg'd will not drink,
To the base from the brink,
A health to the King and the Queen here.

Next crown the bowl full
With gentle lamb's-wool,   20
Add sugar, nutmeg, and ginger,
With store of ale too;
And thus ye must do
To make the wassail a swinger.

Give then to the King   25
And Queen wassailing,
And though with ale ye be whet here,
Yet part ye from hence
As free from offence
As when ye innocent met here.   30

1039. CAUTION IN COUNCIL.

KNOW when to speak; for many times it brings
Danger to give the best advice to kings.

1069. GENTLENESS.

THAT prince must govern with a gentle hand,
Who will have love comply with his command.

1071. TO JULIA.

HELP me, Julia, for to pray,
Matins sing, or matins say;
This I know, the Fiend will fly
Far away, if thou be'st by;

Bring the holy water hither;
Let us wash, and pray together;
When our beads are thus united,
Then the foe will fly affrighted.

1076. ANOTHER ON THE SAME.

[1075 is on Obedience.]

No man so well a kingdom rules as he
Who hath himself obey'd the sovereignty.

1104. WAR.

IF kings and kingdoms once distracted be,
The sword of war must try the sovereignty.

1105. A KING AND NO KING.

THAT prince who may do nothing but what's just,
Rules but by leave, and takes his crown on trust.

1125. THE MOUNT OF THE MUSES.

AFTER thy labor take thine ease
Here with the sweet Pierides.
But if so be that men will not
Give thee the laurel crown for lot,
Be yet assur'd thou shalt have one
Not subject to corruption.

1126. ON HIMSELF.

I'LL write no more of love, but now repent
Of all those times that I in it have spent;
I'll write no more of life, but wish 'twas ended,
And that my dust was to the earth commended.

1127. TO HIS BOOK.

Go thou forth, my book, though late;
Yet be timely fortunate.
It may chance good luck may send
Thee a kinsman or a friend,
That may harbor thee, when I   5
With my fates neglected lie:
If thou know'st not where to dwell,
See, the fier's by.   Farewell.

1128. THE END OF HIS WORK.

PART of the work remains, one part is past;
And here my ship rides, having anchor cast.

1129. TO CROWN IT.

MY wearied bark, O let it now be crown'd!
The haven reach'd to which I first was bound.

1130. ON HIMSELF.

THE work is done; young men and maidens set
Upon my curls the myrtle coronet,
Wash'd with sweet ointments; thus at last I come
To suffer in the Muses' martyrdom,
But with this comfort, if my blood be shed,   5
The Muses will wear blacks when I am dead.

1131. THE PILLAR OF FAME.

FAME'S pillar here at last we set,
Out-during marble, brass, or jet;
  Charm'd and enchanted so
  As to withstand the blow
      Of overthrow;
      Nor shall the seas,
      Or OUTRAGES
      Of storms o'erbear
      What we uprear;
      Tho' kingdoms fall,
  This   pillar   never   shall
  Decline   or   waste   at   all,
But stand for ever by his own
Firm and well-fix'd foundation.

To his book's end this last line he'd have plac'd :
JOCUND HIS MUSE WAS, BUT HIS LIFE WAS CHASTE.

MR. ROBERT HERRICK: HIS FAREWELL UNTO POETRY.[1]

I HAVE beheld two lovers in a night
Hatch'd o'er with moonshine from their stol'n delight
(When this to that, and that to this, had given
A kiss to such a jewel of the heaven,
Or while that each from other's breath did drink   5
Healths to the rose, the violet, or pink),
Call'd on the sudden by the jealous mother,
Some stricter mistress or suspicious other,
Urging divorcement (worse than death to these)
By the soon jingling of some sleepy keys,   10
Part with a hasty kiss; and in that show
How stay they would, yet forc'd they are to go.
Even such are we, and in our parting do
No otherwise than as those former two
Natures like ours; we who have spent our time   15
Both from the morning to the evening chime,
Nay, till the bellman of the night had toll'd
Past noon of night, yet were the hours not old
Nor dull'd with iron sleep, but have outworn
The fresh and fairest flourish of the morn   20
With flame and rapture; drinking to the odd
Number of nine which makes us full with God,
And in that mystic frenzy we have hurl'd,
As with a tempest, nature through the world,
And in a whirlwind twirl'd her home, aghast   25
At that which in her ecstasy had past;
Thus crown'd with rose-buds, sack, thou mad'st me fly
Like fire-drakes, yet did'st me no harm thereby.

[1] This poem is not in the *Hesperides*, but is reprinted by Hazlitt,
Grosart, and Pollard from the Ashmole MS. 38, p. 108, Art. 121.
Hazlitt's text is somewhat confused: Grosart's is almost literatim. I
follow, except in a few words, Pollard, who has corrected the spelling.

O thou almighty nature, who did'st give
True heat wherewith humanity doth live   30
Beyond its stinted circle, giving food,
White fame and resurrection to the good:
Soaring them up 'bove ruin till the doom,
The general April of the world doth come
That makes all equal, — many thousands should,   35
Were 't not for thee, have crumbled into mould,
And with their serecloths rotted, not to show
Whether the world such spirits had or no,
Whereas by thee, those and a million since,
Nor fate, nor envy, can their fames convince.   40
Homer, Musaeus, Ovid, Maro, more
Of those godful prophets long before
Held their eternal fires, and ours of late
Thy mercy helping, shall resist strong fate,
Nor stoop to th' centre, but survive as long   45
As fame or rumor hath or trump or tongue;
But unto me be only hoarse, since now
(Heaven and my soul bear record of my vow)
I my desires screw from thee, and direct
Them and my thoughts to that sublim'd respect   50
And conscience unto priesthood.   'Tis not need
(The scarecrow unto mankind) that doth breed
Wiser conclusions in me, since I know
I've more to bear my charge than way to go,
Or had I not, I'd stop the spreading itch   55
Of craving more, so in conceit be rich;
But 'tis the God of nature who intends
And shapes my function for more glorious ends.
Kiss, so depart, yet stay a while to see
The lines of sorrow that lie drawn in me   60
In speech, in picture; no otherwise than when,
Judgment and death denounc'd 'gainst guilty men,

Each takes a weeping farewell, rack'd in mind
With joys before and pleasures left behind,
Shaking the head, while each to each doth mourn, 65
With thought they go whence they must ne'er return.
So with like looks, as once the ministrel
Cast, leading his Eurydice through hell,
I strike thy love, and greedily pursue
Thee with mine eyes or in or out of view. 70
So look'd the Grecian orator when sent
From's native country into banishment,
Throwing his eyeballs backward to survey
The smoke of his beloved Attica;
So Tully look'd when from the breasts of Rome 75
The sad soul went, not with his love, but doom,
Shooting his eyedarts 'gainst it to surprise
It, or to draw the city to his eyes.
Such is my parting with thee, and to prove
There was not varnish only in my love, 80
But substance, lo! receive this pearly tear
Frozen with grief and place it in thine ear,
Then part in name of peace, and softly on
With numerous feet to hoofy Helicon;
And when thou art upon that forked hill 85
Amongst the thrice three sacred virgins, fill
A full brimm'd bowl of fury and of rage,
And quaff it to the prophets of our age;
When drunk with rapture curse the blind and lame
Base ballad mongers who usurp thy name 90
And foul thy altar; charm some into frogs,
Some to be rats, and others to be hogs;
Into the loathsom'st shapes thou canst devise
To make fools hate them, only by disguise.
Thus with a kiss of warmth and love I part, 95
Not so but that some relic in my heart

Shall stand for ever, though I do address
Chiefly myself to what I must profess.
Know yet, rare soul, when my diviner muse
Shall want a handmaid (as she oft will use),   100
Be ready, thou for me, to wait upon her,
Though as a servant, yet a maid of honor.
The crown of duty is our duty: well-
Doing's the fruit of doing well.   Farewell.

HIS NOBLE NUMBERS

OR,

HIS PIOUS PIECES,

Wherein (amongst other things) he sings the Birth of his CHRIST: and sighs for his Saviour's suffering on the cross.

HIS NOBLE NUMBERS.

1. HIS CONFESSION.

Look how our foul days do exceed our fair;
And as our bad more than our good works are,
Ev'n so those lines, penn'd by my wanton wit,
Treble the number of these good I've writ.
Things precious are least num'rous; men are prone   5
To do ten bad for one good action.

2. HIS PRAYER FOR ABSOLUTION.

For those my unbaptized rhymes,
Writ in my wild unhallowed times,
For every sentence, clause, and word,
That's not inlaid with Thee, my Lord,
Forgive me, God, and blot each line   5
Out of my book that is not Thine.
But if, 'mongst all, Thou find'st here one
Worthy Thy benediction,
That one of all the rest shall be
The glory of my work and me.   10

7. GOD'S ANGER WITHOUT AFFECTION.

God, when He's angry here with any one,
His wrath is free from perturbation;
And when we think His looks are sour and grim,
The alteration is in us, not Him.

33. AN ODE OF THE BIRTH OF OUR SAVIOUR.

IN numbers, and but these few,
I sing Thy birth, O JESU!
Thou pretty Baby, born here,
With sup'rabundant scorn here,
Who for Thy princely port here,   5
        Hadst for Thy place
        Of birth, a base
Out-stable for thy court here.

Instead of neat enclosures
Of interwoven osiers,   10
Instead of fragrant posies
Of daffodils and roses,
Thy cradle, Kingly Stranger,
        As Gospel tells,
        Was nothing else,   15
But, here, a homely manger.

But we with silks, not crewels,
With sundry precious jewels,
And lily-work, will dress Thee;
And as we dispossess Thee   20
Of clouts, we'll make a chamber,
        Sweet Babe, for Thee,
        Of ivory,
And plaister'd round with amber.

The Jews they did disdain Thee,   25
But we will entertain Thee
With glories to await here
Upon Thy princely state here,
And more for love than pity;
        From year to year   30
        We'll make Thee here
A freeborn of our city.

37. SIN SEEN.

WHEN once the sin has fully acted been,
Then is the horror of the trespass seen.

38. UPON TIME.

TIME was upon
The wing, to fly away;
    And I call'd on
Him but a while to stay;
    But he'd be gone,   5
For aught that I could say.

He held out then
A writing, as he went,
    And ask'd me, when
False man would be content   10
    To pay again
What God and nature lent.

An hour-glass,
In which were sands but few,
    As he did pass,   15
He show'd, and told me too
    Mine end near was,
And so away he flew.

41. HIS LETANY, TO THE HOLY SPIRIT.

In the hour of my distress,
When temptations me oppress,
And when I my sins confess,
    Sweet Spirit, comfort me!

When I lie within my bed,   5
Sick in heart and sick in head,
And with doubts discomforted,
   Sweet Spirit, comfort me!

When the house doth sigh and weep,
And the world is drown'd in sleep,   10
Yet mine eyes the watch do keep,
   Sweet Spirit, comfort me!

When the artless doctor sees
No one hope, but of his fees,
And his skill runs on the lees,   15
   Sweet Spirit, comfort me!

When his potion and his pill,
Has or none or little skill,
Meet for nothing but to kill,
   Sweet Spirit, comfort me!   20

When the passing-bell doth toll,
And the furies in a shoal
Come to fright a parting soul,
   Sweet Spirit, comfort me!

When the tapers now burn blue,   25
And the comforters are few,
And that number more than true,
   Sweet Spirit, comfort me!

When the priest his last hath pray'd,
And I nod to what is said   30
'Cause my speech is now decay'd,
   Sweet Spirit, comfort me!

When, God knows, I'm toss'd about,
Either with despair or doubt,
Yet, before the glass be out,   35
    Sweet Spirit, comfort me!

When the tempter me pursu'th
With the sins of all my youth,
And half damns me with untruth,
    Sweet Spirit, comfort me!   40

When the flames and hellish cries
Fright mine ears and fright mine eyes,
And all terrors me surprise,
    Sweet Spirit, comfort me!

When the Judgment is reveal'd,   45
And that open'd which was seal'd,
When to thee I have appeal'd,
    Sweet Spirit, comfort me!

47. A THANKSGIVING TO GOD FOR HIS HOUSE.

LORD, Thou hast given me a cell
    Wherein to dwell,
A little house, whose humble roof
    Is weather-proof,
Under the spars of which I lie   5
    Both soft and dry;
Where Thou, my chamber for to ward,
    Hast set a guard
Of harmless thoughts, to watch and keep
    Me while I sleep.   10
Low is my porch, as is my fate,
    Both void of state;

And yet the threshold of my door
  Is worn by th' poor,
Who thither come and freely get   15
  Good words or meat.
Like as my parlor so my hall
  And kitchen's small;
A little buttery, and therein
   A little bin,   20
Which keeps my little loaf of bread
  Unchipp'd, unflead;
Some brittle sticks of thorn or briar
  Make me a fire,
Close by whose living coal I sit,   25
  And glow like it.
Lord, I confess too, when I dine,
  The pulse is Thine,
And all those other bits that be
  There plac'd by Thee;   30
The worts, the purslane, and the mess
  Of water-cress,
Which of Thy kindness Thou hast sent;
  And my content
Makes those, and my beloved beet,   35
  To be more sweet.
'Tis Thou that crown'st my glittering hearth
  With guiltless mirth,
And giv'st me wassail bowls to drink,
  Spic'd to the brink.   40
Lord, 'tis Thy plenty-dropping hand
  That soils my land,
And giv'st me, for my bushel sown,
  Twice ten for one;
Thou mak'st my teeming hen to lay   45
  Her egg each day;

Besides my healthful ewes to bear
      Me twins each year;
The while the conduits of my kine
      Run cream, for, wine.   50
All these, and better Thou dost send
      Me, to this end,
That I should render, for my part,
      A thankful heart,
Which, fir'd with incense, I resign,   55
      As wholly Thine ;
But the acceptance, that must be,
      My Christ, by Thee.

53. TO DEATH.

THOU bidd'st me come away,
And I'll no longer stay
Than for to shed some tears
For faults of former years,
And to repent some crimes   5
Done in the present times ;
And next, to take a bit
Of bread, and wine with it ;
To d'on my robes of love,·
Fit for the place above ;   10
To gird my loins about
With charity throughout,
And so to travail hence
With feet of innocence :
These done, I'll only cry,   15
God, mercy! and so die.

59. TO HIS SAVIOUR, A CHILD; A PRESENT, BY A CHILD.

Go, pretty child, and bear this flower
Unto thy little Saviour;
And tell Him, by that bud now blown,
He is the Rose of Sharon known.
When thou hast said so, stick it there
Upon His bib or stomacher;
And tell Him, for good handsel too,
That thou hast brought a whistle new,
Made of a clean strait oaten reed,
To charm His cries at time of need.
Tell Him, for coral thou hast none,
But if thou hadst, He should have one;
But poor thou art, and known to be
Even as moneyless as He.
Lastly, if thou canst, win a kiss
From those mellifluous lips of His;
Then never take a second on,
To spoil the first impression.

77. TO HIS SWEET SAVIOUR.

Night hath no wings to him that cannot sleep,
And Time seems then not for to' fly, but creep;
Slowly her chariot drives, as if that she
Had broke her wheel or crack'd her axletree.
Just so it is with me, who list'ning, pray
The winds to blow the tedious night away,
That I might see the cheerful peeping day.
Sick is my heart. O Saviour! do thou please
To make my bed soft in my sicknesses;
Lighten my candle, so that I beneath,

Sleep not for ever in the vaults of death;
Let me Thy voice betimes i' th' morning hear;
Call, and I'll come; say Thou the when and where:
Draw me but first, and after Thee I'll run,
And make no one stop till my race be done.　　　15

83.　THE DIRGE OF JEPHTHAH'S DAUGHTER: SUNG
BY THE VIRGINS.

O THOU, the wonder of all days!
O paragon, and pearl of praise!
O Virgin-martyr, ever blest
　　　Above the rest
Of all the maiden-train!　We come,　　　5
And bring fresh strewings to thy tomb.

Thus, thus, and thus we compass round
Thy harmless and unhaunted ground,
And as we sing thy dirge, we will
　　　The daffodil　　　10
And other flowers lay upon
The altar of our love, thy stone.

Thou wonder of all maids, li'st here,
Of daughters all the dearest dear,
The eye of virgins; nay, the queen　　　15
　　　Of this smooth green,
And all sweet meads from whence we get
The primrose and the violet.

Too soon, too dear did Jephthah buy,
By thy sad loss, our liberty;　　　20
His was the bond and cov'nant, yet
　　　Thou paid'st the debt;
Lamented maid!　He won the day,
But for the conquest thou didst pay.

Thy father brought with him along　　　　25
The olive branch and victor's song;
He slew the Ammonites, we know, .
　　　　But to thy woe;
And in the purchase of our peace,
The cure was worse than the disease.　　　30

For which obedient zeal of thine
We offer here, before thy shrine,
Our sighs for storax, tears for wine;
　　　　And to make fine
And fresh thy hearse-cloth, we will here　　35
Four times bestrew thee ev'ry year.

Receive, for this thy praise, our tears;
Receive this offering of our hairs;
Receive these crystal vials, fill'd
　　　　With tears distill'd　　　　40
From teeming eyes; to these we bring,
Each maid, her silver filleting

To gild thy tomb, besides, these cauls,
These laces, ribbands, and these falls,
These veils wherewith we use to hide　　　45
　　　　The bashful bride,
When we conduct her to her groom :
All, all we lay upon thy tomb.

No more, no more, since thou art dead,
Shall we e'er bring coy brides to bed;　　　50
No more, at yearly festivals,
　　　　We cowslip balls
Or chains of columbines shall make
For this or that occasion's sake.

No, no; our maiden pleasures be 55
Wrapt in the winding-sheet with thee;
'Tis we are dead, though not i' th' grave,
  Or if we have
One seed of life left, 'tis to keep
A Lent for thee, to fast and weep. 60

Sleep in thy peace, thy bed of spice,
And make this place all paradise;
May sweets grow here, and smoke from hence
  Fat frankincense;
Let balm and cassia send their scent 65
From out thy maiden monument.

May no wolf howl, or screech-owl stir
A wing about thy sepulchre;
No boisterous winds or storms come hither,
  To starve or wither 70
Thy soft sweet earth, but, like a spring,
Love keep it ever flourishing.

May all shy maids at wonted hours
Come forth to strew thy tomb with flow'rs;
May virgins, when they come to mourn, 75
  Male incense burn
Upon thine altar, then return
And leave thee sleeping in thy urn.

95. ANOTHER GRACE FOR A CHILD.

  HERE a little child I stand,
  Heaving up my either hand;
  Cold as paddocks though they be,
  Here I lift them up to Thee,
  For a benison to fall 5
  On our meat and on us all. Amen.

96. A CHRISTMAS CAROL, SUNG TO THE KING IN
THE PRESENCE AT WHITEHALL.

Chor. WHAT sweeter music can we bring
  Than a carol, for to sing
  The birth of this our heavenly King?
  Awake the voice! awake the string!
  Heart, ear, and eye, and every thing,   5
  Awake! the while the active finger
  Runs division with the singer.

  From the Flourish they came to the Song.

1. Dark and dull night, fly hence away,
  And give the honor to this day
  That sees December turn'd to May.   10

2. If we may ask the reason, say
  The why and wherefore all things here
  Seem like the spring-time of the year?

3. Why does the chilling winter's morn
  Smile like a field beset with corn;   15
  Or smell like to a mead new-shorn,
  Thus on the sudden? 4. Come and see
  The cause why things thus fragrant be.
  'Tis He is born, whose quick'ning birth
  Gives life and lustre, public mirth,   20
  To heaven and the under earth.

Chor. We see Him come, and know Him ours,
  Who, with His sunshine and His showers,
  Turns all the patient ground to flowers.

1. The Darling of the world is come,   25
  And fit it is we find a room
  To welcome Him. 2. The nobler part
  Of all the house here is the heart,

Chor. Which we will give Him, and bequeath
 This holly and this ivy wreath, 30
 To do Him honor, who's our King,
 And Lord of all this revelling.

The musical part was composed by
M. HENRY LAWES.

102. THE STAR SONG; A CAROL TO THE KING.
SUNG AT WHITEHALL.

The flourish of music: then followed the song.

1. TELL us, thou clear and heavenly tongue,
 Where is the Babe but lately sprung?
 Lies He the lily-banks among?

2. Or say, if this new Birth of ours
 Sleeps, laid within some ark of flowers, 5
 Spangled with dew-light; thou canst clear
 All doubts, and manifest the where.

3. Declare to us, bright star, if we shall seek
 Him in the morning's blushing cheek,
 Or search the bed of spices through 10
 To find him out?

Star. No, this ye need not do;
 But only come and see Him rest,
 A princely Babe, in's mother's breast.

Chor. He's seen! He's seen! Why then around
 Let's kiss the sweet and holy ground, 15
 And all rejoice that we have found
 A King before conception crown'd.

4. Come then, come then, and let us bring
 Unto our pretty Twelfth-tide King
 Each one his several offering; 20

Chor. And when night comes we'll give Him wassailing;
  And that His treble honors may be seen,
  We'll choose Him King, and make His mother Queen.

115. HIS WISH TO GOD.

I WOULD to God that mine old age might have,
Before my last, but here a living grave,
Some one poor alms-house, there to lie or stir,
Ghost-like, as in my meaner sepulchre.
A little piggin and a pipkin by,   5
To hold things fitting my necessity,
Which rightly us'd, both in their time and place,
Might me excite to fore and after-grace.
Thy cross, my Christ, fix'd 'fore mine eyes should be
Not to adore that, but to worship Thee.   10
So here the remnant of my days I'd spend,
Reading Thy Bible and my book; so end.

121. THE BELLMAN.

ALONG the dark and silent night,
With my lantern and my light,
And the tinkling of my bell,
Thus I walk, and this I tell:
Death and dreadfulness call on   5
To the gen'ral Session,
To whose dismal bar we there
All accounts must come to clear.
Scores of sins w'ave made here many,
Wip'd out few, God knows, if any.   10
Rise, ye debtors, then, and fall
To make payment while I call.
Ponder this, when I am gone;
By the clock 'tis almost one.

215. PREDESTINATION.

PREDESTINATION is the cause alone
Of many standing, but of fall to none.

221. CHRIST.

To all our wounds here, whatsoe'er they be,
Christ is the one sufficient remedy.

228. TO KEEP A TRUE LENT.

Is this a fast, to keep
     The larder lean,
        And clean
From fat of veals and sheep?

Is it to quit the dish   5
     Of flesh, yet still
        To fill
The platter high with fish?

Is it to fast an hour,
     Or ragg'd to go,   10
        Or show
A downcast look, and sour?

No; 'tis a fast, to dole
     Thy sheaf of wheat
        And meat   15
Unto the hungry soul.

It is to fast from strife,
     From old debate,
        And hate;
To circumcise thy life.   20

To show a heart grief-rent;
To starve thy sin,
Not bin;
And that's to keep thy Lent.

230. HIS MEDITATION UPON DEATH.

BE those few hours which I have yet to spend,
Bless'd with the meditation of my end;
Though they be few in number, I'm content;
If otherwise, I stand indifferent;
Nor makes it matter Nestor's years to tell,   5
If man lives long, an if he live not well.
A multitude of days still heaped on
Seldom brings order, but confusion.
Might I make choice, long life should be withstood,
Nor would I care how short it were, if good;   10
Which, to effect, let ev'ry passing bell
Possess my thoughts, next comes my doleful knell;
And when the night persuades me to my bed,
I'll think I'm going to be buried;
So shall the blankets which come over me,   15
Present those turfs which once must cover me,
And with as firm behavior I will meet
The sheet I sleep in as my winding-sheet.
When sleep shall bathe his body in mine eyes,
I will believe that then my body dies;   20
And if I chance to wake, and rise thereon,
I'll have in mind my resurrection,
Which must produce me to that gen'ral doom
To which the peasant, so the prince must come,
To hear the Judge give sentence on the throne,   25
Without the least hope of affection.

Tears at that day shall make but weak defence,
When hell and horror fright the conscience.
Let me; though late, yet at the last, begin
To shun the least temptation to a sin;   30
Though to be tempted be no sin, until
Man to th' alluring object gives his will.
Such let my life assure me, when my breath
Goes thieving from me, I am safe in death,
Which is the height of comfort; when I fall   35
I rise triumphant in my funeral.

Of all the good things whatsoe'er we do,
God is the ΑΡΧΗ and the ΤΕΛΟΣ too.

NOTES.

NOTES.

—◆◆—

To the Most Illustrious, etc. Dedicatory verses to illustrious persons were fashionable in Herrick's day, and in this opening poem Herrick follows the fashion. We need not doubt that Herrick was devotedly and heartily loyal, — the general tone of his poetry is enough to assure that he was, — but we cannot detect much more than perfunctory feeling in this poem. Herrick had celebrated the birth of Charles in a *Pastoral* (213), and had written some other poems to him. As to how far Charles could properly be called " the creator " of the poet's work (cf. the dedication of Shakespeare's *Sonnets* : " the only begetter "), one may form some opinion by comparing those poems that have any reference to Charles, or any other of the royal family, and those that have not.

1. *The Argument of his Book.* " One inhales with sense of relief from mephitic air," says Dr. Grosart (I. cxii), " the freshness of the outburst that succeeds the verse-dedication." This very pleasant little poem would seem to have been written by Herrick at some time when he was thinking over his poems, perhaps with a view to publication. Dr. Grosart considers it to have been especially intended as a sort of Table of Contents to an intended edition (I, cxiv and cxxi). Although it is not necessary to go as far as this (*Diss.* pp. 10–12), it is of interest to see how many of the poems of the *Hesperides* are here referred to either directly or by implication. The second line refers, perhaps, to *The Succession of the Four Sweet Months* (70) ; the third to *The Maypole* (697), the *Hock-Cart* (250), *The Wassail* (478), *The Wake* (763). The fourth would refer to a whole class of poems, the Epithalamia, of which that on the marriage of Sir Clipseby Crew (283) is a good specimen. See also *The Bride-cake* (807). The tenth refers to *How Roses came Red* (258, 708) and *How Lilies came White* (190), and, it may be, to a number of other poems on subjects very like. With line 11 cf. *To Groves* (451) and *Twilight* (860, 1048). Line 12 refers to 223, 293, 444. The last two lines may refer to the *Noble Numbers:* it is possible, indeed, that they were added when the poem was put in its present place.

1 3. *I sing of Maypoles*, etc. Some account of the country customs here alluded to will be found in the notes on the poems just mentioned.

1 8. *Of Balm*, etc. Herrick's fondness for perfumes is one of his noteworthy characteristics. Cf. *Introd.*, p. xxxiii.

2. *To his Muse.* The antithesis of village and court, and the mention of *the poor man's cell* strike a note not uncommon. E.g. 106 (80–90), 213, 494, 546, 554, *N.N.* 47.

2 9. *And with thy Eclogues.* The precise distinction here drawn between Eclogue and Bucolic is not wholly clear to me. Professor Kittredge suggests that Herrick may take "*Eclogue* as a discourse of shepherds and *Bucolic* as a discourse of neatherds." There is a hint of such distinction in ll. 7–13; and 494, *An Eclogue* (where the subject is of shepherds), and 718, *A Bucolic: or Discourse of Neatherds*, would point in the same direction.

3. *To his Book.* There are a good many of these little poems addressed by Herrick to his book (*Introd.*, pp. xxviii). 59, 84, 194, 605, 846, 901, 962, 1127.

3 3. *Wantonly to roam* may refer to the custom which was then in vogue of passing about copies of verse in MS. A number of Herrick's poems exist in MS.; collations of the important ones will be found in the notes of Mr. Pollard's edition.

8. *When he would have his verses read.* In the light of this cheerful command it seems quite wrong to put any study at all on Herrick's poetry. His poems were to be read only at a favorable time: nor could he write them except at a favorable time (716). Pollard compares the poem with Martial, x. 19, which is somewhat longer. The last part of our poem is a good translation; the rest merely catches the idea.

14. *To Perilla.* There are two other poems addressed to Perilla (154, 1022), neither of them as fine as this one, which has a grave beauty equal almost to any other one of Herrick's. The last line is especially remarkable. The ceremonies prescribed are doubtless ideal (*Introd.*, p. xxxvii). The use of salt as emblem of the soul is noted by Mr. Pollard and by Brand, II. 234. The strewings are of flowers, as frequently in the *Hesperides.* Brand (II. 302–312) mentions many variations of the custom.

22. *To Anthea.* These ceremonies, too, come from a mind for which such observances had a strong fascination. Wholly different from those of 14, they are quite as noteworthy as indicating the delicate fancy which always twines in with the thread of Herrick's seriousness. Excepting the poems to Julia, which are far more numerous, those to Anthea are more interesting on the whole than the verses to any other one of Herrick's " many dainty mistresses."

25. *The Difference*, etc. This poem is worth noting for its possible bearing on Herrick's opinions. We must, however, remember the remark of Mr. Pollard that in these Gnomic Couplets Herrick is almost as likely to express ideas which he had come across in reading or otherwise that seemed susceptible of epigrammatic statement, as to put forth any settled opinions of his own.

29. *Love, what it is.* Cf. 841.

35. *His sailing from Julia.* The remora was the sea-lamprey, which, according to ancient belief, attached itself to ships and so delayed their course.

39. *Upon the Loss of his Mistresses.* Julia is, of course, the chief, the best known of those to whom Herrick wrote. Judging from the poems we have, we should have expected to find Anthea second and Perilla next. But one cannot insist on rigid rule and order in such matters.

47. *The Parcæ.* This has the tone of having been written to three actual lovely sisters.

51. *Discontents in Devon.* Mr. Pollard's note is as follows: " This poem is often quoted to prove that Herrick's country incumbency was good for his verse, but if the reference be only to his sacred poems or *Noble Numbers* they would only prove the reverse." It would be an error, however, to attempt to prove much of anything from such a poem. It may well have been written on a rainy day when parishioners were bothersome; and as to the last lines, the effect of Herrick's stay in Devonshire is so marked that it needs no special proof.

55. *To Anthea.* In some parishes of England it was in Herrick's day still the custom for some of the clergy, and the people too, to march in procession at certain times of the year around the parish boundaries. The object was not only to pray for a blessing on the fruits of the earth, but also to maintain the legal boundaries and rights. This "processioning," as it was sometimes called, took place on one of the days before Holy Thursday. The "Gospel tree" here spoken of would have been one of the trees under which the minister paused to read the service during the march around the bounds. See Brand I. 197–207.

70. *The Succession of the Four Sweet Months.* Cf. *The Argument*, 1, 2.

77. *To the King.* In the summer of 1644, after the affair at Cropredy Bridge, Charles found himself disembarrassed of Sir William Waller and turned his attention to the West. He marched into Devonshire with a view of joining Prince Maurice and giving battle to the Earl of Essex. The hopes of our poem were to some extent fulfilled, for the King succeeded in surrounding the army of Essex at Lostwithiel in Cornwall and captured the greater part of it. The campaign came between Marston Moor and the second battle of Newbury. Clarendon's book viii gives a detailed, interesting, and rather confused account.

77 2. *Universal genius.* General protecting power.

77 10. *Access.* Coming.

77 11. *White omens.* Fortunate auspices.

81. *The Cheat of Cupid.* Herrick is here translating Anacreon, 31 [3], as Greene had done before him.

82. *To the Reverend Shade,* etc. The full meaning of this poem can hardly be made out: line 6 is as hard to understand as any. There was suspicion of suicide attaching to the death of Herrick's father, and it may be that he was not buried in consecrated ground. Herrick was very young at the time, and it is possible that he had never till 1627 (seven lustra after 1592) really known where his father had been buried. On the other hand, it is not improbable that the language is wholly imaginative. The time of writing was about that of his going to Devonshire. These years may have been years of change of heart for the poet (cf. *The Farewell to Poetry*, p. 133), and it may be that he then reproached himself for carelessness of his father's memory.

86. *Dean Bourn.* It was the tradition (*Quarterly Review* for August, 1810, p. 171) that Herrick uttered these verses when he left Devonshire on being deprived in 1648. The hope of the first lines was not fulfilled, for he did return thither after the Restoration, and lived there until he died. Dean was the name of the parish; Dean Bourn was the river; Dean Prior, Dean Combe, Dean Church were the villages, and Dean Court the manor-house.

88. *To Julia.* A Dardanium, explains Herrick in the original edition, was "a bracelet, from Dardanus so called."

97. *Duty to Tyrants.* This agrees with some of Herrick's utterances elsewhere, and disagrees with others.

106. *A Country Life.* This poem may be compared with *The Country Life* (664), addressed to Endymion Porter. It is perhaps but a fancy, but it seems to me that this latter has by far the more

genuine ring to it. This present poem so full of Horatian wisdom, of Horatian ceremony, and of Horatian reminiscence, lacks the realistic touches of the other. It is more spun out and less vital. It is written in the free versification which I believe to be characteristic of Herrick's earlier poetry, while the other is quite particular as to overrun lines. The references in the present poem to "damask'd meadows" (43), to "fields enamelled with flowers" (46), to "millions of lilies mix'd with roses" (48), have not the genuine character of the "breath of great-ey'd kine" (33) or the "crowns of daffodils and daisies" (51), though it must be confessed that 664 is not without its slight touch of enamelling (29). But 106 has more the tone of being written from the city, perhaps after a visit.

Mr. Pollard (I. 267) notices the many Horatian snatches, and quotes a few. We may add one or two more beside that remarked in the Introduction, p. xx. The simple fare of 111 recalls

> " me pascunt olivae
> me cichorea levesque malvae,"   *Od.* I. xxxi. 15.

while l. 130 was suggested by

> " Auream quisquis mediocritatem
> Diligit," etc.   *Od.* II. x. 5.

111. *A Lyric to Mirth.* This poem bears the earmarks of Herrick's years in London between Cambridge and Devonshire. The general Bacchanalian tone and the references to Horace and Anacreon appear to be more characteristic of this period than of his life in Devonshire.

111 4. *Dollies* was a cant term for sweethearts.

111 8. *Bite the bays.* The laurel of the poets is bay-laurel.

111 13. *Wilson and Gotiere.* "Dr. John Wilson, the singer and composer, one of the King's musicians. Jacques Gouter, a French musician at the court of Charles I." P.

128. *His Farewell to Sack.* This poem, *The Welcome to Sack* (197), *His Mistress' Shade* (577), and the *Farewell to Poetry* (p. 133), have a sort of common quality which makes it seem as though all were written at about the same time, — a time which the last mentioned (perhaps also the last written) would fix at about 1627. There is certainly about all of them a lack of that fine restraint and sureness of expression characteristic of Herrick's best work.

Of these two poems on Sack, the *Farewell* would seem to have been written first. Like many of the rest of us, Herrick had his righteous periods in which he would forswear the flowing bowl. But with Herrick it would seem that these periods sometimes came to an end.

128 4, 5. *Life to quick action.* Dr. Grosart conjectures, "to quick *our* action," which certainly makes better metre. We may, however, read *quick* as a verb without inserting the pronoun.

128 23. *Thy mystic fan* Mr. Pollard explains as a translation of the "mystica vannus" (*Georgics*, i. 166) borne in the Eleusinian processions.

128 36. *Worthy cedar and the bays.* The *bays* are of course in the poet's crown. Cedar-oil was used in the preservation of manuscripts. In one of the few poems that we have of Herrick's, not published in the *Hesperides*, is a couplet with the same allusion:

> "O volume worthy, leafe by leafe, and cover,
> To be with juice of cedar wash't all over."
>
> *Upon Master Fletcher's Incomparable Plays.*

Reprinted in G. iii, 109, from Beaumont and Fletcher's works, 1647. So also in *To Cedars* (165):

> "If 'mongst my many poems, I can see
> One only worthy to be washed by thee," etc.

197. *The Welcome to Sack.* 11. "*The heaven's Osiris* is the sun." Original note. At one time Egypt seems to have had a certain fascination for Herrick. There is a curious allusion to the Egyptian worship in this poem (57) which I cannot explain. We have also *the heavenly Isis* (52), which Herrick explains as the moon. *A Song to the Masquers* (15) ends with this stanza:

> "As goddess Isis, when she went
> . Or glided through the street,
> Made all that touch'd her, with her scent,
> And whom she touch'd, turn sweet."

So in *Love perfumes all parts* (155):

> "Goddess Isis can't transfer
> Musks and ambers more from her."

197 30. *Sulphur, hair, and salt.* Salt was used by the Romans in almost all their sacrifices. Cf. *Saliente mica*, Hor. *Od.* III, xxiii, 20. The hair was sometimes offered. It was due, for instance, to Proserpina. Cf. Virgil, *Aen.* iv, 698. But I know of no example of such a use of sulphur.

197 61. *Cassius.* There is a writer on medicine of this name, called sometimes Iatrosophista, sometimes Felix, to whom Dr. Grosart refers. It is more probable that Herrick was thinking of that Cassius who, according to Cæsar, had "a lean and hungry look." *Julius Cæsar*, i. 2, 94.

197 62. *The wise Cato* was the synonym for a rigid virtue. Herrick often had him in mind (8 10).

178. *Corinna's going a-Maying.* This fine poem seems to have been the product of Herrick's earlier years, of his life in London or Cambridge. It is written as though by a participant, and one cannot well imagine Herrick the vicar actually carrying into effect these delightful precepts, whereas, it is just what we might expect of the student of St. John's or the poet of the Tribe of Ben. The versification would incline one to place it among the earlier poems. May-day was of course celebrated in the city as well as in the country. "In London," says Brand (I. 231), "May-day was once as much observed as it was in any rural district."

178 2. *The god unshorn* was Apollo, the sun-god, who was regularly represented with unshorn locks. Cf. Tibullus, ii. 5, 121 : "Sic tibi sint intonsi, Phoeb₃, capilli."

178 4. *Fresh-quilted.* The figure may have been borrowed from the variety of colors in stuffs quilted together.

178 28. *Few beads.* The original meaning of "bead" is "prayer," and so it is here. But by Herrick's day the word in the sense of "prayer" was almost always used with some thought of the rosary, whence the modern meaning of the word.

178 29 foll. On the morning of May-day everybody went out early and returned with "birch, bowes, branches of trees" (Stubbes: *Anatomy of Abuses*), with which they adorned the houses inside and out.

178 35. White thorn was also among the spoils, being highly esteemed for its efficacy against witches.

181. *A Dialogue.* Mr. R. Ramsay was organist of Trinity College, Cambridge, 1628-1634. P. The poem is translated from Hor. *Od.* III, ix.

186. This poem, which for solemn beauty may remind one of Catullus (ci.), follows immediately upon one written after the death of his brother to Endymion Porter. This latter, in its obsequious tone, shows an ill side of the poet's character as the present shows a good one. It begins with a fine line, however:

> " Not all thy flushing suns are set,
> Herrick, as yet."

201. *To Live Merrily and to Trust to Good Verses.* This pleasant exercise in the classics I take to be a university poem, or it may be of London origin. The climax is noteworthy; as genius wanes he needs more wine; a health to Homer, a cup to Virgil, a goblet to Ovid, an "immensive cup" to Catullus, a tun to ·Propertius, and a flood to Tibullus. Here he pauses with a moral reflection.

201 32. *Bite the bays.* Cf. 111 8. The priests of Apollo ate bay-leaves to give them prophetic inspiration. The notion is carried over to the poets, as in Juvenal, *Sat.* vii, 18, 19:

> " nectit quicunque canoris
> Eloquium vocale modis laurumque momordit."

205. *To Violets.* The turn at the end is common to many of Herrick's amatory verses.

208. *To the Virgins.* This poem may owe a part of its popu-larity to its having been early set to music by William Lawes. It is certainly one of the best known of Herrick's lyrics, though by no means the best, for there are not a few less known which are quite as exquisite.

211. *His Poetry his Pillar.* This poem may be compared with a number of others (v. *Introd.*, pp. xxvii, xxviii), and especially with *The Pillar of Fame* (1131).

213. *A Pastoral.* This poem is a good illustration of the length to which poets of Herrick's time were willing to go for the sake of a compliment to royalty, and of how far the divinity that doth hedge a king could blind a clergyman to decency. This poem on the birth of Charles II. is of course a distinct adaptation of the events accompanying the birth of Christ. We have the shepherds and the star as in the Gospels, the simple shepherd's gifts as in the popular tradition and the miracle plays; we even have the same line used in honor of Charles that Herrick elsewhere uses in honor of Christ (as pointed out by Mr. Pollard : "And all most sweet, yet all less sweet than he"; found also in *The New Year's Gift, N.N.* 97 10). All the grace of the fancy and diction cannot render the poem pleasing to a modern mind, the feeling throughout is so intensely vulgar.

213 20. *A silver star.* This was the compliment of the time: the star appeared again at the Restoration. Cf. Dryden, *Astræa Redux,* 288–291 :

> " That star that at your birth shone out so bright,
> It stain'd the duller sun's meridian light,
> Did once again its potent fires renew,
> Guiding our eyes to find and worship you."

216. *A Meditation for his Mistress.* The mood wherein these stanzas end is not uncommon. Sometimes Herrick meditates on his mistress' death, sometimes on his own : here on both, as at the end of *The Changes*, 252.

218. *Lyric for Legacies.* Herrick loved to think of the circle of his friends, and loved also to think of the verses which he had written to celebrate his friendship for them. As he often prophesies immortality for himself (211, 366, 1131), so does he often promise it to his friends (445, 666, 806). Cf. 509, *Upon Himself :*

> " Th'art hence removing, like a shepherd's tent,
>   And walk thou must the way that others went :
>   Fall thou must first, then rise to life with these
>   Marked in thy book for faithful witnesses."

223. It seems best to put the three chief fairy poems together, for they are obviously connected. Whether they were written at one time or not may be doubtful ; but they were undoubtedly written with thought of each other. It is possible that the *Feast* and the *Palace* were first written and the *Temple* afterward. In favor of this view it may be remarked that the versification of the *Temple* differs decidedly from that of the other two, that the *Temple* is dedicated, not to Shapcot for whom the two others were written, but to another, and that the *Feast* and the *Palace* refer to each other but not to the *Temple*, whereas the *Temple* does refer to the *Feast.* It may be that Herrick wrote the two secular poems before ordination, and afterwards turned his attention to the state of ecclesiastical matters among the fairies. But the matter is not important ; whenever written, the three poems should be read together.

Critics have busied themselves by looking about to see where Herrick got hints for these poems. Mr. Edmund Gosse mentions Jonson's *Oberon*, but Dr. Grosart shows that this must be an error. Grosart himself thinks of Drayton's *Nymphidia*, and Mr. Pollard concurs. It may be, of course, that Herrick gained inspiration from some especial source. But it must, I think, be allowed that this fanciful way of imagining the surroundings of Oberon and Mab was more or less of a poetic commonplace at just this time. We need not believe that Herrick borrowed his idea from Shakespeare, — so far as we can see, he was singularly uninfluenced by the great dramatist, — but certainly the fancies of Titania's orders (*M. N. D.*, iii, 1) and of Mercutio's speech on Queen Mab (*R. & J.*, i, 4, 59 ff.) are distinctly of the same nature as those on which these fairy poems are based. The difference is in treatment; with Shakespeare the idea is but a passing fancy, while Herrick develops it to its utmost.

There is much lore about these poems which may be found in G., I, clix–clxv, and P., II, 306–311. In a little volume of a dozen pages, published in 1635, of which the only copy known is in the Bodleian, are two poems, *A Description of the Kings* (sic) *of Fayries Clothes, brought to him on New-Yeares day in the morning, 1626, by his Queenes Chambermaids,* and *A Description of his Diet.* Both may be found reprinted in P., II, Appendix II. The second is evidently a first draught of *Oberon's Feast,* containing about two-thirds of the lines in slightly varying form and order. The other poem, which is in precisely the same manner, is conjectured by Mr. Pollard to have been written by Sir Simeon in answer to *A New Year's Gift* (319). Several questions are here raised. Mr. Pollard says of Herrick's Fairy poems : "All three were probably written in 1626 and cannot be dissociated from Drayton's *Nymphidia,* published in 1627, and Sir Simeon Steward's *A Description of the King of Fayries Clothes* " (P., II, 306). As above, however, I believe *The Temple* to have been written later.

223 4. *The halcyon's nest* has been dear to the poets since Ovid (*Metam.* x). It floated upon the waters while the kingfisher hatched out her brood, the fourteen days before the winter solstice. During these days the winds were quiet, for Æolus their king had been the father of Alcyone in mortal shape.

223 9. *House of Rimmon.* II *Kings* v, 18.

223 29. *Mab's state, i.e.,* her chair of state.

223 41. *Favor your tongues. Favete linguis,* Horace, *Od.* III, i, 2.

223 43. The *procul este profani* of the *Aeneid,* vi, 258, *profane* meaning merely the uninitiated.

223 47. *Odd, not even pairs.* Perhaps because there's luck in odd numbers. "Numero deus impare gaudet." Virgil, *Ecl.* viii, 75.

223 51. This allusion (to the sacrifice of the mass) is one of those which strike a modern ear as blasphemous. The *Holy Grist* seems to be the sacred wafer.

223 52. *In mood and perfect tense.* In perfect manner and time.

223 59. *Points.* A point was a lace with a metal tag on the end used for fastening the clothes.

223 117. *Fasting spittle.* The spittle of a fasting person was vulgarly held to be of exceptional value in charms and ceremonies. Probably Herrick had also in mind the use of saliva in some of the sacraments of the Roman Catholic Church.

223 131. *The Lady of the Lobster.* This is a coarse burlesque of such terms as Our Lady of Loretto. The lady of a lobster is a sort of calcareous substance in the stomach, which assists digestion.

293. *Oberon's Feast.* There are two MS. copies of this poem. Mr. Pollard collates that in the British Museum (I, 295). The differences are very interesting as showing the care that Herrick took in perfecting his work.

293 10. *Grit* is usually the coarser part of the meal.

293 11. *Nice.* Delicate, exquisite.

293 15. *To stir his spleen.* The spleen was supposed to be the seat of different passions. The word is common, meaning *melancholy*, or often *risibility*, which comes nearer the mark here.

293 28. *Cuckoo's spittle*, "the white froth which encloses the larva of the cicada spumaria." G.

293 33. *Sag* seems to be for sagging. The meaning is clearly *heavy*, but the form is out of the way. Cf. however, "came too lag to see him buried." *Rich. III*, ii, 1, 90.

293 43. *Mandrake's ears.* The root of the *Mandragora* was supposed to resemble a man and to have life. Popular tradition usually went no further than its vocal organs; it cried out lamentably when torn from the ground. Cf. *R. & J.*, iv, 3, 47.

293 44. *Slain stags.* Such as served Jaques for his moralizing, *As You Like It*, ii, 1, 41. It was a common notion that the stag or hart wept when he received his death-wound.

444. *Oberon's Palace.* There are three MS. versions of this poem which give not only a number of variants but also a passage of twenty-seven lines not in the *Hesperides*. It is in precisely the same humor as the rest, and may be found in P., I, 309.

444 14. *Carries hay in's horn* (foenum habet in cornu). Is dangerous.

444 28. *Lemster ore.* The special riches of Leominster was wool.

444 34. *Wild digestion.* Cf. *wild civility*. 83 12. The flowers are digested or arranged, but in a natural carelessness.

444 36. *Love's sampler.* It is possible that the present generation do not remember that a sampler is a piece of worsted work. Cf. 256 2.

444 37. *Citherea's ceston.* Venus' girdle of beauty.

444 57. *Toadstones.* It was the superstition of the day that the toad bore a precious stone in his head; cf. *As You Like It*, ii, 1, 14.

444 60. A wart may be sold to any one who will give a penny for it. The warts pass from the hand of the seller to the buyer. These seem to have got stolen on the way.

444 82. *Winds his errors up.* Brings his wanderings to an end.

225. *Plaudit.* The call for applause at the end of the play; short for the imperative *plaudite.*

250. *The Hock Cart.* Mildmay Fane, second Earl of West-moreland, was a patron of Herrick's, as appears from 112. It was customary throughout England to celebrate the gathering in of the harvest in various ways. The Hock cart was the last cart in from the fields. We find in Brand (II, 16–33) an account of the different customs which obtained in different parts of England. Our poem hardly needs any comment, so fresh and vivid is its picture of the festivity.

250 2. *Wine and oil* is a little conventional as addressed to Eng-lish farm laborers.

250 5. It may not be superfluous to caution American readers against trying to conceive of ears of Indian corn used in this man-ner.

250 13. *Swains and wenches.* The former word became a very elegant term in the next century, the latter quite the reverse.

250 34. *Frumenty* is made of wheat boiled in milk, with black currants in it.

250 41. *Wheaten hats* were twisted from the straw. Cf. the rye-straw hats of the reapers in the masque in the *Tempest,* v, 1.

256 2. Cf. 444 36.

256 6. *Hearse-cloth* does not refer to a hearse as we use the word to-day. It means here simply the covering for a corpse or a coffin.

256 21. *Virgil's gnat.* The *Culex* was then generally held to be by Virgil. Spenser translated it, and Herrick refers to it again (499 9).

258. *How Roses came Red.* There are a number of other poems giving us Herrick's views on Evolution, as illustrated in his garden. He changed his views on Roses (cf. 708).

262. *To the Willow Tree.* This poem is good comment on the expression "wearing the willow," the symbol of the deserted lover. Cf. Desdemona's song in *Othello,* iv, 3.

267. *To Anthea.* This is one of the best known of Herrick's poems, but I do not think it can compare with 447, a poem of its own kind, or many others of different feeling (*e.g.,* 316, 89), which are by no means so famous.

267 2. *Protestant.* The word is curiously used. But *His Protes-tation to Perilla* (154) gives us the probable meaning. He will live to assert his devotion to her,

269. *Obedience in Subjects.* This is one of the Sentences which express Herrick's loyalty. He was neither the first vicar nor the last who held strongly to the divine right of kings.

278. *To his Household Gods.* This is one of the poems which have given rise to the feeling that Herrick hated his life in the country and always longed to be elsewhere. The most probable course of feeling on his part, entirely aside from any evidence but human nature in general, would be that at first, when fresh from London, he greatly missed his old surroundings, and found it hard to accustom himself to new ones. That then, after some years, he made himself at home and fairly contented with his lot. Toward the end of his holding his vicarage the old feeling of hatred of his surroundings, coupled now with the monotony of years, might have made him once more discontented ; and with Herrick, who was decidedly a man of moods, it would not have been at all unnatural that now and then, even in happier times, he should have periods of discontent (v. p. xxx). In wholly different mood did he write *His Content in the Country*, 554.

283. *A Nuptial Song.* This is the most elaborate and finest of the several Epithalamia that we have from Herrick. It was written in 1625 on the marriage of Sir Clipsby Crew, who seems afterward to have been a friend and patron of the poets. There are a number of poems to him in the *Hesperides*, as well as an epitaph upon his wife (980).

283 6. The seven planets of the Ptolemaic system counted the sun and the moon, as in *Paradise Lost*, iii, 481–483. The addition here mentioned has hardly been so permanent as those of Herschel and Leverrier.

283 16. *Chaf'd air.* The original reading is *Chafte-Air.* Mr. Morley reads *chaste.* It seems to me probable that the word *chaf'd* was suggested to Herrick by the mention of amber immediately before. Cf. 375 16, " amber chaf'd between the hands." That the air, like amber, should give forth fumes of Paradise upon being chafed is rather a far-fetched idea, but not, I think, too remote for Herrick.

283 25. The phœnix, when it felt that its time to die was at hand, made for itself a pyre of precious woods and gums, and so expired in a thick glory of incense.

283 29. *Bestroking fate.* Influencing, compelling fate, for from the ashes was born the new Phœnix. For the noun *stroke*, with kindred meaning, cf. Holland's *Livy* (1600), p. 109 : " Appius was the man that bare the greatest stroke."

283 31. *Hymen, O Hymen.* The cry to the god of marriage. Cf. Catullus, 61.

283 32. *Marjoram.* The *amaracus* of the Romans, which was connected with the idea of Love. Catullus (61 8) calls on Hymen to wreathe himself "floribus suave olentis amaraci." Cf. also *Lucretius*, iv, 1179.

283 46. Wheat, like rice, is typical of fertility.

283 54. *Nice.* Delicate, refined, and so in this case modest, retiring.

283 84. Gloves, scarves, and laces were given at weddings. The bridegroom gave the points of his dress to be scrambled for, and the bride her laces.

283 82. *A siren in a sphere.* Cf. 577 52.

299. Cf. 577 52, *Farewell to Poetry*, 17 (p. 133), and *N.N.* 121.

299 2. *Benedicite.* The word is to be taken as an imperative with the meaning, "Bless you (or us) from murders." Cf. "Bless thee from whirlwinds." *Lear*, iii, 4, 60. On *benedicite* as an exclamation to protect oneself on the appearance of ghosts, evil spirits, see Kaufmann, *Trentalle Sancti Gregorii*, p. 55 (*Erlanger Beiträge*, III).

302. *Upon Prudence Baldwin.* She was his maid or housekeeper, and (perhaps owing to this prayer) recovered and lived a long time afterward in spite of the epitaph her master wrote for her (784).

302 5. A cock was the proper vow to Aesculapius, when one had recovered from an illness. Cf. the *Phaedo*, 155.

306. *On Himself. Pilgrim* seems to have been the general term, but *Palmers*, named from the palms they brought back, were properly such only as had visited Jerusalem. *Scallop's shell.* The scallop was a sign that one had visited the shrine of St. James of Compostella. Here as elsewhere we have an intimation that Herrick had his·times when the Christian's life appeared to him as a Pilgrim's Progress.

313. *The Entertainment.* A part of the wedding ceremony was formerly gone through at the church door. Cf. the wife of Bath in Chaucer's *Prologue*, l. 640. The marriage, for which we have here the *Porch Verse* and the *Goodnight*, is recorded at Dean Prior as celebrated September 5, 1639.

313 12. *Fishlike.* The fecundity of fishes did yeoman service to Herrick as source of simile or metaphor. Fishes were convenient as rhyming with wishes. Cf. 283 and 697.

314 8. *Ravish.* Carry him away as the nymphs carried off Hylas.

319. *A New Year's Gift.* It is not easy to say just what events may be referred to in the opening lines. No English navies were burned at sea during the time of Herrick's activity, and there were too many proceedings that might have been called *closet plot* or *open vent*, or outbreak. The expression *late-spawned Tityries* refers to the bands of riotous young men who paraded the streets of London at night, committing all manner of atrocities upon such unfortunates as happened to be abroad. They were the predecessors of the Mohocks of Queen Anne's day, the Hectors, and others of that ilk. Their name was properly the "Tityre tu's," being, for some strange reason, borrowed from Virgil's *First Eclogue.* It has usually been supposed that the origin of these bands was at a period later than the publication of the *Hesperides.* But Mr. Pollard quotes a poem in *Musarum Deliciae,* entitled *The Tytre-tues,* by Mr. George Chambers, clearly written in the time of Archbishop Abbot (*ob.* 1633). The *Century Dictionary* quotes John Taylor's Works, 1630. Mr. Pollard dates this poem circa 1627 (II, 306). We have no difficulty then in supposing that it is to the historical Tityre tu's that our poem refers. Unfortunately it does not throw any light on the reason for the name.

319 6. It hardly needed an astrologer to see that the kingdom was a little under the weather.

319 7. *Wring the freeborn nosthril :* the figure is from [w]ringing the nostrils of a bull; Herrick may have intended the double meaning.

319 14. *Fox-i'-th' hole* was a Christmas game.

319 16. *Shoe the mare* (or the wild mare) was another.

319 17. The custom has not yet passed away of hiding a pea and a bean in a Twelfth-night cake, of which the finders are hailed as queen and king. Cf. *Twelfth Night,* 1037.

319 22. Dr. Grosart says that this kind of divination is more common on St. Agnes's Eve.

319 23. *Crackling Laurel.* Cf. Tibullus, ii, 5, 81 :

> " Et succensa sacris crepitet bene laurea flammis,
>   Omine quo felix et sacer annus erit."

319 28. It is of course the consumer who becomes buxom and capers. From the spelling *bucksome* it may be that Herrick would have derived buxom from *buck.* The earlier meaning is *obedient,* but by Herrick's day it had got to the present meaning which the poet may have developed a little.

319 42. *Liber Pater.* The Latin deity of the fields and vineyards. But the name was commonly used as synonymous with Bacchus.

319 47. Although we commonly think of the bagpipe as a distinctly Scottish instrument, it is used in many other countries, and was common in England in Herrick's time.

323. *The Christian Militant.* 2. *To dead* as a transitive verb occurs once or twice elsewhere in Herrick, and, although not used by Shakespeare, may be found in the works of other Elizabethans.

323 4. *Sedition* would here seem to mean treachery, or perhaps disturbance.

323 5. *That's counter-proof*, etc. Equally undisturbed by the evil chances of country or city.

327 5. *Balm.* Ultimately the same word as *balsam*, and indeed both words are used at present with a very general meaning. Herrick alludes to a particular kind of balm, an oily resinous substance which came to Europe from Syria and Arabia. *Myrrh*, the well-known perfume from the Arabian myrtle. *Nard*, short for spikenard, a somewhat traditional ointment of ancient times. The name is given to various modern productions, but Herrick probably had the old spikenard in mind. Concerning perfumes in Herrick's poetry, v. *Introd.*, p. xxxiii.

333. *To Lar.* In this poem, written we may suppose after Herrick had been dispossessed from his vicarage, he seems to bid farewell to the Household God with whom he had been at home so long.

336. *His age.* John Wickes, or Weeks, to whom this poem is addressed, was a Royalist wit and a popular preacher. G. With the beginning compare the well-known "Eheu fugaces," Horace, *Od.* II, xiv, 1–8.

336 26. Mr. Pollard, always rich in such reference, calls attention also to *Od.* IV, vii, 14.

336 28. *Infernal Jove.* Pluto, the ruler of the lower regions.

336 34. See 327 5, note.

336 48. The peculiar excellence of these lampreys came from their being fed on human flesh.

336 52. Herrick probably had in mind the arched roofs of the great Gothic halls. The word therefore conveys the idea of great richness and magnificence.

336 54. *Baudery*, smut. Herrick transfers the word from the moral to the material, or he may have used it without thought of the moral meaning. The older word *bawdy* meant *dirty*, probably unconnected with *bawd*.

336 68. *Less circular.* Less united.

336 83. *Baucis.* The wife of Philemon. The visit of Jupiter and Mercury to the old couple is told by Ovid, *Metam.* iii, 631.

336 89. *Pussy's ear.* Many people are now so dependent on the weather predictions of the Signal Service as to have forgotten that the cat's washing her face is a sign of change of weather, and so a *calendar*, though we should rather say *almanac*, nowadays.

336 92. *Gripings of the chine.* The chine was properly the backbone. These gripings may have been rheumatism.

336 122. *Wild apple.* For the wassail-bowl. For a recipe, see 1037.

Mr. Pollard collates, and prints a portion of, a MS. version of this poem. It contains a good many variants and some additional verses, of which the last is perhaps worth reprinting : —

> " Then the next health to friends of mine
> In oysters and Burgundian wine,
>   Hind, Goderiske, Smith,
> And Nansagge, sons of clune and pith,
>   Such who know well
> To board the mighty bowl, and spill
> All mighty blood, and can do more
> Than Jove and Chaos them before."

345. *The Power in the People.* Herrick's comment on Hampden and others of like convictions.

359. *To the Right Honorable Philip, Earl of Pembroke and Montgomery.* Philip Herbert, Earl of Montgomery (1584–1650), was the brother of William Herbert, the friend of Shakespeare, and succeeded him as Earl of Pembroke. These two were "the incomparable pair of brethren" to whom the *First Folio* of Shakespeare was dedicated. Philip Herbert was rather a rough character, but in a measure a patron of literature.

366. *Upon Himself.* "Non omnis moriar," Horace, *Od.* III, iv, 6.

371. *His Lachrimæ.* Evidently written in a gloomy time, when the old days in London seemed the only days of joy.

375. *To Mrs. Anne Soame.* This is one of the most fragrant of all Herrick's poems; v. *Introd.*, p. xxxiv.

375 9. *Factors.* The word commonly means a sort of steward, or agent. Herrick uses it then in the sense of "doers."

375 16. *Amber*, when warmed, becomes fragrant.

375 23. *Warden.* A kind of pear.

386. *A Vow to Mars.* Herrick has six other poems almost exactly similar to *Æsculapius* (302), *Apollo* (303), *Bacchus* (304), *Neptune* (325), *Venus* (337), and *Minerva* (532). This one seems written merely with the desire to fill up the list, and with a recollection of the "relicta non bene parmula" of Horace (*Od.* II, ii, 10).

393. *Lar's Portion.* This is one of the poems which give a notion of the worship of the gods of home, which was the subject of the frequent imagining of Herrick. Cf. 278, 324, 333.

413. *The Mad Maid's Song.* No comment is needful to bring out the serene and pathetic beauty of this, one of the most perfect of Herrick's poems.

439. *Policy in Princes.* This may well refer to Strafford, whose fall had an ill effect on the fortunes of his master. It is, however, by no means an idea original with Herrick. It was a commonplace which he picked up and turned into verse, as doubtless he did many another. Mr. Pollard has pointed out that we cannot infer much of Herrick's opinion from these distiches. See note on 25.

447. *To Œnone.* "The brilliant simplicity and pointed grace of the three stanzas to Œnone recall the lyrists of the Restoration in their cleanlier and happier mood." Swinburne, in P., I, xiv.

451. *To Groves.* This poem is extremely interesting, as giving us a hint of the Calendar of Saints in the poet's cult of the god of Love. The story of Phyllis, martyr and saint, l. 23 (cf. Ovid, *Heroides,* Ep. ii, and *To the Maids,* 618 13), was very like that of Dido, and may be read also in Chaucer's *Legend of Good Women,* viii. The lot of Iphis, l. 24, was happier. Born a woman, but changed by Isis to a man, (s)he was a witness rather of the power of love than its suffering. Cf. Ovid, *Metam.* bk. ix. The story of Iphis is not one of the best known, but I fancy it caught the fancy of Herrick through its connection with Isis. Cf. 197 11, note.

475 8. *Cock's first crow.* All ghosts and fiends vanished at daybreak. So the ghost in *Hamlet* and the *Apparition,* 577.

478. *The Wassail.* "There was an ancient custom, which is yet retained in many places on New Year's Eve : young women went about with a Wassail Bowl of spiced ale, with some sort of verses that were sung by them as they went from door to door. . . . It were unnecessary to add that they accepted little presents on the occasion from the houses at which they stopped to pay this annual congratulation." Brand, I, 1. The composition of the wassail "was ale, nutmeg, sugar, toast, and roasted crabs or apples." *Ib.*

488. *Loss from the Least.* Compare 704.

499. *Upon a Fly.* 5. *Took state.* Was proud.

499 9. *Virgil's gnat.* Cf. 256 21.

499 11. *Martial's bee.* Cf. *Epig.*, 10, 32 (P.).

499 15. *Phil* was Herrick's sparrow. Cf. 256.

517. *His Winding-sheet.* Of all Herrick's more serious pieces this is the chief. But the absence of any Christian thought on immortality is certainly noteworthy. Even such thought as there is has hardly the genuineness of the rest. The last ten verses seem hardly of the same piece as the others.

517 19. Cf. Job, iii, 17.

517 27, 29. The Star Chamber and the Court of Requests were abolished in 1641.

517 46. The Platonic year is that wherein everything shall return to its original state. It is the year in which the cycles of the seven planets are fulfilled on the same day. Cf. Plato, *Timæus*, cap. 33.

523. *To Phillis.* One compares, of course, with Marlowe's *Possionate Shepherd*, which will possibly be preferred as more perfect in its self-restraint. Herrick makes no attempt to control the exuberance of fancy which the country life calls up.

523 26. *Themilis* is a pastoral name which I do not find elsewhere. Milton uses Thestilis in *L'Allegro*, 88.

523 30. *The hayes* was a winding country dance. Cf. Sir John Davies's description in his *Orchestra*, st. 53:

> " Of all their ways I love Meander's path,
> Which to the tunes of dying swans do daunce:
> Such winding sleights, such turns and tricks he hath,
> Such creeks, such wrenches, and such dalliaunce,
> That whether it be hap or heedless chaunce,
> In his indented course and wriggling play
> He seems to daunce a perfect hay."

Cf. also *ib.*, st. 47.

526. *Upon her Eyes.* 4. *A baby there.* Herrick has the figure of babies in the eyes many times. Cf. Pollard's note to 38. 6. *Intelligence.* A ruling spirit.

527. *Upon her Feet.* The reader will probably award the palm to Sir John Suckling's better known

> " Her feet beneath her petticoat,
> Like little mice, stole in and out
> As if they feared the light."

532. *A Vow to Minerva.* 1. *An art.* The use is peculiar, and I find nothing to compare with it.

541. *To Julia.* Cf. *Introd.*, p. xxxvii. The last two lines may be compared with the poem on the birth of Prince Charles, 213. It would be rather hard for us to imagine a clergyman writing them (and the poem may be an early one) were it not for much more of the same sort in Renaissance literature.

541 3. The *inarculum* is explained in the original edition as "a twig of pomegranate which the queen priest did use to wear on her head at sacrificing."

547 2. *One lip-leaven.* That which leavens the lips, permeates the speech. These men are of the same ruling tendency of thought.

547 9. *Prefer* in the older sense, meaning *to put forward.*

554. *His Content in the Country.* This poem is quite as genuine in feeling as those which express his loathing of Devonshire. The poems may have been written at widely distant times, but it may also be believed that at about the same time Herrick would have been sometimes in one mood, sometimes in another.

577. *The Apparition of his Mistress.* Mr. Pollard (ii, 276) prints a collation of the text with that of the 1640 edition of Shakespeare's poems. Some of the variants are worth mention. For instance, that for *Beaumont and Fletcher* we have not unnaturally *Shakespeare and Beaumont.* In my study of the chronology of Herrick's poems I endeavored (*Diss.*, pp. 37, 38) to show reasons for holding that this poem was not written after the death of Jonson, but that the allusion to Jonson in Elysium was jocularly complimentary. I had not at that time seen Mr. Pollard's collation which (l. 57) for "In which thy father Jonson *now is* placed" reads "*shall be* placed," which certainly seems as though Jonson had been alive at the time of writing. By the time of the publication in the *Hesperides* he was dead, and Herrick changed the wording.

It is characteristic that Herrick thinks first of the delightful fragrance of Elysium. Less characteristic are the spangles, tinseling, gilding, and enamel. This artificiality, which appears to us at present as rather bad taste, was common in Herrick's day, but Herrick himself was much freer of it than most of his contemporaries.

577 30. *The incantation of his tongue.* Cf. "The holy incantation of a verse," 8 2.

577 43. *Sharp-fanged* and *snaky* are far more appropriate epithets for Martial and Persius than is *towering* for Lucan. Lucan was,

however, highly esteemed in Herrick's day.   We may also compare
Adonais, 404.

`577 52.   *In their spheres.*   The Ptolemaic astronomy conceived
of the earth as surrounded by a number of spheres, — those of each
planet, including the sun and moon, that of the fixed stars, and so on.
Cf. Plato, *Timæus*, cap. 11, and Milton, *Paradise Lost*, iii, 481–484.

577 53.   *Evadne.*   The heroine in *The Maid's Tragedy*, by Beaumont and Fletcher.

577 62.   Cf. *The Bellman*, 299.

618.   *To the Maids.*   5.   *Draw-gloves.*   Brand (II, 416) quotes
243 *Draw-gloves*, but gives no other description, nor do I find one
elsewhere.   Mr. Pollard's note is "talking on the fingers," Dr. Grosart's "a now unknown game," neither of which is of much help.

618 12.   *Philomel* and *Phillis.*   These two unfortunates were favorite subjects of ancient and mediæval story, — Philomel betrayed by
Tereus, Phyllis by Demophon.   Their stories may be found, to mention one of many places, in Chaucer's *Legend of Good Women*, where
the excellent poet sympathises loudly with them.

618 24.   *Bays and rosemary* were used at weddings and sometimes
gilded (*Brand*, II, 119).   The *posy* was the inscription within the
ring.   The giving of gloves and laces (ribandings) to the guests
at weddings was once as common as the present custom of giving
cake.

619.   *His own Epitaph.*   A *buttoned staff* seems to be merely one
with a knob to it.

626.   *Poets.*   This distich should be learned by heart by every one
who would know what manner of man was Herrick.   It is probably ·
as true of him as of Ovid (*Tristia*, ii, 353, 4).   Cf. note on the last
couplet in the *Hesperides*.

636.   *To his Lovely Mistresses.*   One of the ceremonies which
Herrick loved to imagine when his mind dwelt on his dreamy cult
for the gods of Love and Death.   The word *reverend* has been
already used in this sense in speaking of "his religious father," 82.

645.   *The Hag.*   This has a fine movement, but seems to need no
comment.

664.   *The Country Life.*   This is the finest of Herrick's Bucolics,
except for its incomplete ending.   It is very appropriately dedicated
to Endymion Porter, who seems to have been a man generously dis-
posed to poets and to literature in general.   Herrick wrote to him
various other poems not in his best vein, among them *An Eclogue or
Pastoral between Endymion Porter and Lycidas Herrick* (494), in

which the poet with oaten pipe endeavors to attract his patron from the coùrt to the country, promising him the attentions of Jessamine, Florabel, and Drosomel, of Tityrus, Corydon, and Thyrsis. In this poem, however, a far more sincere note is struck.

664 23. *The best compost for the lands.* Cf. 773, 8, and Hazlitt, *English Proverbs*, p. 369 (ed. 1869): "The foot of the owner is the best manure for his land."

664 31. *A present godlike power.* This touch seems hardly natural in Herrick.

664 28. *The kingdom's portion is the plow.* The idea is not wholly obvious, but Herrick probably had in mind the thought of the plow as the support of the nation, as in the old poem *Speed the Plough*.

664 38. *Mummeries* were maskings, usually at Christmas time. A party of merry-makers would go masked from house to house, a favorite representation being that of St. George and the Dragon.

664 46. *For sports, etc.* Herrick has celebrated most of these events in the country calendar by special poems. On wakes, v. 763; on maypoles, 697; on harvest home, 250; on the wassail bowl, 478, 789; on Twelfthtide kings and queens, 1037; Christmas revelings, 786, 787. *Quintal* is here but another form of *quintain*. It consisted of a bar set up on a pole so that it could swing round. On one end was a mark, on the other hung a weighted bag. The game was to run at the mark, hit it, and escape before the bar had swung round and struck you in the back. The *Morris* dance was a favorite pastime, most common on Mayday. The name comes from the word *Moorish*, but the characters personated in the dance were not Moorish at all, being very commonly Robin Hood and his followers, cf. 763 8.

664 54. *Whitsun ale.* Church ales were festivals in which the whole parish contributed to a brewing, the ale being on tap sometimes even in the church. Whitsuntide was the favorite season, although not the only one. The practice had by Herrick's day given rise to great abuses, but it was not wholly done away with till much later.

664 62. *Nut-brown mirth and russet wit.* The adjectives are suggested by nut-brown ale and russet gowns.

697 12. *Like to fishes.* Cf. 313 12, note.

704. *Mean Things overcome Mighty.* This reflection may well have been occasioned by the assassination of Buckingham by John Felton, August 23, 1628. Cf. 488.

714. *Laxare Fibulam.* Dr. Grosart subjoins to the word *bashfulness*, "*i.e.*, in greed to take more and still more." I should rather take the couplet to be a versifying of Herod. i, 8: ἅμα δὲ κιθῶνι ἐκδυομένῳ συνεκδύεται καὶ τὴν αἰδῶ γυνή.

726. *His Grange.* 6. As to Prue, cf. 302 and 784.

726 25. *To these.* In addition to these.

726 13. This special excellency of the goose is quite as likely to be due to a reminiscence of Rome as to a feeling for realism.

726 26. *Tracy* was the name of his spaniel, for whom he wrote an epitaph, 969. It used to be said that Herrick had also a pig whom he taught to drink out of a tankard; but if such were the case he seems to have considered the pig no fit subject for poetry.

732. *Charon and Philomel.* Charon was the ferryman who bore the souls of the dead over the Styx. Philomel was the sister of Procne (cf. line 15) and the victim of Tereus. See the note to 618 12.

753. *Our own sins unseen.* The idea, of course, is not original with Herrick. Cf. *Phædrus*, iv, 10, for the fable of Jupiter's giving man two wallets, the one to be worn before, the other behind.

763. *The Wake.* The wake was an annual church festival, held on the day of the saint for whom the church was named.

763 8. *Marian.* Maid Marian was one of the characters of the Morris as well as Robin Hood, Little John, Friar Tuck, and Will Scarlet. So also (provided it were not forgotten) was the Hobbyhorse.

763 12. *Base in action.* These barn-stormers were as badly off for costume as for art in their acting.

763 17. *Coxcomb.* The object of cudgel-play (single-stick or backswording) was to "break the head," — *i.e.*, to cause the blood to flow.

784. *Upon Prue his Maid.* This epitaph was only sportive, for Prudence lived on till 1678, long after the *Hesperides* was published.

786. *Ceremonies for Christmas.* These poems are themselves so descriptive as to need no comment.

787. *Christmas Eve.* 3. *Flesh-hooks* = hands.

846. *To his Book.* There are one or two other poems in which Herrick trembles for the fate of his book. Cf. 962, 1127.

851. *Satisfaction for sufferings.* Herrick's version of the well-known *Forsan et haec olim meminisse juvabit. Aen.* i, 203.

853. *To Mr. Henry Lawes.* The friend of Milton, who set the songs in *Comus*, and himself acted the part of the Attendant Spirit. *Wilson, Gotire*, cf. *A Lyric to Mirth*, 3. "Nicholas *Lanier* was appointed Master of the King's Music, 1626." P.

872. *The Sacrifice.* Cf. *Introd.*, p. xxxvii.

894. Candlemas day is February 2d; the eve is the day or evening before. Another poem on the same subject is 982.

894 7. It was a common superstition that the sun danced on Easter Day in joy of the Resurrection. Cf. Suckling, *Ballad of a Wedding.*

> " And oh, she dances such a way !
> No sun upon an Easter Day
> Is half so fine a sight."

Sir Thomas Brown, however, held that "we shall not, I hope, disparage the Resurrection of our Redeemer if we say that the sun doth not dance on Easter Day." *Pseudodoxia Epidemica*, bk. v, ch. 23, § 14.

895. *The Ceremonies for Candlemas Day.* 1. *The Christmas brand.* Cf. 786.

912. *Upon Ben Jonson.* Jonson was in the time of Herrick's stay in London the great poet of England. In his own day he had an inordinate reputation for scholarship, wit, and genius.

913. *An Ode for Him.* The *Sun,* the *Dog,* the *Triple Tun* were taverns of which Jonson was a great frequenter. But the "Mermaid" and the "Apollo" are the two taverns especially connected with the name of Jonson. The "Mermaid" was the scene of the traditional wit combats with Shakespeare. It was for the "Apollo," however, that he seemed to have most affection, and for which he drew up the rules for the Tribe of Ben.

913 17. *That talent spend.* Herrick had perhaps the parable of Matthew xxxv in mind; there, however, there is no question of spending the talent.

962. *To his Book.* Cf. 846, 1127. Absyrtus was the brother of Medea. When she fled from her father with Jason, after the winning of the Golden Fleece, she took Absyrtus with them. On being closely pursued by the Colchians, she killed Absyrtus, and cutting his body to pieces she strewed them on the waves. Her angry father, on finding the fragments, returned to Colchis to give them burial, and the lovers escaped.

1028. *Saint Distaff's Day.* Work began on the day following Twelfth Day, after the Christmas holidays.

1030. *His Tears to Thamesis.* Richmond, Kingston, and Hampton Court are all on the Thames, just above London, and now, as in Herrick's day, are favorite places of resort.

1037. *Twelfth Night.* Epiphany. For some other Twelfth-Night customs, v. Brand, I, 21.

1131. *The Pillar of Fame.* The writing of poems in the actual shape of some object was one of the artificial elegancies of the time. Thus, *N.N.* 268 is in the form of a cross. See *Introd.*, p. xxviii, note. With the poem, cf. Horace, *Od.* III, xxx.

With the last couplet compare the distich *Poets*, 626, and *Martial*, i, 5, 8 :

> " Lasciva est nobis pagina : vita proba est."

His Farewell to Poetry. The poem has a number of difficult and doubtful passages, arising probably from its never having received final correction for the press. Some of these I pass unnoticed, there being no sufficient means for determining the true meaning or reading. In some cases I call attention to the difficulty, as in l. 75. The whole poem is to be compared with those to *Sack* (128, 197) and *The Apparition* (577).

2. *Hatch'd o'er with moonshine.* To *hatch* is to overlay small and numerous bands on a ground of different material.

17. *Bellman of the night.* Cf. 299, 577 53, *N.N.* 121.

21. *Drinking to the odd number of nine.* *Nine* is Mr. Pollard's emendation for the MS. *wine.* He refers to *A Bacchanalian Verse* (655):

> " Well, I can quaff, I see,
> To th' number five
> Or nine,"

where the allusion is to the number of cups.

22. *Full with God.* Filled with the poetic inspiration. Cf. *infra*, l. 42.

27, 28. These two lines only are addressed to Sack. In the previous lines and those succeeding the subject is poetry.

28. *Fire-drakes.* Here probably meteors, though the word also means will-o'-the-wisps.

34. *The general April.* Probably the day of judgment, a day of smiles and tears.

67. *The minstrel.* Orpheus, who succeeded in bringing his bride Eurydice out of Hades, but lost her just as they were reaching the upper air, by turning to look back at her.

71. *The Grecian orator* was Demosthenes.

75. *Breasts of Rome.* Dr. Grosart reads *brooks*, but neither reading seems to make sense. Not having access to the MS., I have

not attempted a conjectural reading. It seems, however, that *beasts* would be better than either.

84. *Numerous feet.* The word *numbers* was later an elegant synonym for poetry. So Pope "lisped in numbers for the numbers came." *Hoofy Helicon.* The reference is, of course, to Pegasus, the winged horse of the muses.

THE NOBLE NUMBERS.

1. *His Confession.* In spite of Herrick's regret for the lines penned by his wanton wit, he printed them in the same volume with these more pious effusions. The Noble Numbers have, however, a separate title-page, and are dated 1647, a year before the *Hesperides*. It is just possible that Herrick at first contemplated the publication of his religious poems only. They were in all probability the last written, and it has never been explained why they should have been the first printed.

2. *His Prayer for Absolution. My unbaptised rhymes.* Whether he means the whole *Hesperides*, or merely poems written in London before taking orders, is hard to say. *Here* means in the *Noble Numbers*.

41. *His Litany.* 13. *Artless*, in the obvious but little-used meaning, without art.

41 21. The *passing-bell* was tolled as a person was dying. Brand, II, 202.

47. *A Thanksgiving.* 4. *Weather-proof*, cf. 336 52. As to Herrick's humble fare, we have already referred to Horace : "Chicorea levesque malvae," *Od.* I, xxxi, 16.

59. *To his Saviour.* It is this poem and *An Ode* (33) that led Mr. Gosse to write of the *Noble Numbers:* "He succeeds best where he permits himself to adorn a celestial theme with the picturesque detail of his secular poems ; he is happy if he be allowed to crown the infant Saviour with daffodils, or pin a rose into His stomacher." Ward's *English Poets*, II, 128. I should say, however, that 41, 47, 77, 95 were superior to this poem ; they represent a vein of genuinely serious thought, to be found also in *His Winding Sheet* (517), and not a few other poems in the *Hesperides*.

GLOSSARY.

———◦◇◦———

.

THIS Glossary has been made not so much to explain unfamiliar words occurring in the text[1] as to exhibit the peculiarities of Herrick's vocabulary. With this view, a good many words have been introduced which do not occur in the poems selected for this edition. On the other hand, there are a good many omissions in the present list as will be seen at once by comparing with Grosart's Glossarial Index. Matters of spelling are excluded for one thing, as *baptime, bodies, bucksome.* A good many words have been considered rather matter for an Index to the Notes than a Glossary, as *ash-heaps, barley-break, blue-ruler, buttoned staff.* A number of things seemed to belong rather to syntax, as *for and, all and some.* A number more were rather matters of expression than of vocabulary, as *abbey-lubbers, ale-dyed, blush-guiltiness.* Some matters which belong more properly to grammar will be found in the *Introduction,* pp. lix, lx. Within these limits, however, it is hoped that the Glossary will be found, though not complete, at least of value.

References are made by poem and line.

Access, 1 5, admission, and so opportunity. 77 10, arrival.

Aches, 336 87 (as a dissyllable).

Admiredly, 821 6. There are contemporary examples of this word, but the form is very uncommon.

Adulce, 672 6, to sweeten. The common spelling is *addulce.*

Affection, N.N., 230 26, partiality. The word was obsolescent, even in Herrick's day.

Affrightment, N.N., 263 21, fright.

Ark, 274 6, basket.

Armilet, 47 4. Apparently coined from the Latin diminutive armilla. See p. lx.

Aromatic, 375 14, 444 44. The word is very rare as a noun.

Artless, N.N., 41 13, without art.

Attent, 250 23, bent upon.

Auspice, 900 9. The singular, although uncommon, may be found even in the present century.

Auspicate, 963 10, auspicious.

[1] The readers for the *Century Dictionary* have gone over Herrick very thoroughly. It contains a great number of those words which occur only in Herrick, and there are very few words in Herrick which it does not have.

Babyship, 213 26. **See p. lx.**

Barbel, 336 46, a kind of fish.

Batten, 554 13, to thrive, to get fat.

Baudery, 336 54, smut.

Benizon, 725 4, a blessing, benediction.

Bents, 894 17, 223 95. The name *bent-grass* is given loosely to any stiff grass.

Be-, compounds in. See p. lix.

Be-strutted, 293 34. See *to strut*.

Bishop, *vb.*, 168 10. Dryden, *Cym. and Iphig.*, 243, has an example as here, of "confirmed and bishoped."

Blacks, 1130 6, black garments.

Blaze, 283 160, to blazon.

Blitheful, 657 1, 718 1, joyful.

Blouze, 774 23, a cant term for beggar's wench.

Boar-cats, 1124 9, he-cats.

Brass, 106 24, money.

Brave, 128 14, admirable, splendid.

Bruckel'd, 223 58, begrimed.

Bucketings, 61 4, pouring water from buckets.

Bulging, 71 2, the staving in of a ship; connected with *bilge*.

Burl, 596 2, 108 10, to cleanse (especially cloth).

Candid, 445 5, 900 6, white. So *candidate*, 817 2, and *candor*, 3 1, *N.N.*, 128 11. See *white*.

Candle-baudery, 336 54, smut caused by candles.

Carcanet, 34 2, 88 5, properly a necklace of jewels.

Carouse, 336 127, to drink deeply.

Cates, 106 109, dainties.

Cense, 444 45, *N.N.*, 97 6, 98 15, to burn incense.

Cess, 100 3, assessment, here rather property.

Ceston, 444 37. *Cestus* is the more common form. Herrick may have got this form from Ben Jonson.

Chalcedony, 88 12, chalcedony, a beautiful quartz, milky in color, with opaque veins.

Chit, 640 13, to sprout.

Chives. In 223 133, the meaning seems to be *shreds*. It may be also in 333 6 and 676 4, though in these it seems more naturally to mean *chive garlic*, a potherb.

Circum-, verbs compounded with. See p. lx.

Circumstants, 197 85, bystanders.

Cirque, 382 5. Here used for *theatre*.

Cittern, 1038 6, a kind of guitar. More commonly spelt *cithern*.

Civility, 83 12, polish, good-breeding.

Cock-all, 223 59. The knuckle-bone, with which the boys played as at dice.

Cocker, 106 26, 359 15, to pamper, to spoil.

Cockrood, 664 66, a run for snaring woodcocks.

Coddled, 283 61, boiled or stewed (not the word meaning pampered).

Codlin, 223 61, an apple.

Colewort, 106 113, a cabbage.

Commended, 293 53. To *commend* is to bring to the mind of; "commend me to So and so." Here it is curiously used in the passive. In 618 35 it means to give.

Compartiement, 654 8. The same word as *compartment*. Here it seems to be the pattern of the tooling on the cover.

Complexion, 197 72, disposition.

Comply, 444 98, 577 40, to embrace.

Comportment, 458 5, 949 1, manners.

Consenting, *vb. int.*, 106 32, according, agreeing with.

Continent, 506 2, 742 3, that which contains. Used in 506 of a vase, in 742 of an apron or petticoat.

Convince, 197 7, p. 1 34 40, to overpower.

Cornish, 223 20, cornice.

Counterproof, 323 5, proof against.

Coxcomb, 763 17, a slang term for the head, like mazzard, sconce, etc.

Creeking, 726 10. Apparently the same word as *creaking*, although somewhat curiously used of the noise of a hen.

Cunctation, 746 2, 922, delay.

Currish, 86 11, like a cur, rude.

Dandillion, 444 86. The connection with *lion* is wholly obscured by the penultimate accent.

Dardanium, 88 8. See note.

Dead, *vb. tr.*, 120 2, 204 12, 323 2, 788 4. The verb is now obsolete, except intransitively in student's slang.

Decurted, 900 8, cut off, abridged.

Delicates, 106 110, now obsolete as a noun.

Denounced, 128 47, proclaimed.

Designment, 926 1, design ; cf. *affrightment*.

Determine, 577 66, to come to an end.

Dingthrift, 424 3, spendthrift.

Disacquainted, *N.N.*, 56 18, unacquainted. The word, though rare, is to be found elsewhere.

Discruciate, 701 2, to torture ; cf. *excruciate*.

Disease, *vb. tr.*, 1030 21, to disturb.

Disgustful, 6 5, violently offensive. The word was not uncommon.

Disparkling, 444 29, sparkling round about.

Disport, 1030 9, recreation.

Disposeress, 718 12. Apparently coined.

Distraction, 83 4, confusion.

Divorcement, 197 2, divorce.

Dollies, 111 4. A cant term for sweethearts.

Dolor, *N.N.*, 154 2, pain, distress.

Domineer, 894 6. The word is used without the bad sense now common.

Dukeship, 266 1. The word is also found in contemporary writers.

Effused, 82 8, 636 4, poured out. So *effusion*, 629 5.

Enfriezed, 444 67, having a frieze ; cf. 223 21.

Enstyled, 444 92, called.

Entertainment, 313, reception.

Epithalamy, 271 8, 283, 900 12, *N.N.*, 232 12, a wedding song.

Err, 83 5, 336 63, *N.N.*, 233 4, to wander.

Errors, 444 83, wanderings.

-ess, feminines in, see p. 73.

Excathedrated, 168 4, judged ex cathedra.

Excruciate, *N.N*, 227 2, to torture ; cf. *discruciate*.

Factor, 375 9. See note.

Fantasy, 106 47, fancy.

Farcing, 561 2, stuffing.

Fardel, 753 2, a burden : the word was already going out of use.

Fat, 250 40, vat.

Fetuous, 223 68, more properly *featous*, neat.

Filleting, 22 6, 900 1, *N.N.*, 83 42, a band tied about the head.

Firstling, 36 3. For such diminutives, see p. lx.

Flosculet, 318 7, diminutive from *floscule*, itself a diminutive.

Fond, 732 10, foolish.

Fondling, 23 5. There are contemporary examples of this word in the sense of one fondled.

Footpace, 223 132, a dais; here rather a pedestal.

Fore-, nouns in, see p. lx.

Frippery, 223 21, worthless adornment.

Frolic, 913 10, sportive.

Frumenty, 250 34, a country dish.

Fuzz-ball, 293 29, a puff-pall.

Genius, 106 115, the guardian spirit.

Gin, 283 70, 319 7, engine, trap.

Glade, 664 66, an opening in the wood useful for snares.

Glib, 467 5, *glib temptations;* smooth, as ice, and therefore here applied to something likely to make one fall.

Gossamore, 444 95, gossamer,

Grit, 293 10, ·the coarse part of the meal.

Handsome, 238 13, 494 31. The 17th century use of the word was somewhat different from our own. Here the word is applied (238) to anger and (494) to hands.

Handsel, *N.N.*, 59 7, 90 2. The handsel was a first gift, as at New Year, or a first payment on making a bargain.

Hearse, 82 15, tomb.

Heave-offering, *N.N.*, 258 4. See Exodus xxix, 27.

Heyes, 523 30, a country dance.

Hind, 664 13, a rustic.

Hispid, 559 24, shaggy (*hispidus*).

Holy-rood, 306 13, the Cross.

Horrid, 323 14, more forcible than as used to-day, but not in the Latin sense.

Huckson, 640 11, the hock, the lower part of the leg.

Humor, 197 31, moisture, fluid.

Hypostatical, *N.N.*, 207 2, pertaining to a distinct person.

Illustrious, 128 14, giving light.

Immensive, 201 25, 687 2. See pp. lxi, lxii.

Inapostate, 1102 16, attentive.

Inarculum, 541 3, "a twig of pomegranate which the queen priest did use to wear on her head at sacrificing." Note by Herrick.

Incanonical, 1102 4. Not found elsewhere.

Inconveniency, 700 2, inconvenience.

Incivility, 86 2, lack of civilized manners.

Incurious, 763 14. The word usually means *indifferent*. Here it seems to mean that the villagers were simple, or not curious in their tastes.

Indignation, 871 2, unworthiness.

Ingression, 654 2, entrance.

Injeweled, 283 2, inlaid with jewels.

Inly, 128 46, inwardly, and so, secretly.

Instant, 319 40, 546 22, present, current.

Intelligence, 526 6, presiding spirit.

Inter, verbs compounded with, p. 74.

Intext, 654 6, text, contents.

Jet, *N.N.*, 123 66. To *jet* it, to strut, to assume a haughty carriage.

Junket, 763 4. The word has a special meaning, but is here used in a general sense for delicacy.

Justments, 82 4, the things which are due : not noted elsewhere. Dr. Grosart derives it from Lat. *justa*, obsequies.

Ken, *N.N.*, 51 9, to recognize. The word seems to have been in current use in Herrick's day.

Kingship, 213 43. Cf. babyship, etc., p. 73.

Kitling, 106 124, 293 24, 336 146, 444 74, a kitten.

Lar, 106 106, the household deity.

Larded, 106 111, run through with lard, as with certain richly cooked meats, and so, as here, luxurious.

Lations, 133 4. Formed from Lat. *latum*, used as p.p. of *fero*. The meaning is hard to determine. Perhaps *bearings*, in the sailor's sense, would come as near Herrick's idea as anything else.

Laureate, 359 6. Rare as a verb.

Lautitious, 785 3. Apparently coined from Lat. *lautitia*, splendor.

-let, diminutives in, p. lx.

-ling, diminutives in, p. lx.

Lust, 128 12, energy.

Lustre, 82 1, a period of five years.

Manchet, 478 4, a small loaf of the finest white bread.

Mantle-trees, 333 3, used here probably for mantelpiece.

Margent, 577 14, margin, border.

Marmalet, 654 14, marmalade.

Maukin, 250 9, a sort of mop.

Maund, 1070 7, a basket,

Maundy, *N.N.*, 123 29. The meaning here seems to be *alms received*, probably on account of the dispensations on Maundy Thursday.

Mel, 370 4, honey.

-ment, nouns in, p. lx.

Miching, 726 24, sneaking, skulking.

Mickle, 444 6, 640 3, great, large.

Napery, 283 68, table linen.

Nard, 872 7, an aromatic unguent.

Near, 478 27, stingy.

Neat, 106 30, elaborately prepared.

Neatherdess, 986 3, one of Herrick's feminines.

Nectarel, 54 4, for nectareal.

Needihood, 640 16, neediness.

Nervelets, 41 8, a diminutive, cf. p. lx.

Novity, *N.N.*, 244 2, newness.

Nosthrills, 319 8. The form recalls the etymology.

Null, 508 14, to make void.

Orient, 123 11, 178 22, eastern.

Outduring, 1131 2, outlasting.

Outred, 23 4, to surpass in redness.

Paddock, *N.N.*, 95 3, a frog or toad.

Pannicles, 716 4, the membranes enclosing the *cella phantastica*. Cf. *pia mater* in Shakespeare.

Pap, 201 7, often meaning *pulp*, seems here to be used for *sap*.

Parley, 11 7, conference.

Peccant, 270, 1064 8, offending.

Peeps, 444 49, the pips on playing cards.

Peltish, 444 17, angry, from *pelt*, anger.

Perking, 130 7. To *perk* is to be jaunty or pert.

Perplexity, 444 24, intricacy; rarely found in just this use.

Perpolite, 968 2, highly polished.

Perspire, 644 9, to breathe through.

Picks, 444 48, the diamonds on playing-cards.

Piggin, *N.N.*, 115 5, a small wooden vessel.

Pill, 97 3, to rob, pillage.

Pipkinet, *N.N.*, 130 3, a little pipkin.

Placket, 1028 7. The *placket-hole* is the opening in the side of a petticoat.

Poetress, 265 10. The word occurs also in Spenser.

Poise, *N.N.*, 16 2, weight.

Posset, 618 32, a mixture of hot milk and wine or ale.

Prank, 250 20, 494 32. *To prank it*, *N.N.*, 123 67. *Be pranked*, 523 44. To *prank* is to decorate.

Precomposed, 839 3, made beforehand.

Prefer, 547 9, to bring forward.

Premonished, *N.N.*, 43 5, warned beforehand.

Prevaricate, 197 87, to swerve from.

Prevent, 106 21, to come before, get ahead of.

Profuser, 691 1, one who is profuse, lavish.

Progermination, 747 8, origin, birth.

Propulsive, 450 1, propelling. The word does not commonly occur before the 19th century.

Protestant, 267 2, see the note.

Proto-notary, *N.N.*, 72 2, chief notary.

Purfling, 577 14; to *purfle* is to embroider on the edge.

Purl, 494 4, to make a murmuring sound. Generally used of water, but here of the oaten-pipe.

Purslane, *N.N.*, 47 41, a potherb.

Pushes, 596 1, pustules.

Quarelets, 75 8, diminutive of *quarry*, a square or lozenge.

Quick, vb., 128 5, to enliven, strengthen.

Quick, 499 12, alive.

Quickened, 78 6, given life.

Quintal, 664 52, quintain, see the note.

Rape, 106 126, capture.

Rapt, *N.N.*, 112 1, snatched, taken by force.

Re-, verbs compounded with, see p. lx.

Reaved, *N.N.*, 123 22, reft, taken by force.

Rectress, 1082 15, is more correct as a form than *poetress*.

Redeem, 444 26, to regain.

Regredience, 658 2, return.

Reiterate, 1030 3, to walk over again.

Religious, 14 8, 22 5, 82 2, 138 3, sacred.

Remora, 35 4, a delaying seamonster; see the note.

Repullulate, 336 23, to bud again. So *repullulation*, 796 4.

Repurgation, 510 4, a clearing.

Requesters, *N.N.*, 30 3, petitioners.

Resident, 521 4, remaining.

Respasses, 375 20, raspberries.

Retorted, 201 12, twisted back (from the forehead).

Ribbanding, 618 28, 986 26, an ornament of ribbons.

Rubylet, 654 10, a coined diminutive.

Russet, 664 60, of a reddish brown color, hence *homely, rustic,* country-made cloth being (or having been) of the russet color.

Sack, 128, 197. In Herrick's time the name was given to almost any white wine, except Rhenish.

Sag, 293 33, heavy.

Saintship, 223 33, 498 3. See p. lx.

Salvages, 86 12, 278 4, savages.

Saturity, *N.N.,* 138 2, repletion.

Scarlets, 23 7, pieces of scarlet cloth.

Sciography, 347 2, a picture. The N.L. *sciagraphia* is first remarked, 1650.

Securely, 106 35, safely.

Shagged, 128 15, shaggy.

Shepherdling, 2 12, 523 36. See p. lx.

-ship, nouns in. See p. lx.

Skills, 823 6, avails.

Slit, 336 86, sleet.

Slug-a-bed, 178 5. Cf. *Romeo and Juliet,* iv, 5, 2.

Smallage, 82 9, the celery plant, especially when wild.

Smirk, adj., 283 67, 377 72, smart, spruce.

Smirk, vb., 504 3, *smirking,* 250 36. Exactly what idea Herrick had in mind in using this word with wine would be hard to say. He probably meant either that the wine made others cheerful, or that it looked so itself.

Snugging, 78 3, snuggling.

Souce, 640 7, pickle.

Sparables, 650 2, nails used in cobbling.

Spars, *N.N.,* 47 5, beams.

Spartaness, 142 8. See p. lx.

Speed, 36 13, outcome. Generally of good fortune, but not so here.

Sphering, 336 148, passing round about.

Spiceries, 375 2, places where spices are kept.

Spirt, 8 5, 106 60, apparently means to *sputter.* In 106, one of the MSS. reads *crackling.*

Starve, 81 12, 115 16, *N.N.,* 83 70, to die (or make to die) of cold. In 293 14, it means to deprive of sustenance.

Statist, 490, statesman.

Still, 763 4, 923 2, always.

Stomacher, 83 6, the lower part of the bodice in front.

Storax, ·577 8, a sweet-smelling gum.

Strut, 672 21, to swell, to bulge out.

Suppling, 377 51, tender.

Supremest, 14 6, 327 2, 840 6, 1030 1, last.

Swerved, 81 10, wandered.

Swinger, 1037 24, as we should say, *a good one.*

Tardidation, *N.N.,* 137 6, delay; Lat. *tardidatio.*

Teem, vb. tr., 257 5, to bring forth.

Teend, 786 12, 788 2, 895 5, to kindle; cf. tind, tinder.

Tersely, 106 27, without extravagance.

These-like, 197 84. Cf. *such-like.*

Thronelet, 821 8, coined. See p. lx.

Thyrse, 111 8, 201 32, 336 135, 546 9, the staff symbolic of the worship of Bacchus.

Tiffany, 283 8, a kind of thin silk.
Tincture, 23 8, 193 32, color, tint.
Tityries, 319 2, roisterers. See note.
To, 223 97, in addition to.
Tods, 769 1, bunches.
Toning, 452 4, sound.
Trammel-net, 664 65, 883 2, commonly used of a kind of fishing-net, but not so here.
Transpire, 375 17, 577 7, to exhale.
Transshift, 1 9, 594 3, to interchange.
Tucker, 596 2, a fuller.
Turbant, 223 138, a turban.
Tyrant, 97 5, with the classical meaning of *usurper*.

Un-, adjectives in, see p. lx.
Unfled, *N.N.*,47 22, not mouldy (?).
Unsluice, 35 10, to open the floodgates.
Unsmooth, *N.N.*, 137 4, rough.
Unthrift, 274 17, a prodigal.

Volumed, 331 4, enrolled.

Wantonness, 1 6, 83 2, sport, sportiveness.
Warden, 375 23, a kind of pear.
Watched, 223 73, 284 3, watchet, a pale blue.
Weed, 306 2, garment.
Whenas, 178 13, and *passim*, when, or sometimes whenever.
Whipping-cheer, *N.N.*, 265 8, chastisement.
White, 77 11, 313 2, 336 40, 758 12, *N.N.*,128, auspicious, lucky. So *whiter*, 106 71, 547 8, *N.N.*, 128 9.
Whitflaws, 444 59, a whitlow, felon.

Yerk, 377 21, 1052 1, to irk, annoy.

Zonulet, 114 3, diminutive from *zonule*, which is itself a diminutive from zone. Cf. *flosculet*.

INDEX TO FIRST LINES.

— ◦◦ —

THIS Index has been prepared to facilitate reference not only to this selection, but also to the editions of Grosart and Pollard. To the former, the references are by volume and page; to the latter, and to this selection, the reference is by number. Each of the editions named has its own index, but it seems convenient to have all three together.

THE BEST HISTORIES.

MYERS'S Eastern Nations and Greece. — Introduction price, $1.00. With full maps, illustrations, and chronological summaries.

"Far more interesting and useful than any other epitome of the kind which I have yet seen." — Professor BECKWITH, *Trinity College.*

ALLEN'S Short History of the Roman People. — Introduction price, $1.00. With full maps, illustrations, and chronological synopsis.

"An admirable piece of work." — Professor BOURNE, *Adelbert College.*

MYERS AND ALLEN'S Ancient History for Schools and Colleges. — Introduction price, $1.50. This consists of Myers's Eastern Nations and Greece and Allen's Rome bound together.

MYERS'S History of Rome. — Introduction price, $1.00. With full maps, illustrations, tables, and chronological summaries.

"Though condensed, the style is attractive and will interest students." — Professor SPROULL, *University of Cincinnati.*

MYERS'S Ancient History. — Introduction price, $1.50. This consists of Myers's Eastern Nations and Greece and History of Rome bound together.

MYERS'S Mediæval and Modern History. — Introduction price, $1.50. With a full series of colored maps.

"Sure to be liked by teachers and pupils and by the general reader." — Professor SNOW, *Washington University.*

MYERS'S General History. — Introduction price, $1.50. With full maps, illustrations, tables, and summaries.

"The best text-book in universal history for beginners that we are acquainted with." — Professor STEARNS, *University of Wisconsin.*

MONTGOMERY'S Leading Facts of English History. — Introduction price, $1.12. With full maps and tables.

"I have never seen anything at all equal to it for the niche it was intended to fill." — Professor PERRY, *Princeton College.*

MONTGOMERY'S Leading Facts of French History. — Introduction price, $1.12. With full maps and tables.

"It is a marked advance on any available work of its scope." — *The Nation.*

MONTGOMERY'S Leading Facts of American History. — Introduction price, $1.00. With full maps, illustrations, summaries of dates, topical analyses, tables, etc.

"The best school history that has yet appeared." — Principal RUPERT, *Boys' High School, Pottstown, Pa.*

EMERTON'S Introduction to the Study of the Middle Ages. — Introduction price, $1.12. With colored maps, original and adapted.

"An admirable guide to both teachers and pupils in the tangled period of which it treats." — Professor FISHER, *Yale College.*

And many other valuable historical works.

GINN & COMPANY, Publishers, Boston, New York, Chicago, and London.

BOOKS IN HIGHER ENGLISH.

AND OTHER VALUABLE WORKS.